★

"It was his face! When he looked up at me...his face was white and blotched. His skin looked decayed... and his eyes were black.... He looked...he looked—"

"Mrs. Pearson," Ransom said firmly, cutting her off for fear that she would work herself into a frenzy, "the thing is, you weren't seeing a ghost. What you were seeing was a real person, so we have to take into account the possibility that your husband has come back and is pulling this nonsense on you for some reason."

Abigail stared blankly, then her face ran through a series of changes, from fear to anger with several more indistinguishable emotions in between. "No. No, that's too fantastic. I can't believe it's him."

"But before you were so sure it was him," Ransom said after a beat.

"I know, but I thought I was seeing...some sort of ghost or something. It was horrible. But if it's a real person, then I just can't believe... How could he do such a thing?"

"That's what we need to find out," said Ransom, looking none too pleased.

★

"Hunter deserves high praise for bringing us face to face with our own prejudices and creating an exceptionally sensitive portrait of two elderly women."

—*Booklist*

FRED HUNTER

RANSOM UNPAID

WORLDWIDE.

TORONTO • NEW YORK • LONDON
AMSTERDAM • PARIS • SYDNEY • HAMBURG
STOCKHOLM • ATHENS • TOKYO • MILAN
MADRID • WARSAW • BUDAPEST • AUCKLAND

RANSOM UNPAID

A Worldwide Mystery/November 2000

First published by St. Martin's Press, Incorporated.

ISBN 0-373-26365-1

Printed in U.S.A.

For Molly Weston, who provided the title

ONE

ABIGAIL PEARSON WAS excessively fond of hats. She considered herself blessed that she had been born with a perfectly oval face, her head neither too big nor too small, so that she looked good in almost every style of headgear, from cloche hats to wide brims, to the man's fedora, complete with a wide black band, that she'd sported during the late sixties and early seventies, much to the dismay and embarrassment of her children. But it had been her subtle form of support for the women's movement. The only kind of hat she had never much cared for were hats that tied under the chin. She had an aversion bordering on phobia to feeling bound in that way, whether it was under her chin or around her neck, no matter how sheer the material. Even the softest silk scarf, draped around her neck rather than knotted, made her feel as if she were suffocating.

As Abigail had grown older, she'd lost much of her affection for small, tight hats, although she still enjoyed seeing them on other women. She'd let her hair grow into a long mane that was half steel-gray and half white, believing that a luxurious train of hair lent an air of stateliness to an elderly woman.

She sat on the small chair at the vanity she'd had since she was young. She called it her "powder puff" chair because the seat was round, soft, and white. It brought to mind the large, fluffy puff that came inside the first circular box of powder she received one Christmas as a child. She had loved the softness of it against her skin, and the white clouds of dust it sent into the air whenever she applied the powder. She had kept it in the box on the side of her vanity for months after the powder was gone.

A variety of hats were piled to her left and right on the vanity. In the still of the night she had been seized with one of those flurries of activity where, unable to sleep, one finds oneself unaccountably compelled to scrub the kitchen floor, or clean out the closets, or rearrange all the wall paintings. Abigail's particular craze was to retrieve her collection of hats from the shelves in the closet between her bedroom and bath, and sort through them to decide which to keep and which to discard.

She looked at herself in the perfectly round mirror mounted on the back of the vanity and sighed. She looked tired and she certainly looked old, even if she didn't feel it. The lines around her eyes had deepened so that they no longer gave her character, but instead made her look as if her flesh were being slowly carved away. She picked up the silver-handled brush her mother had given her many years ago and ran it through her long hair, brushing it back behind her ears. She replaced the brush, picked up the hat from the top of the pile on her right, and placed it carefully on her head. The hat had a very wide floppy brim and was lime green with a pale band. She considered it in the mirror.

"What was I thinking?" she said with a grimace at her reflection. "Honestly!"

She snatched the hat from her head, tossed it on the floor and picked up another. This one was also wide brimmed, tan with a dark brown ribbon and a small cluster of berries and flowers on the left side.

"Maybe without the foliage," she said as she removed the hat, placing it on the pile to her left.

The next was a small white hat with a black band and abbreviated brim. A tiny broken feather stuck out from the band. The hat was faded and smudged beyond the ability to be cleaned, but Abigail tried it on anyway. There was something mannish about the hat, though it remained feminine. The color, coupled with the slight point at the back, made her look like a sort of mafioso sprite. She smiled at herself in the mirror. Her husband would have hated this hat. Then again, he would have hated anything she bought for herself. That was partly the point. She took the hat off and tossed it on the floor.

She was just reaching for another when both the overhead light and the boudoir lamp on the vanity flickered in unison. Abigail looked at each of the offending lights in turn and wondered what could have made them unstable. It wasn't entirely out of the ordinary to lose power during a storm, but the weather was calm that night. There was only an occasional gust of warm wind, which caused a branch of the tree outside her window to scrape against the glass. To Abigail it sounded like fingernails. She reminded herself to tell Gregory to trim the branch when she saw him next.

The ancient grandfather clock at the foot of the stairs began to loudly chime midnight. It was a comforting sound that usually made her feel she wasn't alone in the house, although there were times when the loud, insistent ticking made her feel as if her life was being ticked away.

When the clock struck the final note of twelve, the lights flickered again, then went out. Abigail sat motionless, staring straight ahead where her reflection had been, letting her eyes adjust to the darkness. She told herself that she shouldn't be frightened, although it would have been more effective if she could have thought of a reason why the lights would go off on their own.

Slowly she became used to the change, and the shadows around her formed into the things with which she had a lifelong familiarity: the bed with its high, oak headboard, the small nightstand and reading lamp, and the low chair in which she sat every morning to slip into her shoes. Once she had taken stock of these things, drawing a sense of peace from her precious possessions, she began an internal debate as to whether or not she should venture down to the kitchen to try to find a spare fuse, and then into the hollow basement which might have unnerved her at the best of times. There was something about going down the narrow stairs into the cellar that was a bit too much like descending into the belly of the beast. She didn't even relish the idea of doing it in the daylight.

No, she thought with a sigh, *I'll just leave it until morning and go back to bed. There's no sense in trying to find my way around now.*

She pushed herself back in the chair, placing steadying hands on either side of the vanity to brace herself as she rose. It was then that she heard a loud creak that seemed to come from somewhere in the center of the house. She froze in place, her fingers poised like spiders beside each pile of hats.

After a moment of straining her ears against the silence, she shook her head and chuckled at her own skittishness. Had the lights been working she would have thought nothing of the popping and snapping to which one is subjected in an old house as it settles. Abigail wasn't about to let those sounds worry her now. She got up and pushed the chair under the vanity as neatly as she could in the darkness, and stood for a moment resting her hands on the chair's back.

Then she heard it again. This time the sound rang out more deliberately than before. She wondered briefly why it seemed so familiar, then she realized it was the sound that the floorboard in the downstairs hallway made whenever anyone chanced to step on it.

Abigail suddenly became aware of a drumming in her ears that coincided with the pounding in her chest. There was definitely someone in the house, and there was nothing in the bedroom she could use to defend herself should the intruder decide to venture to the second floor. She did a quick mental inventory of where the few paltry items that could be considered valuable were, and wondered if the intruder would settle for what he found and leave quickly, or better yet, decide that there was nothing of real value at all. Her worst fear was that he might take to exploring the rest of the house to see if there were any hidden treasures.

Hidden treasure, she thought with a sudden, ironic smile. *If he only knew.*

It seemed to Abigail that she had been standing for hours in that attitude, her mind feverishly going from one possibility to the next then back again, when the silence was once again broken by a loud snap from the floorboard below.

The repetition of the noise caused a puzzled frown to appear on Abigail's face. Surely whoever was down there should have noticed by now that he was risking discovery by continuing to trod on the one space in the hallway floor that would bring him notice. It was almost as if the intruder was walking back and forth across the board purposely. This caused another shock of fear for Abigail: It would be worse to be faced with an intruder who actually *wanted* to rouse the house.

The pounding in her chest increased its speed and drew her attention back to itself. She had every reason to be afraid, but her heart felt as if it might run out of control. For this, at least, she was prepared. As carefully and quietly as she could, she pawed the vanity till she found the handle of the top right-hand drawer. She slid it out, then felt for the small bottle of pills she kept there. Once she had it in her grasp, she twisted the cap, trying not to allow the pills to rattle. She extracted one, put it under her tongue, and set the bottle down.

She stood with her eyes closed against the darkness, laying her hands back on her chair as the pill took effect. There was a general relaxing as her pulse began to slow. It was then that something happened that almost made her heart stop. Out of the silence came a voice that sounded far off and muffled, but still clear enough to be understood. It said only one word: "Abigail!"

For several seconds she stood immobilized, her eyes wide with terror. She tried to convince herself that she had been imagining things, but she could feel the blood rushing through her veins, and her nerve endings tingling. She listened again, but could hear nothing over the renewed pounding in her ears. When the sound was not repeated after a wait of over a minute, she started to think she actually *had* imagined it. She was tempted to go out in the hall and investigate, but knew that was a crazy thing to contemplate. But after a few more moments of continued silence, her curiosity began to get the better of her. *After all,* she thought, *I can't stand here like this forever.*

Drawing upon some of the bravery and foolhardiness she had known in her younger days, she quietly made her way across the room to her bedroom door. She pressed the tips of her fingers against the knob and cautiously turned it. The door unlatched with a click that was almost inaudible, though to Abigail it sounded loud enough to be heard in the next county. She waited for a moment, listening intently for approaching footsteps, but there was nothing. She pulled the door open and stepped out into the second-floor hallway.

Her room was the first in the hall. The hall ran directly back from the top of the stairs. She stood there for a while, trying to discern any further movement below. She was met with the rushing wind of silence that permeates the ears of anyone who tries too hard to listen. She was just about to cross to the newel post at the top of the stairs when suddenly she heard it again.

The dim voice, seeming to come to her from a great distance, once again called out: "Abigail."

She felt her heartbeat increase, and at the same time could feel her eyebrows knitting together. She was afraid and confused. There was something familiar about the voice.

"Abigail!" it called again in its far-off whisper.

Despite herself, Abigail felt compelled to go and look over the railing at the landing. She lurched across the hall and laid hold of the post for support.

"Who's there?" Her voice sounded cracked and dried. There was no answer, but she soon heard slow, deliberate footsteps coming down the first-floor hallway from the back of the house to the front.

Abigail had to struggle to keep herself from crying out when he came into view. From her bird's-eye position and with the darkness below, she couldn't really make out much more than a dark suit and silver hair, but his overall carriage made her sure she knew who the intruder was.

He didn't pause or look up at her. Instead he made his way to the front door. He seemed to slowly glide or float rather than walk, and he opened the door and went out without a word, closing the door behind him.

"Phillip?" Abigail said softly.

Then the darkness folded around her, and she knew no more.

TWO

"WE'RE GOING TO keep her overnight," said Dr. Frederickson, "to run some further tests and monitor her heart, but unless we find something more than we already have, she'll be released tomorrow."

"Tomorrow?" JoAnna Pearson said, her face drooping as if the weight of this development were dragging it down. Her cheeks were already pale enough without the aid of the additional stressful news, and her dark red hair was shot through with gray that seemed to add ten to her forty-plus years.

"Yes," said Frederickson. "Is there anyone who can look after her?"

JoAnna stared at the third button from the top of the doctor's long white coat. The end of a loose thread protruded from one of the tiny holes in the button, and in the midst of her jumbled thoughts, JoAnna found herself irrelevantly thinking that if he wasn't careful, he'd lose the button.

"Miss Pearson?"

"What? Oh, no, there isn't. I suppose...I suppose I could find someone, but there isn't any time, is there?"

The doctor hesitated, then said, "You know, of course, that she has angina. We don't know what caused this episode, but we haven't been able to find any damage to the heart. There may be some other reason for what happened, but we haven't discovered anything else wrong with her. I don't know that she needs a nurse, if that's what you're thinking, but I don't think she should be left on her own." Here he paused for a moment. "Has she shown any signs of anything else lately?"

JoAnna tried very hard to focus her attention on him. It was difficult, though, because she kept finding her concentration interrupted by a stream of thoughts such as *What am I going to do?* and *How am I going to handle this?* She kept coming back to the idea that she might have to move back in with her mother, but even thinking about it was almost too much to bear. She knew that if someone had to live with her mother, the responsibility would fall to her. She couldn't count on Gregory to be any more help than he ever was. And even if she could bring herself to move back, it still wouldn't be a solution. She had to work, and that would mean hiring someone to come in during the day, and she didn't even know where to start. And then her life would no longer be her own. Her existence would be reduced to going to work, then coming home to stay with her mother. Not that her life amounted to much more than that at the moment, anyway.

"Miss Pearson?" the doctor said, once again trying to gain her full attention.

"Oh. I'm sorry," she replied with a distressed smile, "I'm just... There's so much to do."

"I understand. Now, can you tell me if your mother has shown signs of anything unusual lately?"

"What do you mean?"

"Has she been more absentminded, forgetful? Has she been more tired than usual or has she suffered from loss of appetite?"

"No. No, not that I've noticed."

"Would you notice?"

Although there was no accusation in his tone, JoAnna looked up at him, her cheeks reddening. Like so many people who try to do their best, she always harbored the secret fear that her best was not good enough.

"Of course I would notice. What do you mean?"

"Nothing," Frederickson said, quickly backpedaling. "All I meant was that when you see somebody on a regular basis, it's easy to miss changes that take place gradually, over a period of time. It's much easier to notice these things if you haven't seen the person for a while."

"Of course," JoAnna replied sheepishly. She looked down in an effort to hide how deeply she was blushing. "I see my mother almost every day. A day doesn't go by that I don't visit her to make sure she's all right. I think I would notice this type of change you're talking about. Why do you ask?"

Frederickson shrugged. "Just looking for some explanation for the way you found her."

"I can't...I can't help you there," said JoAnna, shaking her head slowly, at a loss for her own inability to answer. "Is it all right if I see her now?"

"Certainly," said the doctor. He took his leave of her and went down the hall, intently scribbling notes on a clipboard. He was so distracted he narrowly missed being broadsided by a massive food cart that was veered out of the way at the last moment by the alert hospital employee who was pushing it.

JoAnna went through the door, which closed behind her with a muffled thud. Her mother lay on the bed, arms at her sides and palms up. Her head had lolled sideways, and her jaw had gone so slack it looked as if it might skew off the bottom of her head like a loose platen on an antique typewriter.

It was a semi-private room, and JoAnna was thankful to find the second bed empty. She tiptoed across the scuffed tile floor and pulled a chair out of the corner, positioning it so that she could more easily view her mother's face. Once she was seated, she adjusted her purse on her lap, folded her hands on top of it, and sighed. Her mother's face seemed to have taken on a gray tinge and her long hair was flared out helter-skelter, making her look like a wild thing that had fallen asleep without warning. Far from the solid rock on whom JoAnna had always relied, Abigail now looked frail and broken.

JoAnna was struggling so hard not to cry that she absently brushed her fingers across her right cheek, unaware that her tears had not yet begun to flow.

I suppose it's this way for all children, she thought. *You always know that one day your parents will die but you never really think it will happen.*

"I'm not dead yet." The weak voice came from the bed.

JoAnna was startled not so much because the voice was unexpected but because it seemed to be reading her thoughts.

"Mother!" she said anxiously. "Are you all right?"

Abigail managed a half-smile. "I think so." The smile quickly faded as she turned her head to look at the room. "Where are we?"

"The hospital."

"What am I doing here? What happened?"

"Mother...I found you this morning. On the upstairs landing. You were just lying there. I couldn't get you to wake up."

Abigail stared at her daughter with unwavering intensity. "I was on the landing?"

JoAnna nodded.

Abigail relaxed the muscles in her neck and allowed her head to roll back onto the pillow. She stared up at the ceiling as if it were a distant eye chart she was being asked to read. "The landing...now what was I doing there?"

"I don't know." JoAnna sounded slightly embarrassed. She had enough respect for her mother that any intimation that she was losing her faculties was difficult.

"The lights..." Abigail said quietly, "the lights went out."

"The lights in the house? They were on this morning. Is that it? The lights went out and you were frightened?"

"Yes...no.... Someone was there...." She stopped and turned to her daughter with a look of utter amazement. "JoAnna! I saw him!"

"You saw who?"

"Your father!"

JoAnna's jaw dropped and it was a few seconds before she could recover herself enough to respond. "You saw Daddy?"

Abigail nodded slowly.

"But that's not... You couldn't have!"

"He called to me. I heard him call my name. And I went out to the landing. And I saw him!"

JoAnna took two deep breaths to calm herself, then she reached out and laid a plumpish hand across her mother's skeletal fingers. "Mother, Daddy's been gone for a long, long time. You couldn't have seen him."

Abigail searched JoAnna's eyes with mounting confusion, then snatched her hand away. "I know what I saw!"

For a while JoAnna continued to try to get her mother to elaborate, but Abigail was so displeased with having her word doubted that she turned away and limited her responses to a series of uncommunicative grunts. Finally she drifted off to sleep again, and JoAnna quietly went out into the hallway.

She rested briefly against the door to her mother's room, and looked down the hall to the right, then to the left, as if she literally didn't know which way to turn. She remembered seeing a pop machine as she had passed through the visitor's lounge by the elevators, and decided it might help to get something cold to drink, sit for a while, and try to gather herself together. As she went toward the lounge, the hallway seemed to elongate and grow narrower, as it did in the nightmares she had experienced in which she tried to flee from some unseen pursuer only to find the door to salvation getting further and further away. Nurses and orderlies passed her by, talking with one another and paying no attention to her, as if everything were perfectly normal.

But nothing was normal for JoAnna now. The jolt she had received when she went to check on her mother only to find her in a crumpled mass at the head of the stairs was nothing compared to the shock of her mother's declaration. At first JoAnna had only been worried about her mother's medical condition; now she was worried about her mother's mind. And it wasn't the first time that the idea of Abigail's failing faculties had occurred to her. There had been other instances at home. This thought brought her back to the doctor's questions before she had gone in to see her mother. On reflection, it seemed to JoAnna that he, too, had suspected Abigail of some mental deterioration, and had been trying to gently direct her to an admission of the situation. After her mother's startling statement, JoAnna was sure that those fears were founded.

She finally reached the lounge and bought a Coke from the machine. She knew the caffeine might not be the best thing for her at that moment, but thought at least the sugar would sustain her. She settled herself in a chair by the window and sat for a while sipping the drink and gazing out over the park outside the hospital.

Across the room to her right a young woman sat next to an elderly woman in a wheelchair. The young woman kept up a steady, subdued stream of chatter, each part of which began with "Do you remember?" followed by short anecdotes, some apparently meant to be amusing, some not. The elderly woman stared dumbly at the window as if she could see the glass but nothing beyond. To JoAnna, it was like getting a glimpse of her own future.

"I came as soon as I could," said a voice directly behind her.

JoAnna started, spilling a few drops of the drink onto the thin-piled carpet.

"Oh. Greg," she said, casting a glance over her shoulder at him. "I'm sure you did."

"What's that supposed to mean?" He came around in front of her. He wasn't very tall, but between her seated position and feeling as if she were collapsing into herself, Gregory Pearson seemed to tower over her.

"It's been almost three hours since I called you," she said.

"I was at work," Gregory replied evenly. "This was the earliest I could get away."

"Of course." JoAnna took another sip of Coke.

He sighed and pulled up a chair beside her. JoAnna noted that he sat on the edge of it, as usual. He always gave the impression that he was about to bolt up out of his seat and rush off to something more important.

"How's she doing?" he asked.

"I don't know."

"What do the doctors say?"

"They don't know, either. They haven't found anything wrong with her yet. But when I found her... You should have seen her."

Gregory was silent for a few moments. "What were you doing there so early?"

JoAnna closed her eyes and sighed. Beads of condensation had formed on the can, which she raised and pressed against her forehead. "I called her this morning. A couple of times. Just to check on her. I was so tired. I usually visit her after work, but I thought I might just skip today and call instead. She didn't answer the phone and I got worried."

"That didn't mean anything. You know how Mother is. She might just not have been answering the phone."

"I was worried." She looked him in the eyes as pointedly as she dared, hoping to get the point across that any child would have been—or should have been—worried under the same circumstances.

He chose to ignore her. "So you went over and found her...."

"She was lying in a heap on the landing. Right at the top of the stairs. God, Greg. If she'd been a foot or so further along when she fell she would've gone right down the stairs and...that would've been that."

"Hmm," Gregory said, drawing back slightly. He looked as if this was the first time it had occurred to him that today's episode might have been fatal, and it gave

JoAnna some satisfaction to see that he seemed moved at the prospect. "I didn't realize it was that serious."

JoAnna put the Coke down on a magazine on the table by her chair and absently rubbed the armrests with her palms as she continued.

"It's worse.... It may be worse than that."

"What do you mean?"

"There might be something wrong with... I think there's something else wrong with her."

She stopped, and Gregory impatiently prompted her. "Go on."

"While I was waiting for the ambulance to get there, I looked in her room. Her hats...her hats were all over the place, on the vanity, in piles...and some were on the floor. All of her hats...I can't imagine what she was doing with them."

"So her hats were out. Big deal."

"But it looked so... Why on earth would she have pulled all her hats out in the middle of the night?"

"How do you know she did it in the middle of the night?" Gregory replied with a shrug.

"I was there yesterday. They weren't there then."

He looked at her with a frown. "You're a very dutiful daughter, aren't you?"

"She's my mother," JoAnna replied accusingly. "I check on her as often as I can."

Gregory gave a solitary "Hmph," then said, "I still don't see what the big deal is."

"Then we got her to the hospital, and the doctors started their tests, and they haven't been able to find anything physically wrong with her—other than her angina. One of them asked me if...well, about how she's been acting lately."

"So what? That's what they're supposed to ask you."

JoAnna dug her fingernails into the armrests, then leaned over to Gregory, whispering, in case the other occupants of the hospital should hear her. "He sounded as if he thought there might be something wrong with her...*wrong* with her. And then I went in and talked to her. She couldn't explain why she was there on the landing—''

''She might have—''

''Wait! She said that...she said she saw Daddy.''

Gregory finally sat back in his chair, although his back remained so rigid he didn't seem to be aware of the support. ''She said what?''

''She said she saw Daddy!''

After a pause, Gregory sat forward again and dismissed this with a wave of his hand. ''She must've been dreaming.''

''Out on the landing?''

''Yes,'' Gregory replied testily. ''She could've passed out or whatever when she was on the landing and dreamed she saw him.''

JoAnna looked at him with wide eyes. This was a scenario that hadn't occurred to her. And it made sense, and was much easier to deal with than what she'd been fearing.

''You really think so?''

''Of course I do,'' Gregory said carelessly. ''What else could it be?''

JoAnna hesitated, then said, ''Well, the way she described it...''

''What?''

''It sort of...explained the way I found her. I mean what she would've been doing out there on the landing to begin with. She said he called to her, and she went out there. It made sense. That's the way it seemed when I found her...like she'd seen something that scared her.''

''It made sense? Oh, for Christ's sake, you could tell all that by the way she was lying on the landing?'' Gregory exclaimed as he got up and began to pace in the small space in front of her. ''You watch too many goddamn movies!''

''It was what Mother said happened,'' JoAnna said defensively. ''I didn't say I believed her!''

"The only thing that makes sense is that she dreamed the whole damn thing!"

JoAnna glanced around the room to see if they'd drawn anyone's attention. The young woman who JoAnna had noticed earlier was still chatting at the old lady, although her eyes were fixed on Gregory.

"Lower your voice!" JoAnna said in an anxious whisper.

"You just make me so goddamned mad when you do this!" Gregory continued, making no attempt to comply. "You have to use your brain now and then instead of letting your imagination run wild! If you were old, like Mother, I could halfway understand it. But you're young enough that you should be able to get your brain working!"

"I'm sorry!" JoAnna said hurriedly. "Mother just sounded so sure when she said it."

Gregory stopped his pacing and looked down at her with something bordering on contempt. He looked as if he were disappointed that he couldn't think more highly of his younger sister. He dropped back down onto the chair beside her.

"It's all right," he said, making an abortive attempt to pat her hand. "Mother can be very compelling. Even when she's not at her best. But you have to *think*, JoAnna. She saw our father? That's not possible!"

She turned to him. "Isn't it?"

"Of course not!" Gregory exclaimed, his volume rising again. "It's been over thirty years, for Christ's sake!"

"He walked out on us," JoAnna replied more sharply than she ordinarily would have dared. "He didn't die."

"And thirty years later he showed up in the house in the middle of the night. Use your head, Jo!"

There was nothing left for her to say. Of course, Gregory was right. The whole idea was ridiculous. But this realization did nothing to relieve her apprehensions. Her mother was so certain she had seen their father. If that wasn't possible it was just further proof to JoAnna that there was something desperately wrong with her mother.

GREGORY STOOD propping open the door to his mother's hospital room. His impression of her was much the same as JoAnna's had been, but his concern seemed less emotional and therefore more grave. To an onlooker he would have appeared to be disinterestedly assessing a complete stranger, were it not for the marked resemblance between mother and son. Although his face had fewer lines than Abigail's (and in fact, fewer than JoAnna's, though he was the elder), he had the same oval face and perfectly shaped head, and eyes that became crescents on the rare occasion when he smiled.

Abigail's eyelids fluttered, then opened slightly. When she saw Gregory backlit in the doorway she tensed, and her eyes widened.

"Phillip?" she said hoarsely.

"No, Mother. It's me."

"Oh, Gregory!" she said, putting her right palm to her forehead. "Of course. Your father's hair, it was gray...."

He stepped through the doorway, continuing to grip the handle as the door closed, then crossed the room and sat in the chair his sister had occupied earlier.

"How are you doing, Mother?"

"I'm tired. I feel like I haven't slept in weeks."

"You seem to have been active last night."

She drew her hand away from her forehead and draped it across her midriff. "I was?"

"Yes. What were you doing with your hats?"

"My hats?" she said, furrowing her brow.

"Yes. JoAnna said they were all over the place."

"Oh!" said Abigail, noticeably relieved to remember. "I couldn't sleep. I decided to sort through them and throw out the ones I didn't like anymore."

"I knew there was a logical explanation," Gregory mumbled.

"What was that?"

"Nothing." He looked at her, searching her face for some indication of whether or not he should proceed, but there was nothing there. He decided to go on anyway. "Mother, JoAnna tells me you saw something last night."

Abigail turned away from him and stared straight ahead as if picturing the scene over again.

"I saw your father."

"That's what JoAnna said. But that isn't likely, is it?"

She turned back toward him. "Are you saying I don't know what I saw?"

Gregory met her gaze without flinching. "Did you see his face?"

"No. I saw him from the landing. The top of his head. But it was him."

"How can you be so sure?"

"I was married to him. Do you think I wouldn't recognize him?"

Gregory heaved a heavy sigh. "That was a long time ago. I think it's more likely you were asleep and dreaming."

She shook her head obstinately. "I heard him call my name. I went out to the landing and then I saw him...." She started to falter. "I don't remember anything after that.... Not until I woke up here."

There was a lengthy pause during which Gregory stared straight into her eyes. "Mother," he said at last, "I don't believe for a minute that you saw Daddy, but if you saw *something,* if somebody broke into the house with you there, then clearly it isn't safe for you to stay there. I think it's time we talk about your living arrangements."

"My living arrangements?" Abigail repeated apprehensively.

"Yes. Maybe you shouldn't be living on your own anymore."

Her jaw hardened and her eyes narrowed. "What are you getting at?"

Gregory sighed. He felt he was being pressured to put this more bluntly than he would have liked. Still, he made an effort to choose his words carefully. "Maybe we could find you some place to live where you'd have other people around in case anything happened. Someone to look after you."

Abigail's lips formed a thin flat line. She barely moved them when she said, "Like a nursing home?"

"Not necessarily," Gregory said quickly. "Perhaps a retirement home."

"I'm not moving out of my house!"

"You could have been hurt last night. Or worse!"

"I'm perfectly all right!"

"Mother, you're in a hospital!" Gregory replied. He was quickly losing the ability to hide his frustration.

"That doesn't mean a thing!" Abigail said, taking an angry swipe at the air with her hand. "I'm fine. Ask the doctors."

"But Mother—"

"I'm not leaving my house," she said with finality.

Gregory sighed again. "I know how you feel about it, but the place is a crumbling castle. It's much to big for you to keep up and it has been for years."

"I have Nedra."

He shook his head. "Once a week. And she's hardly any help when she's there. You've said that yourself."

There was a long pause during which Abigail gazed at her son's face so intently that it almost made him lose his composure. "What do you want me to do," she said at last. "Sell the house? Give you the money?"

"That's the *last* thing I want you to do!" He managed to sound indignant. "You know that better than anyone. But I'm worried about you living there alone!"

"That house is the only thing I have," she said hotly, "And I'm going to keep it in our family. I have no intention of giving it up!"

"For Heaven's sake, Mother! Nobody's asking you to!"

There was a tense silence, then Abigail folded her hands on her stomach. "I never should have told you what I planned to do. But I wanted you to know. I didn't want you to find out after I was gone and think I was punishing you or something. I didn't want you to think I was disinheriting you. And now you hate me."

"I don't hate you, Mother."

"You've been surly to me ever since. Surlier than usual, I should say. I would've thought you'd be happy that I'm leaving the house to Robert."

Gregory clenched and unclenched his jaw. "I think it is a very nice gesture." It sounded like a painful admission.

"After all, he's just barely starting out in life. He can *use* a house. You've already made your way in the world. You have everything you need."

"That's not the issue and you know it! Robert's *my* son, and I think I know what's best for him. And I think I know him better than you do. If something should happen to you and Robert gets his hands on that house, he'll sell it in a minute, and you know what that means!"

She looked at him for a moment in disbelief. "Robert wouldn't sell it. He knows how I feel about it."

"The only way to ensure that it stays in the family is to leave the house to me. That's the only way you can know that everything will be taken care of." He stressed the last few words in an attempt to get through to her, but it had no effect.

"Robert will not sell the house," Abigail said stubbornly. "He's a good boy."

"Mother," Gregory said, losing all patience, "he'll have it on the market before your body is even cold. Look at you now! You're in a hospital, and nobody knows what's wrong with you! Don't you realize that something could happen to you and then it will be too late to change your mind?"

"How can you..." Abigail began. Her face was still as stern as granite, but her voice quavered. "How can you talk to me like that when I'm in here? Don't you know I'm not supposed to be upset? What are you trying to do?''

For the first time Gregory looked unsure of himself. "I didn't... I'm sorry...."

"Please go! *Please* go! I'm so tired...." Her voice had become a hoarse whine, and Gregory gave her a look of distaste before rising from the chair.

"Very well. I didn't mean to upset you. I'm sorry." He went to the door and was about to open it when she called to him.

"Gregory!" She seemed to have regained some of her composure. "It doesn't matter now, anyway. Despite what you may think, I have a few years left in me. And I'm never going to leave that house. Not as long as I'm alive!"

ROBERT PEARSON loosened his tie when he left Merchandise Mart, the mammoth home of manufacturer's showrooms that sits on the edge of the Chicago river like a monolith left by an earlier civilization. He worked for Marlac Fixtures, a company that specialized in ornate plumbing fixtures for people with more money than taste. He spent most of his time guiding representatives of decorating firms around displays of every possible variation of faucet. It was a boring, dead-end job, but it was all he had been able to get after graduating college with his bachelor's degree, and even this nothing job had been procured through a series of connections so long and labored he wasn't sure to whom he was indebted for it. To make matters worse, business was so sparse that he had plenty of time to ponder what had become of his aspirations. The problem was that at the tender age of twenty-two, when hopes for the future still should have been burning brightly in his heart, he couldn't remember ever having any. He had made his way through college without developing a particular interest in anything, and had graduated even more directionless that he had begun. What he did have was a nagging feeling that he *should* want to get ahead, muddled by a persistent vagueness about

where he wanted to go and how getting there could be
accomplished.

Robert had a long wait on the El platform, followed by
an even longer ride in the cramped train up to the Edge-
water apartment he shared with Leslie—affectionately,
Les—the girl he had married during his last year in college
because he hadn't been able to think of a good reason not
to.

Les is all right, Robert thought, feeling slightly disloyal
for even entertaining the idea that there might have been a
lack of passion in their relationship, or a question about the
efficacy of his marrying at an early age. Certainly his father
thought the latter was true.

It took almost forty-five minutes in the suffocating,
crowded train car to get to the Argyle stop. When Robert
emerged from the train his shirt was soaked with sweat and
his hair was so damp it looked closer to brown than the
ash blond it really was. He pulled the red-and-blue striped
tie the rest of the way off, then rolled it up and stuck it in
the pocket of his sports coat. He then unbuttoned the top
three buttons of his shirt.

The four-block walk to his apartment on Kenmore felt
like a parade through the desert. The sidewalk was so hot
that he imagined steam would rise from it in the unlikely
event of rain. The block on which he lived had definitely
seen better days. A couple of the buildings, elegant in their
time, had been boarded up and were awaiting demolition
or gentrification, depending on which special interest group
got to them first. It didn't seem to matter. The late sun was
beating down on the buildings at an angle that sent their
shadows creeping into the street, but the shade provided no
relief from the heat.

Robert's building was on the corner. It took up almost a
fourth of the block and was flush against the sidewalk, brick
against concrete, which gave a sterile, unfriendly atmosphere to the place. There were no flower beds and no room

for grass or any other natural vegetation. One couldn't imagine plants surviving there, let alone humans.

Robert went up the musty staircase to their third-floor apartment. There was an old elevator—the kind with a gate you had to pull closed—which had been out of service so long the janitor had taken to using it as a broom closet. The third-floor hallway smelled like wet carpet and burned meat. As usual, many of their faceless neighbors had made it home before him and were in the process of burning dinners that were too heavy for the heat anyway.

When Robert reached his door he unlocked the dead bolt and the doorknob jiggled in his hand as he turned it.

"Les? Are you home?" he called out as he struggled to pull the key from the lock. After turning it back and forth and pulling at it firmly, he let out a sigh that seemed to deflate him. He then gave the key one last, gentle tug and it popped out of the lock as if there had never been any problem. He stuck the key in his pocket and closed the door.

"Les?" he called again.

Leslie Pearson emerged from the bedroom. She was a painfully thin young woman with long, straight blond hair. Her skin was so pale she looked as if exposure to the sun might cause her to burst into flames. Her small mouth, which tended toward an attractive pout, was turned down at the corners.

"Oh, Bobby!" she said, slipping her arms around his neck and pressing the side of her face against his shoulder.

"What is it?" he said disheartenedly. He never knew what to expect from her when he came home anymore, and right then he felt that the only thing that could add to the oppressive heat and stagnant air would be a scene.

"Oh!" she exclaimed, pulling back slightly, "You're soaking!"

"Is something wrong?"

"It's your grandma. She's in the hospital. Your mom

called and left a message on the machine. I heard it when I got home."

"In the hospital? Is it serious?"

"She said she didn't think so. She didn't really know. Don't you think you should call her?"

He looked into her eyes. She was so young and innocent, and yet there was a searching quality in her eyes that made her seem wise beyond her years.

"Yes, of course," he replied.

He kissed her lightly on the forehead, then disappeared into the bedroom. Leslie went into the tiny kitchen to finish making their dinner, which would consist of a cold salad into which she had mixed some canned chicken. As she sliced a pair of tomatoes to put on top, she could hear the low mumblings of Robert's half of the telephone conversation. After a few minutes, she heard him hang up. He then appeared in the doorway clad only in a faded pair of paisley boxer shorts. His skin glistened with sweat.

"She's okay," he said.

"Oh! That's great!" Leslie heaved a relieved sigh. "What happened?"

"Nothing, really, I guess," he said as he retrieved a tumbler from the cabinet over the sink. "Gran just passed out or something. JoAnna found her this morning."

"She just passed out? They don't know why or anything?"

"Nope." He took a pitcher of water from the refrigerator and poured himself a glass. "But it doesn't look serious."

Leslie was about to go back to slicing the tomatoes when she was stopped by something in his tone. "You don't sound happy about that."

"Of course I'm happy about it," he said crossly. "Why wouldn't I be?"

"I don't know," she said, turning away. "I didn't mean anything."

There was a pause, then Robert said, "I know you didn't. I'm sorry."

"I can't say anything!" She fought to hold back tears, but she was losing the battle. The knife trembled in her hand as she cut into the last tomato.

"Don't let's fight."

"It's just...I was never off the register today, the store was so busy! I was on my feet all day. I'm tired!" She dropped the knife and buried her face in her hands.

Robert crossed behind her and put his hands on her shoulders.

"I'm sorry I snapped at you," he whispered.

"I'm acting crazy," she said, giving him a weak smile over her shoulder. "It's just so hot!"

"You were right anyway." He released her and took a seat at the scarred, secondhand kitchen table. "I probably did sound disappointed. I probably was. You'll think I'm a terrible person."

"What? What are you talking about?"

"Anybody else who heard their grandmother was sick, they'd be upset. And I am upset, I really mean that. But you know what was the first thing that popped into my head when you told me?"

"What?"

He looked at her for a moment before answering. Her expression told him that she couldn't believe ill of him, no matter what. "I thought how badly we could use that house of hers."

"Her house?" Leslie looked as if she almost thought that was funny.

He nodded. "You know Gran is going to leave me the house. Boy, we could use it now!"

"That old barn?" Leslie said, squinching her face up. "I wouldn't want to live there! It's like some dusty old museum!"

"Not to *live* in it, honey. To sell it."

"Oh, your Gran wouldn't like that. She loves that old dump. And you promised, remember?"

"I know, I know, but she'll be gone. It won't matter to her anymore."

She stopped and looked at him. "It doesn't really mean anything to you—that house?"

He shook his head. "No. Why should it? I wasn't brought up there. Sure, I spent a lot of time there when I was little, but it wasn't our house. You know that."

"It doesn't mean anything to you that it's so important to her? You love your Gran, I know you do."

He gazed at her for a beat. "There's more important things than that."

There was a long pause during which Leslie seemed to be calculating something in her head. "You think you'd get very much for it? The neighborhood is a little iffy, isn't it?"

"We'd get enough for us to last for a while, anyway. Maybe enough to live off for a couple of years. Is it so terrible to want that? It's not like I *want* Gran to die or anything."

"No," Leslie replied thoughtfully. "You just want to take care of us." She put her hands on his shoulders and rested her head atop his.

"Bobby, do you think we were right to go to your grandmother?"

He pushed her away. "I wasn't begging!"

"I know, I know," Leslie said, her eyes brimming with tears. "But...don't you think you should tell your father?"

"Oh, Christ, no! I know what he'd say and I'm not putting myself through that!"

"But Bobby—"

"No!" he said sharply. "Things are bad enough!"

JOANNA DIDN'T GET HOME to her Clark Street apartment that evening until long after seven o'clock. She was so hot and exhausted that she wavered as she stepped onto the elevator. She pressed the button for her floor and slumped against the wall. There was an elderly man on the elevator with her. He had a head shaped like a walnut and skin the approximate shade and consistency of its shell. His thin lips were sucked in, as if he had forgotten to wear his teeth. Despite the heat he was carrying a sweater over one arm. He gave JoAnna a slow, sidelong glance, apparently curious about her but far too cautious to address a stranger. When the doors opened on the eleventh floor, JoAnna straightened herself up with some effort and stepped out. She could feel the old man's eyes riveted to her back until the doors closed.

Her limbs felt heavy and awkward as she walked down the hallway to her door and rummaged through her purse for the keys. She unlocked the door and went in, quickly switching on the hall light before closing and locking the door behind her. Normally, if she had known she was going to be out so late, she would have left the hall light on. She wasn't afraid of the dark, but she really hated coming home to a dark apartment. Even more than coming home to an empty one.

Oh God, not tonight, she thought as this crossed her mind.

But the uncertainty of her mother's health had triggered a wave of personal ambivalence that caused her to look at her life, and she didn't like what she saw. The divorce she had obtained years ago had been necessary. She knew that. To this day whenever she thought of her ex-husband she refused to call his name to mind, as if it was safer to think of him only as an amorphous entity with which she had at one time been unfortunately yoked. She had dropped her married name—Bellman, of all things—and readopted her maiden name right after the divorce was final, as if determined to wipe the entire experience out of her life.

But what do I have now? she asked herself silently. *An empty apartment, a job, a few friends, and a daughter who never calls. I'm alone. Was it really that bad with him?*

She dropped her purse and listened to the silence for a

few seconds, as if someone might give her the answer. Then she sighed. She already knew the answer.

She went into the bathroom, splashed some warm water on her face, and looked at herself in the mirror as she dabbed one of the rose-colored towels to her cheek.

Christ, I look old, she thought.

She went out to the kitchen and opened the door to the refrigerator, knowing before she did it that it would be futile. She had meant to shop after work, but after finding her mother she had never made it back to work, let alone to the grocery store. The entire contents of her refrigerator consisted of a tub of margarine, a small container of sour cream, and a half-empty bottle of chardonnay. She pulled the bottle out, popped the cork, and poured herself a glass. She then poked through the pantry until she found a packet of soda crackers. She took them, along with the wine, out to the living room.

JoAnna kicked off her shoes, sat down on the couch, and put her stockinged feet up on the coffee table. She took a healthy drink of wine, then sat back and let out a long, weary sigh. She still had so much to do. She had to find someone to stay with her mother for a while, at least during the day. She originally thought she should hire a nurse, but the doctor didn't seem to think that was necessary. Besides, she didn't have that kind of money and neither did her mother. No money, just that lumbering, ridiculous old house that her mother insisted on clinging to.

"And I'm left to do it all myself," she said aloud.

She had been right—Greg would be no help. In the five minutes he spent with their mother, he had only managed to antagonize and agitate her with all that talk of finding her someplace to live. When Mother told her what had happened, JoAnna was furious. He should have known how it would upset her.

She took another drink and nibbled at a cracker. Then she sighed again, this time with frustration. Greg was right: The house was too big for Mother to keep up and she really shouldn't be living on her own, anyway. This latest episode was proof of that. But Mother was Mother, and once her mind was made up there was no changing it, no matter how hard you tried.

One of these days, JoAnna thought, *I'm going to go over there and find her dead. She'll have died and nobody will know about it. And I know I'll be the one to find her—Greg doesn't go over there unless he has to, and Robert only visits when the whim strikes him.*

She glanced at the phone on the end table beside the couch. She knew she would have to start calling soon if she ever hoped to find anyone to stay with her mother. She also knew she was going to miss another day's work. She couldn't possibly find someone to be there on such short notice.

Why did this have to happen on Monday? she thought. *Now I'm going to be scrambling all week to find somebody to help.* She had a sudden, intense longing for the whole thing to be over so she could resume her normal life—what little of it there was.

As she reached for the phone she thought, *"Or maybe I could just finish off the rest of the wine. Drink myself to sleep and pretend none of this ever happened."*

"HI, GRANDMA!" said Robert, poking his head into Abigail's room. There was a broad, unconcerned grin across his face.

"Robbie!" Abigail exclaimed, brightening for the first time since waking up in the hospital. "Get in here!"

He obeyed immediately. Unlike his father and his aunt, he ignored the guest chair and thoughtlessly sat beside Abigail on the bed.

"I'm sorry I'm so late," he said. "Visiting hours are almost over. But I didn't find out you were here until I got home from work, and then there was everything to take care of there before I came here."

Abigail beamed at him. If it entered her mind that he

might have waited to visit her so that his visit could, by hospital rules, be cut short, she didn't show it.

"Where's that wife of yours?"

"At home. In bed. She's not feeling too well today."

Abigail frowned. "She's taking care of herself, isn't she?"

"Of course she is. Of course. She just had a long day at work, and got overtired. She'll be all right."

"She shouldn't have to work." Abigail's tone was stern but not accusing.

"You got the wrong generation, Grandma," Robert said lightly. "Things have changed. Now, tell me what you're doing in this hospital! You don't look any sicker than I do!"

She curled her lips. "I just fainted, is all."

"Fainted? How did that happen?"

She studied his face for a moment, trying to decide whether or not she should tell him the full story. She decided he had enough on his mind without her adding to it. "It wasn't anything.... It's too long and too damn silly to go into."

"No, Grandma, you tell me," he said with genuine concern.

She shook her head. "My heart was just a little tricky. I took one of my pills. Sometimes I think they work too fast. It just slowed me down too much. That's all. Nothing to worry about."

"Nothing could slow you down," he said playfully. It was one of those lies sometimes shared between people who love each other. Both of them knew it wasn't true. Since Abigail rarely left the house, Robert didn't know of anything she would have to slow down from.

"Go on," she said, laughing. After a moment, her expression grew more serious. "Robbie, you *are* taking care of Leslie, aren't you?"

"Of course I am," he replied. He looked anything but pleased to revert to this topic.

"You need to take care of her, you know. It's your job."

"I know." He tried not to sound testy, but it was difficult.

"And you'll get help from me in the future, you know. I told you that. The house will be yours when I'm gone."

"You old thing," he replied, readopting his playful attitude. "You get out of here! You're going to be with us forever!"

"I don't know. My heart isn't what it used to be. And—well, I won't dwell on it. It's nothing to worry about." The deeply troubled look on her face belied her words.

"Grandma, what is it?" Robert asked, because he thought he should.

"Oh…it's nothing. Your father was here tonight."

"Oh."

"We had a bit of a fight."

"Both of you? Or did he do this one alone?"

Abigail smiled. "You be good now, Robbie."

"Whatever you say. What was this one about?"

"You."

"Me? I haven't seen him in months! What could he have to complain about now?" His forehead creased. "You didn't tell him anything, did you?"

"I told him about the house."

"Oh. I see."

"He's not happy. He thinks like me, you see. He thinks the house should stay in the family."

"So?"

"He doesn't think you'll do that."

"What? He knows how much I love you! Look, this is silly, talking about this stuff while you're in the hospital. It's silly and it's unhealthy. You should only be thinking about getting well."

"I'll be getting out tomorrow."

"See? What did I tell you? That's great! There's nothing to worry about, and nothing's going to happen to you for a long, long time, so it's just stupid to be talking about this now.''

"No, it's not," Abigail said firmly. "Now, Robert, you made me a promise, didn't you?"

"Yes, ma'am."

She reached out and wrapped her fingers around his wrist. "Robbie, I want you to promise me..."

"I already did."

"Again. I want you to promise me again that you'll keep the house in this family. You know why I decided to give it to you. Now I want you to promise me again that you'll hold on to it."

He looked her straight in the eye. "I promise."

THREE

"I'M WELL AWARE THAT you love me," said Emily with amusement, "especially when I'm feeding you."

Tam, the cat that derived her name from the orange-and-black circle that covered the center of her head like a jaunty cap, rubbed herself against Emily's ankle. Tam had been a gift from her friend, Detective Jeremy Ransom, a short time after Tam's predecessor died at a ripe old age. Although Tam had never been a small cat, having arrived on the scene long after her kittenhood had passed, under Emily's loving overindulgence the cat had developed the bottom-heavy pear-shape common to her breed. When she sat on her haunches she looked like a feline Buddha. Ransom had once indelicately remarked on the resemblance between Tam and a doorstop. Emily had clucked her tongue at him, but the smile that accompanied it showed that she didn't entirely disagree.

She emptied the small can of food onto a saucer, then mashed the mound with a fork. Then she carefully placed the saucer next to the bowl of water by the stove, and Tam immediately forgot her affection for her beloved owner in favor of the savory breakfast.

Emily looked down at the animal and spared a gentle "tsk." "You'd think I starved you!"

She dropped the empty can into the garbage can by the door, then filled the teakettle with water and placed it on the stove. She gingerly switched on the burner as if she was sure it would explode, despite the fact that she'd had an electric stove for almost twenty years, then took her blue china cup and saucer down from the cupboard and placed them on the counter. She was just settling herself in her usual seat at the kitchen table when she heard the front door open.

"Good morning!" called a voice down the hallway.

"Good morning, Lynn," Emily responded.

Lynn Francis came into the kitchen like breath of fresh air, carrying with her a large shoulder bag and a paper sack full of groceries. Lynn was in her mid-thirties and had an air of self-confidence that was devoid of self-satisfaction, so that she seemed to brighten any place she happened to be. She was so straightforward and guileless that with one flip of her tawny hair she could sweep a room clear of pretensions.

Emily had grown to be a great admirer of Lynn, partly because the young woman had managed to maintain her bearing through the long illness and eventual loss of her lover, even though her role as caretaker had completely upended her life. And the loss had been devastating. Lynn's ability to overcome hardship showed Emily that she was indeed made of stern stuff.

"Did you have your breakfast?" Lynn asked, checking the sink for dishes.

"Yes," Emily replied with a twinkle in her eyes. Seldom did anything escape her notice. "And I cleaned up after myself. You won't find any dirty dishes."

Lynn laughed. "On the days I'm here to clean, you don't have to do the dishes yourself—I'll do them for you."

"That's really not necessary."

"Are we going to have this discussion again?" She forced a frown. "If you keep cleaning up after yourself, I'm going to feel like I'm taking money under false pretenses!" She placed the bag on the counter and draped the strap of her shoulder bag over the back of one of the kitchen chairs.

"You know I appreciate everything you do. And I appreciate Jeremy for hiring you—"

"Hiring me? Huh!" Lynn uncharacteristically interrupted. "Nobody had to hire me to work for you. I would have done it for free."

Emily smiled. "But it has taken some getting used to, being a lady of leisure. I'm used to being active."

"Nothing will ever keep you from being active," Lynn replied, laughing. "Nobody could."

The teakettle began to whistle and Emily started to rise from her seat, but Lynn waved her back. "Oh, no you don't! I'll get your tea. Here's the paper."

She pulled a newspaper from the grocery bag and handed it to Emily, who smoothed it out with her delicate, wrinkled hands.

Lynn poured the boiling water from the kettle into Emily's old ceramic teapot, then took two tea bags from a jar on the counter and dropped them in, leaving their strings dangling down its side. She placed the pot on a pad within Emily's reach, then busied herself with emptying the paper sack and putting away the groceries.

"Anything of interest?" Lynn asked, referring to the newspaper.

"Nothing out of the ordinary," Emily replied.

"Given the type of nonsense your favorite detective gets you mixed up in, I'd like to know what you *would* find out of the ordinary!"

"Most of life is interesting, if you look at it that way," Emily said with a smile. "But I'll admit, Jeremy does add a certain dimension to it. Of course, when you get to be my age, there's only so many dimensions you need."

Lynn laughed again. She folded up the paper sack and dropped it on the stack of newspapers beside the garbage can. When she straightened up, all of the amusement had gone out of her expression. She brushed her hands on her skirt and sighed.

Emily noticed the change in atmosphere at once. "Lynn? What's the matter? You look troubled."

"Oh. Oh, I'm sorry. It just suddenly struck me—I don't want to sound maudlin—but it struck me that you're very lucky to have Ransom around. He's the type of person who knows how to take care of things."

"Why, of course I'm lucky, dear." Emily kept her attentive gaze trained on the young woman. It hadn't been all that long since Lynn's lover had died, and Emily thought that this might be one of those occasions where an innocent word or gesture had brought back a flood of memories to someone experiencing a loss. "But you haven't told me what's wrong."

As she answered, Lynn bent down and retrieved a bucket and an assortment of cleaning products from the cabinet beneath the sink. "I got a very sad call last night from a woman who was looking for someone to stay with her mother."

"Really?" Emily replied with puzzled interest. "Why would she call you?"

"My name was given to her by a friend of a friend. Her name is JoAnna Pearson."

"But you don't do that sort of thing."

"I know, I told her that. But it was an emergency and she was trying to find anyone who might be free during the day to stay with her mother, at least until she could find somebody proper to do it. Of course, I had to explain to her that I'm not free during the day. A lot of people think that if you're self-employed you're available at the drop of a hat, but I have clients booked every day." She stopped and shook her head. "I felt awfully sorry for her. She sounded so desperate."

"You wanted to help her."

"Yes, I did, as a matter of fact."

Emily smiled. "It does you credit." She reached for the teapot and tilted it over her cup. As she replaced the pot, her expression became slightly distant. "I wonder why..." Her voice trailed off in the absent way that was her custom when pondering a problem.

"Why what?"

"Oh! I wonder why there was a *sudden* need for help?"

"Well, it seems that Mrs. Pearson, JoAnna's mother, may be ill."

Emily's eyebrows formed two high carets. "*May* be ill?"

Lynn nodded, then proceeded to explain the gist of her phone conversation with the worried daughter, which had included the fact that her mother believed she had seen an intruder and who she believed him to be. During the recital, Emily's eyebrows lowered to their usual position, as if the gravity of what she was hearing was pulling them down.

"JoAnna told you all of this?" Emily said when Lynn had finished.

Lynn shrugged. "Like I said, she seemed desperate. And when she thought I was going to refuse, I think she just wanted to try to convince me of how badly someone was needed."

"Yes, I suppose that's possible," Emily said, her teacup poised halfway between the saucer and her lips.

"Not that I needed any convincing. I know what it's like when someone needs to be taken care of. But I couldn't do it."

"It seems very curious...." Emily said vacantly.

"That she would tell me so much?"

"No, no—that the man that Mrs. Pearson saw did nothing more than walk out of the house."

This caught Lynn completely by surprise. She had closed the cabinet and was standing with a bucket and bottle of pine cleaner in her hands. "You think she actually saw someone?"

Emily looked up at the young woman. "I think it's very possible, don't you?"

'Well, I thought she was probably just dreaming, or maybe she's just..." Lynn faltered and her face flushed a dark, attractive red. "I can see I'm digging myself into a hole."

Emily smiled warmly. "It's all right. It's natural to assume when something like this happens to an elderly person that he or she might be confused, or perhaps worse. It's not right, but it's natural. The odd thing about it is that one might be confused at the age of forty without anyone attributing that confusion to being middle-aged.''

Lynn let out a deep, pleasant laugh that seemed to bubble up from an internal spring. ''Yes, that's true.'' She poured some of the pine cleaner into the bucket and put the bucket under the faucet.

''If Mrs. Pearson *were* forty years old and she told you this had happened, what would you think?''

''Well,'' Lynn said as she turned on the water, ''I guess I'd still think she'd been dreaming.''

''Or?''

''Or that she was unstable.''

''There, now! You see?'' Emily said triumphantly. She raised the cup to her lips and took a sip of tea.

Lynn was even more perplexed than before. She turned off the water and came over to the table, taking a seat across from Emily. ''No, I don't see. What are you saying?''

Emily put the cup down, folded her hands, and leaned forward slightly. It was the posture that always put Ransom in mind of a strict schoolmarm, and the one she usually adopted when about to impart something she believed to be important.

''If you would believe that of a younger woman, how much more so would you believe it of an elderly one?''

Lynn thought for a few seconds, then said, ''I still don't get it.''

''I mean that no matter who told you that story, the last thing you would think is that it actually happened. And yet, all of the evidence would indicate that it did.''

''The evidence?'' Lynn said, running her right hand through her long, tawny hair. ''She didn't say anything about there being actual evidence that someone broke in.''

''Of course not. She probably didn't look. I'm talking about the evidence you told me about. Didn't you say that

Mrs. Pearson was found on the landing, right where she would have been if her story had been true?"

"Yes, but—"

"Well, there you are!" Emily said, spreading her upturned palms.

"Where am I?" Lynn said, laughing, as she sat back in her chair.

"Since Mrs. Pearson is elderly, it's easier to believe that she was confused, or dreaming, or simply scatty than it is to believe the obvious." Emily leaned in a little more. "That she went to the landing, saw something that frightened her and fainted."

Lynn lowered her head and sighed, then raised her eyes to Emily. "You're right, and I'm ashamed of myself. After knowing you, you would think I'd know better."

Emily elevated her shoulders slightly. "As I said, it's a natural assumption."

"If what you say is true, then…"

"Then something very peculiar is going on in that house."

"That's putting it lightly," said Lynn.

Emily didn't seem to hear her. She had once again raised her cup halfway to her lips and held it there as she stared off into the distance. After a long silence, she said quietly, "Double, double, toil and trouble…."

"What?"

"Oh, I'm sorry," said Emily, replacing the cup without drinking. "I don't know why that came to mind, except…are you familiar with *Macbeth?*"

"Sure."

"That phrase has always rather haunted me. The three witches. It's so perfectly indicative of stirring up trouble, isn't it?"

Lynn smiled. "Is that what you think is going on? Emily, isn't it more likely—I'm sorry. I really do agree with what you were saying before, but…don't you think it's more likely that Mrs. Pearson just isn't well?"

"I wouldn't rule out that possibility," Emily replied, "But either way, it doesn't sound as if it's safe for her to be in that house alone, does it?"

As Emily took her next sip of tea there was a look on her face that made Lynn fear that she might be sorry she'd ever brought the matter up.

"Emily? What are you thinking?"

She set the cup back in the saucer. "I was just thinking that *I'm* available during the day…although it does seem that the most interesting things are happening there at night."

"You mean you could stay with Mrs. Pearson?"

"One does have to look out for one's own kind, you know," Emily said meaningfully.

Lynn said carefully, "Emily, in all probability there's nothing wrong over there, except for her health. And…I know you mean well, but…I think they're looking for someone who can…"

"Help?" Emily said with a more pronounced twinkle in her eye. Lynn was unsure whether Emily was offering assistance or finishing her sentence. The color returned to her cheeks.

"From what you say, the daughter is just looking for someone to be there, at least for the time being. And when it comes to summoning help in the case of a medical emergency, surely I can dial a phone." Her forehead creased and her smile faded. "Of course, I suppose you're right in a way. It would seem rather unusual…especially staying there at night…and then I would probably need assistance, and that would…" Her voice trailed off as she became lost in thought. At last, she said, "I suppose…yes, I suppose I could say that he's my grandson."

"What?"

"It's much easier than explaining who he really is."

Lynn shook her head and smiled. "Emily, you've lost me again. Who are you talking about?"

She looked at Lynn. "Jeremy, of course." She straight-

ened herself in her chair and folded her hands on the edge
of the table. "Now, I would like you to do two things for
me. First, I'd like you to call JoAnna Pearson and tell her
that you've found someone to stay with her mother, at least
on an interim basis. Then, if you wouldn't mind, I'd like
you to take me to see Jeremy."

The look on Lynn's face went from surprise to concern.
"Emily, you *really* think there's something wrong at Mrs.
Pearson's house, don't you?"

"Oh yes, my dear." She looked into the young woman's
eyes and read the uncertainty there. She leaned toward her
and smiled. "Let me put it this way. If I came to the top
of the stairs in the middle of the night and saw my late
husband walking out of the house, I would think there was
something wrong here, too."

Lynn's lips formed a half-smile as she gazed across the
table at Emily. As usual, Emily had managed to gently but
sharply put the whole matter into perspective: If she was
indeed the one who had told this strange story, Lynn would
have believed her without question. She felt brought up
short at the idea of how easy it was to dismiss the story of
another elderly woman.

"You are a crafty old thing, aren't you?"

Emily innocently lifted her cup to her lips as she said,
"I'm sure I don't know what you mean."

"SO I'M TO BE your grandson, am I?" Ransom tried to
sound skeptical, but the idea brought an unexpected warmth
to his heart that he wouldn't have admitted to anyone. Although he often thought of Emily as his adopted grandmother, this was the first tangible indication that she
thought the same way, even if she only meant it as a ruse.

Emily sat on the hard wooden chair across the desk from
him, her purse at her side and her hands folded neatly in
her lap. It was only the second time in their acquaintance
that she had been in his office. The first had been when
they had met: Emily had come to ask him to investigate

the death of a friend who was believed to have died of natural causes. On that occasion, Ransom had mistaken her for a dotty old woman. It was a mistake he never made again.

"If you're going to stay with the woman for a few days, that's fine," Ransom continued. "But why this cloak-and-dagger business? I don't see any reason to even bring me into it."

Emily replied patiently, "I've told you what happened at Mrs. Pearson's house."

"Yes, and I agree, someone should stay with her. And I can't think of anybody more resourceful than you to do it. But I certainly don't think the law is necessary in this case. It could probably be cleared up with medicine."

"That's entirely possible." Her tone was proper in the extreme, and Ransom was painfully aware that he had come close to crossing an invisible line. "I have no idea what the matter is at the moment, but I would like to be prepared for anything."

"By telling them I'm your grandson?"

Emily nodded. "By preparing them for your possible appearance on the scene as my grandson. It may seem an unnecessary deception, but it would allow you the freedom to visit me if needed without raising suspicions."

Ransom tapped the end of an unlit cigar against the top of his desk. "You realize that you're investigating without a license. And as far as my involvement goes, there's nothing to investigate. I couldn't launch any sort of inquiry unless a crime was actually committed."

"Not officially," Emily replied with a glance at the cigar, "but perhaps in an unpaid capacity?"

Ransom noticed her glance and unceremoniously stuck the cigar in his breast pocket. He leaned back in his chair and sighed heavily. "Emily, why do you want to get involved in this?"

She cleared her throat. "Everyone seems much too willing to dismiss Mrs. Pearson's story out of hand."

"You haven't even met her," Ransom said with a shrug. "They may be right."

"That's just the point, Jeremy." Her tone was severe. It was the nearest she had ever come to sounding as if she were scolding him, and she knit her eyebrows so closely together that she almost looked cross. "I haven't met her, and yet I'm willing to give her the benefit of the doubt."

Ransom laid his palms on the desk. "Emily, I know I couldn't dissuade you once you've made up your mind to do something. I wouldn't even try. Certainly you're not looking for my permission."

Her face relaxed. "No. I'm looking for your assurance that you would agree to the 'cover' I've proposed." She apostrophized the word, making it sound even more quaint than it otherwise would have coming from her. "It will allow me to call on you readily without anyone thinking it is strange for you to be around if I introduce you as my grandson."

"All right," Ransom said with an indulgent smile. "You know I could never refuse you anything. I would mount a protest about the whole thing if I thought there was really any danger, but I'm sure there's not. Unless, of course, Mrs. Pearson becomes a danger herself."

"Jeremy," Emily said coyly, "I suspect you're humoring me."

"Not at all," he replied in a tone that so closely echoed hers the idea of their being related seemed like more than just a ruse.

FOUR

AT FIRST JoAnna had been ecstatic at the news that Lynn had found someone who could stay with her mother for a few days, but her happiness faded noticeably when she learned the age of the proposed caretaker. Lynn tried her best to reassure her that Emily was quite capable, alert, and very reliable—she stopped short of telling her about the number of police cases in which Emily had been involved as an informal advisor, figuring that would alarm JoAnna rather than comfort her. Besides, Emily clearly wished that kept a secret, at least for the time being. But for all Lynn's efforts over the phone, JoAnna sounded only marginally convinced. In the end, she agreed that Emily could serve as a stopgap measure, and had to admit that her mother might find someone nearer her own age a less objectionable companion than someone half a century younger.

Lynn also explained (in a scenario that Emily had worked out with her beforehand) that Emily's one stipulation for taking on the task was that she be allowed to stay in the house rather than traveling home in the evenings. Lynn said that, given the distance to Abigail's house, it would be more convenient all the way around if Emily could just stay there. JoAnna wanted to feel relieved by this, because it would save her having to stay at her mother's house at night, but she wasn't too sure that she wouldn't end up taking care of two elderly women rather than one.

She asked tentatively, "Did you tell Ms. Charters what Mother said she saw?"

"Yes."

"And she wasn't scared?"

"Oh, no!" Lynn replied with a throaty laugh. "Emily isn't the type of woman to scare easily. She's more likely to find something like that interesting."

The "Oh" that followed this seemed to indicate that JoAnna didn't find that a promising reaction.

It was agreed that Lynn would bring Emily over later that day. Lynn spent the earlier part of the afternoon helping Emily pack a small case with enough linens and dresses to last her a few days, a small notebook and an aged, dog-eared copy of Macbeth she intended to reread if time and circumstances allowed.

Abigail Pearson's house was located on Chase Street at the north end of Rogers Park, just short of the northernmost border of Chicago. It was an awkward drive from Emily's house. Lynn opted for driving over to Lake Shore Drive and heading north until the Drive gives way to Sheridan Road. From there there was no choice but congested city streets.

Emily spent the time gazing with interest out the window, first silently watching the lake go by, then letting out an occasional "Hmm" as they passed through the various neighborhoods on their way. Her eyes would sometimes follow the line of one of the high-rise apartment buildings, then she would purse her lips and look as if she was deep in thought.

"Has this area changed much since you last saw it?" Lynn asked.

"Well, it's very interesting, you know," said Emily, breathily. "It's been quite some time since I've ridden up this way. It *looks* the same, and yet it seems to have changed, if you know what I mean."

"I'm not sure I do."

Emily furrowed her brow. "It's something like running into someone you haven't seen for a while. Outwardly they may look the same, though a little older, but somehow you sense that inwardly something has changed. Just in the nature of life that person would have had experiences that

you don't know about—they would have grown,
changed...."

"I see...." This set Lynn to thinking about her own life
and the all-too-recent death of her partner, Maggie, after a
relationship of many years. Lynn wondered whether or not,
if she ran into someone she hadn't seen for a long time,
that person would be able to sense the change in her. There
was something disquieting in the notion that she might not
be able to hide a personal tragedy from an acquaintance.

"Here we are," said Lynn as she steered the car onto
Chase.

Emily emitted a longer "Hmm" as she scanned one side
of the street, then the other. Lynn slowed the car to a crawl
as she tried to read the number plates on the buildings. The
street was lined with a wide variety of buildings, all of them
old. There were large, three-story buildings with apartments
big enough to house families; smaller, flat buildings from
the fifties that had more people but less character than their
older sisters; and huge, rambling houses built nearer the
turn of the century, when families were more inclined to
stay together under one roof.

"Oh my!" Emily said quietly as they came to a stop in
front of one of the houses.

"I think this is it," said Lynn. She didn't sound very
happy.

The house was an enormous, dark box with shuttered
windows on the first floor and unshuttered windows on the
second. The front door was dead center between the lower
windows. It had a curved top and a slight overhang that
would barely have provided sanctuary for one visitor
caught in the rain. To Emily, the front of the house looked
like the face of a heavyset woman who had received an
unpleasant surprise. The roof was steeply sloped and had
wide eaves, so that it looked not unlike a witch's cap that
had been pushed down too far on the woman's head. The
roof was topped by an ancient weather vane that had per-
manently rusted in a northeasterly direction.

"Why on earth does she want to keep this place?" said Lynn.

"Sentiment can be a very strong thing," Emily replied, though from the way she was looking at the house one would have thought she believed sentiment to be highly overrated.

Lynn helped Emily out of the car and retrieved the suitcase from the backseat. On the way up the walk, Emily had a chance to give closer inspection to the house and grounds. The structure itself looked sturdy enough, but although much care might have been taken to keep it up in the past, in recent years it had fallen into disrepair. The paint was cracked and peeling and had faded from whatever color it had been originally to a sort of dirty yellow. There were small cracks in two of the windows, and one of the shutters was slightly askew. The lawn had been carelessly mowed, leaving patches of tall grass here and there, and the garden around the front of the house had been allowed to run wild.

Lynn helped Emily up the three steps to the front door, then pressed the bell. Inside they could hear the doorbell ringing out in deep funereal tones. It was only a minute before the door was opened by JoAnna Pearson.

"Are you Lynn?" she said with a worried smile.

"Yes." Lynn extended her hand, which JoAnna shook limply.

"I'm JoAnna Pearson."

"I'm pleased to meet you. I wish it could've been under better circumstances. This is Emily Charters, the woman I spoke with you about."

JoAnna's eyes traveled down to Emily. The smile didn't fade, but it flickered as if it might suddenly go out entirely.

"Oh! How nice to meet you," she said, touching the old woman's hand rather than shaking it. She then cast an uncertain glance at Lynn. "Well...why don't you come in?"

"Thank you," said Emily as JoAnna stepped aside to admit them.

They found themselves in a large, open hallway. There

was a wide archway to the left leading to the living room, and another directly ahead through which the hallway continued to the back of the house. The high ceilings coupled with the lack of light made the interior of the house feel like a series of dark caverns.

The staircase was directly to the right. It had a heavy banister and the last few steps curved into the hall. As JoAnna closed the door behind them, Emily peered up at the landing.

"Yes it is, isn't it?" she said to herself.

"What?" Lynn asked.

"Oh, nothing. I'm sorry. Just thinking aloud."

An awkward silence fell among the three of them. JoAnna continued to look at Emily as if the fears she had entertained earlier—that she would end up taking care of two helpless women instead of one—were about to be realized. At last she took a deep breath, pressed her fingers together, and said, "Well, Mother is upstairs in her room. Should I take you up to meet her?"

"I think that would be best," said Emily with a knowing gleam in her eye that gave JoAnna the uncomfortable feeling that Emily had been reading her mind.

"I don't think Mother will be any trouble," she said a little too cheerfully as she preceded them up the stairs. "She seems to be perfectly...the same. I suppose I wouldn't be so worried about her if the doctors had been able to figure out what caused the...thing to happen."

"Perhaps they will," Emily said lightly, her hand gently resting on Lynn's arm as they ascended the stairs.

JoAnna glanced back over her shoulder at Emily. "I mean, they do say that this sort of thing happens sometimes.... I suppose when you get older, you should expect things to start—that eventually—"

"Yes, they do say that," Emily said.

Lynn looked down at her. Emily had a look on her face that Lynn could only have described as mischievous. She almost laughed.

"She's been just fine since I brought her home. If I hadn't found her here I wouldn't think anything had been wrong—I mean, to see her now, you wouldn't think anything had happened."

They reached the landing, and the three of them looked down into the hallway. It was like looking into a chasm.

"Yes, that's very curious, isn't it?"

JoAnna shot a questioning glance at Lynn, who merely answered with a smile and a shrug.

"Mother's room is over here. The first door on the right."

"I'll wait out here," Lynn said as she set the suitcase down by the railing.

JoAnna hesitated, then said, "Yes, I guess Mother would probably be less upset with just the two of us." She opened the door and led Emily into Abigail's bedroom.

Abigail was lying on the bed, propped up by a pile of pillows that raised her upper body as if on a hospital bed. She was wearing an eggshell-white dressing gown and her hands were folded beneath her breasts. Her long hair had been brushed and straightened, and her head was lying just barely to one side. There was a slight smile on her face. She looked almost as if she were lying in state.

Although Emily didn't know the woman, she thought she could sense telltale signs of the night's unusual activities on her face. Despite Abigail's smile, the lines around her eyes and mouth and across her forehead were deep and taut, as if she were being worried in her sleep. And occasionally there was a nervous twitch in the index finger of her right hand.

"I don't want to wake her," JoAnna whispered.

"I'm awake."

The voice was so deliberate and unexpected that a bolt ran through JoAnna's body. She looked at her mother, but saw no signs of movement. After several seconds, Abigail's eyes popped open.

"I said, I'm awake."

"I'm sorry, I didn't mean to disturb you," JoAnna said meekly.

"You didn't." She rolled her eyes in Emily's direction. "Do I know you?"

"We haven't met," Emily replied.

"Mother, this is Emily Charters. She's going to stay with you for a few days while we...while I try to figure out what you need."

"I need to be left alone!"

JoAnna folded her hands together and held them beneath her nose for a moment. "We talked about this, Mother. I don't think you should be left alone right now. Neither do the doctors. Miss Charters has offered to stay with you until I can arrange for something else. I thought you might—"

"I don't need looking after." Abigail managed to summon up enough energy to convey her anger.

"Of course you don't, Mrs. Pearson," Emily said with a firmness that commanded attention, "but perhaps it would be *safer* if someone stayed with you for the time being."

Abigail stared across the bed at Emily. She looked startled by the tone of her voice. She anxiously searched Emily's face for some indication that she wasn't imagining things. Finally she locked onto Emily's knowledgeable eyes, and an understanding passed between the two elderly women that escaped the notice of JoAnna, who stood by looking perplexed and unhappy.

"Yes," Abigail said at last, "I think it might be nice to have company."

"Thank you," Emily said primly.

There was a noticeable lessening of the tension in the room, and JoAnna released a relieved sigh so expressive of her stored-up anxiety that there was a slight tremolo in the escaping breath.

"Let me show you to your room. It's right next door."

"That would be nice," said Emily. She started to follow the young woman out of the room, but they were both stopped when Abigail called from the bed.

"JoAnna! What happened to my hats?"

"What?"

Abigail gestured toward the vanity, which had been cleared. "My hats! What happened to them?"

"I put them away while you were sleeping. I put them back in the hall closet where they belong."

"All of them?"

"Of course, all of them."

Abigail wearily laid back in the bed and said, "Oh, damn! Now I'll have to start all over!"

With one last worried look at her mother, JoAnna went out into the hallway and closed the door after Emily had passed through.

"Is everything all right?" Lynn asked as she picked up the suitcase.

"Yes," JoAnna replied. "She's agreed to let Emily stay."

"Forgive me," Emily interrupted, "but what was that business about the hats?"

"Oh, that," said JoAnna, her cheeks reddening. She was obviously embarrassed by her mother's foibles. "She dragged all of her hats out last night. She has dozens of them. They were all over the vanity and the floor...everywhere!"

"Did she explain what she was doing with them?"

"She said something about sorting them to decide which ones to get rid of, but who knows what she was *really* doing."

Emily clucked her tongue. "That's a shame."

JoAnna gave Emily a grateful smile, mistakenly taking her words as commiseration. She would have been much more embarrassed had she known what Emily was really thinking.

JoAnna showed Emily and Lynn into the second room along the hallway. It wasn't as opulently furnished as Abigail's, but it was serviceable and clean. A small chest of drawers, about the size one might expect to find in a child's room, was against the far wall. An antique wardrobe was to the left of the door. The bed was large and covered with a quilt that appeared to be an antique: Its design was made up of several series of triangles, and Emily vaguely remembered that the pattern was supposed to represent pine trees. As with Abigail's bed, there was a mountain of pillows stacked against the headboard. A single chair was set at an angle by the window, and outside the moonlight illuminated a huge maple tree that for all intents and purposes blocked the view.

"This used to be my room," said JoAnna.

"I see," said Emily.

JoAnna opened the window to air the room. "I wish we could keep things better. Mother does what she can, which isn't much, and there's a lady, Nedra Taylor who comes in and cleans. She should be here tomorrow morning. But we can only afford to have her here once a week. My brother pays for that." There was an odd note in her voice when she added the last part. Emily sensed there was some animosity between brother and sister.

"This will do quite nicely," she said.

"Will it really?"

Emily turned to the young woman. "Of course."

"Good." JoAnna looked down at the floor, then back up. "I'll leave you to unpack. I'm going to go down and see what I can do about dinner."

"There's really no need," said Emily. "I can manage."

"Oh, no...I couldn't...you're a guest."

"No, I'm here to help. And I might as well start straightaway. I'm sure you could use a rest. This must have been a very trying day for you."

For the first time, JoAnna looked as if part of her burden had been alleviated. But she was too unsure of the situation to entirely let go. "Well I appreciate that. But I'd feel better if I got dinner tonight."

"As you wish," Emily replied with a kind smile. JoAnna was about to leave when Emily said, "Oh! There was one thing I forgot to mention. I have a grandson, Jeremy, who may be stopping by to check on me from time to time." She paused, then added apologetically, "It can be a bother sometimes. He worries about me, you see, and he likes to make sure I'm all right. Just as you worry about your mother. I hope that's acceptable to you."

JoAnna looked uncertain as to how she felt about this development. Lynn decided to help.

"He really is a very nice man. He's the one who hired me for Emily. It would mean you'd have someone else to make sure everything was all right here."

This seemed to ease JoAnna's mind somewhat. "I'm sure that'll be fine." With a glance at Lynn, JoAnna left the room, closing the door behind her.

"That woman is very distressed, if you don't mind my stating the obvious," said Lynn.

"Indeed."

Lynn deposited the suitcase on the bed and opened it. "All right, Emily, what was that all about?"

"I can do that," Emily offered.

"Oh, no you don't!" Lynn replied as she began to unpack. "You may be here to help them, but I'm used to doing for you!" She performed the comic parlor-maid courtesy with which she usually accompanied statements of this nature. "Now, why don't you tell me what that was all about?"

"What do you mean?"

"That business on the landing when we came up. You seemed awfully interested when we were all looking down from there."

"Oh, yes," said Emily, sitting on the edge of the bed. "It is a very interesting view, don't you think?"

Lynn paused in the act of placing some of Emily's neatly folded linen in the top dresser drawer. "Why?"

"Because it's so open."

"Um hm?"

"Well, it just seemed to me that if you were looking

down from the landing, it would be very difficult to mistake what you were seeing.''

Lynn turned away and slowly resumed what she was doing. "I suppose. All things being equal.''

Emily smiled in a way that made her look like some form of ancient gnome. "Don't you mean, all *minds* being equal?''

Lynn closed the drawer. "How did Mrs. Pearson strike you?''

Emily sighed. "She seemed afraid. And angry.''

"Afraid of something here?''

"I don't think so. I think it's something very different from that." Emily shook her head slowly. "But I won't know until I've had a chance to talk with her more. If I were to hazard a guess, I would say that she's afraid of herself.''

"Herself?'' Lynn said as she pulled Emily's dark blue dress from the suitcase.

"You've seen for yourself how she's being treated. When I asked JoAnna about the hats, she said, 'Who knows what she was *really* doing with them?' But why should Abigail have been doing anything other than what she said: sorting them out?''

"In the middle of the night?''

"Why not, if she was awake and wanted to keep busy?''

"I suppose....''

"But more importantly, Abigail has seen something that everyone tells her she hasn't seen. I'm sure she's aware of the possible debilitations one can suffer as one grows older. Most likely she's afraid that something like that may be happening to her. By now she's been properly confused about what actually *did* happen. But she seemed quite relieved when I told her it would be safer to have someone here with her.''

"Safer? So she may be afraid of something more tangible? Then it really might not be safe to stay in this house."

Emily looked intently into Lynn's eyes. "I don't think it's safe for Abigail Pearson to be alone in this house."

FIVE

"HOW COULD YOU do something so stupid?" Gregory barked into the phone.

"Stupid? Why is it stupid?" Joanna was always a bit more willing to challenge her brother over the phone than she was when they were face-to-face. But the minute the words were out of her mouth, she regretted them. She knew that all Gregory would do was reinforce her own fears.

"You've hired some other old lady to go over and watch our mother, and you don't know why that's stupid?"

"I didn't hire her, she offered to do it. It's only until I can find someone else."

"Oh, great work, JoAnna! This Charters woman isn't charging you, so that's all right! What if something happens to her?"

There was an anxious pause before JoAnna said, "What do you mean?"

"What if something happens to her?" He was almost yelling.

"What could happen?"

"Of course, as usual, you haven't thought anything through, have you? Anything could happen, and we'd be liable! She could fall down the stairs. Or worse, Mother could hurt her!"

"Mother?" JoAnna couldn't believe what she was hearing. "She wouldn't hurt anyone!"

"Not if she was in her right mind, but what about now? For Christ's sake, JoAnna! Yesterday she was babbling about seeing Dad! If her mind is really going, there's no telling what she may do!"

"The doctors said they couldn't find anything wrong with her."

"*Physically,* Jo!" Gregory spat back. "Physically! They have no way of knowing if there's something wrong with her brain!"

"Greg, please calm down," JoAnna said, fighting back her mounting panic. These were things she hadn't thought of before, and now that Gregory was bringing them up, she was alarmed by the prospect. The possibility of her mother being in danger, at least due to her health, had been foremost in her mind. The idea that she might be a danger to others hadn't occurred to her. "I'm sure nothing will happen. Mother won't hurt anyone."

"And what if she does? What if she does something to this old woman you've got staying there? She could sue! Don't you realize that? This is the most idiotic thing you've ever done!"

JoAnna could feel her anger rising like bile in her throat. "I had to find somebody right away. Maybe if you could have done it better, you should've handled it."

"Oh, right," Gregory replied. "You've done something totally ridiculous and it's my fault, just like it always is!"

JoAnna could feel herself deflating. *I should've known better,* she thought. *I can never win an argument with him.*

After a long pause, she said, "Well, it's done now, so we're stuck with it. Now I'm going to try to find someone to hire to stay with Mother until we're sure she's all right."

"Um hm," Gregory replied. JoAnna could tell from his tone that there was more trouble to come. "You're going to hire someone, huh?"

"I'm going to have to. I have to work. I can't stay with her all the time."

"Well, I'll tell you something: I'm not paying for it!"

JoAnna was tempted to shoot back that nobody had asked him to, but she knew it would make matters worse, especially since eventually she would have to turn to him for financial assistance.

"It wouldn't be that expensive," she said tentatively. "The doctors didn't think she needed a nurse."

"Well, that's too bad, isn't it?"

JoAnna was completely stumped by this. "What do you mean?"

"Maybe Medicare would've paid for a nurse. I don't know. But I do know I can't afford to pay someone to baby-sit our mother twenty-four hours a day. And I'll tell you something else, JoAnna—something you obviously didn't think of—Medicare isn't going to pay someone to baby-sit, either! If she can't be on her own, she's going to have to go into a home!"

"You're not...serious," said JoAnna. The lump in her throat felt like it was melting. Her face became hot and tears ran down her face.

"You better believe I'm serious! That's all there is to it! There is no choice! Do you get that?"

"How can you—how can you be like this?"

"Like what? What I'm doing is facing facts but that's something you could never do, isn't it? Look, Jo, all your life I've tried to protect you, but I'm not going to be able to do that much longer! You're going to have to start facing facts!"

Unable to bear it anymore, JoAnna slammed down the receiver. It rattled in its cradle as she continued to clutch it with her shaking hand. She put her left hand over her right, closed her eyes, and took several deep breaths. As she slowly exhaled, the shaking in her body started to dissipate. It was a few minutes before she had calmed down enough to release the phone, and even then she thought a glass of wine would be necessary to completely calm her nerves, if that was even possible.

She went to the kitchen and poured some chardonnay into one of the long-stemmed glasses that had been a wedding present many years ago. Her husband hadn't taken them with him after the divorce. He hadn't wanted anything that they had accumulated together, and she had been so eager to get out of the relationship that she had asked for nothing in return. Nothing but the guarantee of his absence. She carried the glass of wine back out to the living room and collapsed on the couch.

It was all happening exactly the way she thought it would, only worse: She'd thought Greg would at least be willing to help financially, but now he'd made it clear he wouldn't. And after this most recent scene, she thought she was better off with him staying out of it. He had always been abusive, but when they were teenagers JoAnna had given him the benefit of the doubt, hoping that some day he'd grow out of it. Even though she was the younger of the two, she had considered herself more mature than he even then.

But there was no excuse for him now, any more than there was an excuse for herself. She couldn't believe she was such a coward. To JoAnna, she and her brother seemed to be growing backward: As he got older, Greg seemed to be getting angrier, while she seemed to be dwindling into nothing. There was a time when she thought she could fight back, but that time was now long past.

What's happening to me? she thought as she let her body sag against the back of her couch and closed her eyes.

THE DINNER JoAnna had provided for the two old ladies consisted of cold pasta and small green salads which they ate on trays in Abigail's room. As much as Emily appreciated having the meal prepared for her, as well as JoAnna's insistence on cleaning up afterward, she had been eager for JoAnna to leave so that she could talk with Abigail alone.

It was after seven when JoAnna finally, reluctantly, left the house. Emily first went to the kitchen to prepare a pot of tea. Like the rest of the rooms, the kitchen had a high ceiling that gave her the feeling of being in the bottom of a pit. The walls were a dark blue, which made the room seem narrower than it was, and there were splatters of grease on them, showing that it had been a long time since anyone had given any serious thought to washing them down.

The appliances were old and familiar: There was an olive-green refrigerator from which some of the enamel had chipped away, and a gas range that was desperately in need of a good scrubbing. But both of them appeared to be in good condition otherwise. Emily found an old-fashioned teakettle in the cabinet under the sink, and after rinsing it out she filled it with water and put it on the range to boil. She found teacups in another cabinet. She laid two of them out on a tray along with a cup of milk and the sugar bowl. When she had finished preparing the tea, she carried the tray up to Abigail's room. Although Emily had professed her abilities earlier, she did find the climb up the stairs a bit taxing. But by taking it slowly she was able to manage with very little trouble. She gave a single knock on Abigail's door, then pushed it open and went in without waiting for an answer.

Abigail was still propped up by the pillows. Her eyes were closed, but she was very slowly drumming her fingers on top of the blanket. A large, steel-framed fan was on a stand by the window, methodically oscillating, blowing warm air around the room.

"I thought you'd like some tea," said Emily as she sat the tray on the bedside table.

"Thank you," Abigail said with a smile. "My daughter would be appalled if she saw this. Hot tea in the summer."

Emily nodded as she poured out. "I like to think it equalizes temperature, don't you?"

"Of course it does."

"Young people don't always know these things." This wasn't the type of thing Emily would normally say, because she was loath to generalize about any person or group. But she thought it would help establish something of a rapport with the other woman. She poured herself a cup of tea and took it with her to the chair on the other side of the bed.

Once she had settled herself, she said, "This is a very nice house."

"Ha! It's old and full of cobwebs. Like me." Abigail blew over the top of her tea, then took a tentative sip.

Emily made a sound something like *tut*.

"We bought the house...it must be over forty years ago. It wasn't perfect even then. Whoever built this place had his head screwed on backward. Seemed to want the type of house where company would be welcome, but didn't do anything to facilitate them. One bathroom in a place this size, if you can imagine! We had to put more in. And the cellar was only half finished. You wouldn't think you'd find a dirt floor in a city like this but we had to finish it ourselves."

Emily nodded. "It seems primitive by today's standards, I'm sure, but there was many a stately home back then built the same way."

Abigail smiled. She seemed pleased to be able to share with someone who remembered how things once were. She warmed to the subject. "The whole house was like that. We did everything: papered the bedrooms, painted the downstairs, laid the carpet. I even sewed curtains. I used to be good with a needle and thread. Oh, I wanted to make this house look beautiful." She paused, and the corners of her mouth turned down. "I don't fool myself. I know the house has run down. But I've lived here for over half my life. It's the only thing I own."

"And you love it. That's perfectly understandable."

A cloud of uncertainty slowly crossed Abigail's face. Emily wondered what had caused it, but even though her intention was to discover what, if anything, was going on in the house and the family, she thought it best to proceed carefully. She was there in the guise of a caretaker, and didn't want to arouse suspicions by appearing too nosey. She decided to let Abigail's interesting reaction go for the time being, hoping that an opportunity to broach the subject might present itself later.

"I suppose…" Abigail began, then interrupted herself to take a sip of tea. As she set the cup back in the saucer on her lap, she continued, "I suppose my daughter told you about what happened?"

"Of course."

Abigail sighed. "My son and daughter think I'm losing my mind. Or my health. Or both. I guess they should know. They're both very smart, my children. JoAnna, she's the regional salesperson for Lavender Cosmetics. It's a very important position, so she says. And Gregory—he's my son, you haven't met him—he's the head of his division at the Gorden Chemical Plant out in the suburbs. Do you know it?"

"No. I'm afraid I don't."

"It's a very big company," Abigail said wistfully, "and he's a very important person. Both of my children are intelligent. And they both think I'm…that there's something wrong with me."

"There are many kinds of intelligence," Emily said after a pause, "and it's possible to be intelligent and still be wrong."

Abigail said slowly. "But…it is crazy, isn't it? To think I saw my husband?"

Emily set aside her cup of tea and folded her hands in her lap. "Why don't you tell me exactly what happened?"

Abigail looked as if she wasn't sure at first whether or not Emily was seriously interested or just humoring her, but after a moment she related exactly what she remembered of the event, while Emily sat forward slightly with her intent gaze fastened on Abigail's face. When she had finished, Emily said, "You didn't see his face?"

Abigail shook her head. "No. Just the top of his head."

"Hmm." Emily fell silent as she mentally ran over the details.

"You don't believe me, do you?" Abigail sounded almost petulant.

Emily looked at her with surprise. "Of course I do. Your

explanation certainly fits the facts as we know them: why you were found on the landing, and why you had collapsed even though there was nothing physically wrong with you, other than your angina. And a bout of angina certainly wouldn't explain what you were doing on the landing.''

"Gregory insists I was dreaming."

"That's the comfortable explanation," Emily replied. "I'm sure there was something dream*like* about what you saw, but that doesn't mean you were dreaming." Emily sat back in her chair and thought for a minute. "You know, when you described what happened it sounded almost as if you were describing a scene from a movie or a play. Like something that was stage-managed."

"How can that be?"

"I don't know, but I think the pertinent question is not *how*, but *why*. The man didn't harm you or take anything from the house. Nor did he run when he heard you. From your account he simply strolled out the door. Which means the reasons for his being here must be very, very curious."

For a moment there was a little hope in Abigail's eyes, but it quickly abated. Her hands tightened around the edge of her blanket.

"There's another explanation," she said.

"Hmm?"

"Maybe Gregory and JoAnna are right. Maybe my mind is starting to go."

Emily shook her head slowly. "You mustn't think like that. I have spent a few hours with you now, and you seem to me to be a perfectly capable woman who has had a shock. If you're guilty of anything at the moment, it is of allowing some well-meaning relations to confuse you. Take away your son and daughter who keep telling you that you couldn't possibly have seen anything and what are you left with? The fact that you saw what you saw. The easiest thing to do is to explain it away by saying it didn't happen. It's much more difficult to explain just exactly why it *did* happen.''

There was a pause, then Abigail reached out and gripped the little woman's hand firmly.

"Thank you, Emily," she said fervently.

Emily returned a gentle smile and said, "Not at all."

Abigail released her hand and slumped back against the pillows. Emily's reassurance seemed to have alleviated Abigail's pent-up tensions, and with that relief came the exhaustion that often accompanies the end of a long period of stress.

Emily wished her good night. Abigail was barely able to reply before she'd fallen asleep.

WHEN EMILY AWOKE the room was pitch-dark, and it was a few moments before she remembered that she wasn't in her own house. She had the groggy, half-waking feeling that her sleep had been disturbed by something other than natural causes. Somewhere dimly in her mind, she thought she'd heard a noise. She lay there listening, all the while feeling her body grow heavier as sleep tried to draw her back into its welcoming arms. She was startled out of this state by a distant rap that sounded like two pieces of wood being knocked together.

Emily sat up, then climbed out of bed. The long gray hair she usually kept neatly in a bun had been unpinned for the night and hung down the back of her sensible white-cotton nightgown. She crossed to the light switch by the door and flipped it, but the ceiling light didn't come on.

"Bother!" she said softly as she opened the door.

The hallway was not completely dark. Moonlight streamed in through a window at the end of the hall, casting four elongated rectangles across the floor. She realized her room had seemed dark because the huge tree outside blocked the reflected light. She could hear a soft shuffling noise which she thought was coming from the direction of the living room.

She started toward the staircase, and chuckled to herself as the moonlight glanced across her nightgown. *Anyone who saw me right now would think I was haunting the place,* she thought.

She stopped at Abigail's door and opened it very quietly. Since the windows in the room were only partially blocked by the tree, there was more light than there was in Emily's room: enough light to see that the bed was empty.

She closed the door and continued to the railing by the stairs. To the left was a light switch for the hallway, which she tried to no avail. The shuffling continued in the living room below.

Emily placed her right hand on the newel post to steady herself, then called out in a clear, distinct voice, "Abigail?"

The shuffling stopped immediately.

Emily was dimly aware of movement, which lasted only a few seconds, followed by a muffled click somewhere at the back of the house. There wasn't as much light on the staircase as there had been in the hall, but it was enough for her to guardedly feel her way down the stairs. She knew there was a certain amount of foolishness involved in what she was doing, but she set aside the admonition concerning fools and angels by reminding herself that she didn't believe in ghosts, and that whoever had paid the earlier visit to the house hadn't harmed anyone.

She reached the bottom of the stairs and crossed to the archway leading to the living room. She felt the walls on either side of the entrance and found the light switch on the right.

I might as well try it, she thought with an inward sigh. Much to her surprise, two floor lamps sprang to life at the flip of the switch. Although neither of the lamps was particularly bright, after the darkness in which she'd groped her way down the stairs, the glow was almost blinding.

When her eyes had adjusted, Emily was further surprised to find that there was apparently nothing wrong with the room. Although not arranged with a great deal of care, the furniture seemed to be placed logically. However, indentations in the carpet showed that some of the pieces had recently been moved.

If only I'd had a chance to look in this room earlier, Emily thought, *I would be able to tell if something had been changed.*

She sighed deeply, then switched off the lights. She was hardly aware of the slow journey back up the stairs, her mind was so occupied with the strange goings-on. She stopped when she reached the top and rested for a moment. She took a deep breath and exhaled, then crossed the hall to Abigail's door. Once again she quietly opened it.

Abigail was lying on her side in the bed. Her mouth hung open slightly and her breathing was slow and steady.

Emily closed the door.

SIX

DESPITE HER NOCTURNAL adventures, Emily rose early the next morning. She wanted to survey the interior of the house before Abigail stirred. After bathing, she put on the navy blue cotton dress that Lynn had hung in the closet for her, then carefully wound her hair into a bun and pinned it at the back of her head. She then embarked on her inspection of the house.

Besides a bathroom, there were only two other rooms on the second floor, both directly opposite the bedrooms that were currently occupied. The first was a bedroom in which all of the furniture had been covered with white sheets. The sheets were coated with a thick layer of dust. Heavy window shades, yellowed with age, were pulled down over the windows. The second room, the one farthest down the hall, was identical to the first with the exception of a recess in the corner to the right of the door. This proved to be a narrow, steep staircase leading to a trapdoor, presumably the entrance to the attic. Emily emitted a gentle "Hmm" as she stared up at the wooden planks that comprised the door.

Although she hadn't touched anything, she absently brushed her hands together as she left the room. She returned down the hall to the staircase and was just about to begin her descent when she was stopped suddenly by a noise from below. Once again she heard what sounded like furniture being moved in the living room. Instead of calling out this time, Emily quietly went down the stairs to see what was happening.

When she reached the bottom, she went to the side of the archway and looked into the room. At the far end was a woman moving a small occasional table to the side of the couch. The woman was well over fifty years old, with blotchy brown skin and hair the color of rust, which she covered with a kerchief tied under her chin. She wore a faded blue jumper and a dingy white apron. Once she had positioned the table to her satisfaction, she grabbed a wing chair and set it in the corner, then went to an easy chair and pushed it a few inches to the right. She worked quickly and efficiently, but she seemed anxious to get the job done, like an elf who had waited a bit too long to help the shoe-maker.

"You must be Nedra," said Emily.

The woman let out a truncated shriek and wheeled around, her right hand flying up to her heart.

"Jesus!" she exclaimed. "Don't be sneaking up on somebody and saying something out of the blue like that! You're like to give a body a heart attack!"

"I'm so sorry," Emily said with amused sincerity.

"Half the time I expect a ghost to come sneaking up behind me here!"

Emily smiled. "It is a very old house."

Nedra fanned herself with her hand for a moment, uttered something like "ooph," then eyed Emily. "Who are you?"

"My name is Emily Charters. I'm Ms. Pearson's guest."

Nedra let her hand drop to her side and sighed. "Pleased to meet you. Like you said, I'm Nedra." She glanced down at the glass-topped coffee table, frowned, and pushed it a little to the left. "Honestly!" she said under her breath.

"Nedra, may I ask what you're doing?"

Nedra shot her a rueful smile. "It's just a little game me and Ms. Pearson play."

"A game?"

"Oh, yes. Ms. Pearson, she likes to rearrange the furniture for me. I just put it back, nice as you please, and act like nothing's happened." She became more confidential. "First I thought she might was just giving me something to do, not like I don't have enough work to do in this big ol' house.''

''I'm sorry,'' Emily said, her expression highly quizzical, ''I don't understand.''

''Don't you!'' Nedra gave an affectionate laugh. ''Neither do I!''

''No—what I mean is, if Ms. Pearson rearranged the furniture, why are you putting it back?''

''Because it upsets her so bad.''

''I beg your pardon?''

Nedra shifted from one leg to the other and put her hands on her hips. ''I came here one mornin' and all the furniture was all moved 'round. When Ms. Pearson comes down, I told her I liked what she did with the room. Well, she went white in the face, and she rushes in here and you would've thought she'd seen a ghost. She yells out, 'What happened here? Who did this?' She looked like she was crazy! Then she told me, 'Put it back! Put it back!' Well, I put it all back like she says, but next week when I come here, all the furniture, it was put in the middle of the room. All bunched up. Ms. Pearson near had hysterics over that. Since then, I don't say nothin' about it. Every week I get here the furniture's been moved around. I just put it back where it belongs, hopefully before she comes down in the morning. She gets down early, and there's something out of place, I just say, 'Oh, no, Ms. Pearson, I moved that myself 'cause I'm gonna clean under it.' That pretty much sets her mind at ease, but she still don't look too happy about it.''

The featherlike creases at the corners of Emily's mouth dropped downward, and her brows slanted in toward the top of her nose. ''Tell me, when did this first happen?''

Nedra shrugged. ''Oh, five, six weeks ago.''

''Five or six weeks ago....'' Emily repeated absently.

''Poor thing,'' Nedra said, shaking her head sympathetically. ''You wanna know the truth, Miss Charters, she's getting up in years and I think she's startin' to give way.''

Emily's eyes widened. "That certainly is possible. Has anything else happened? Other than the moving furniture?"

Nedra glanced at the archway to make sure Abigail wasn't coming down the stairs, then leaned close to Emily. She gave every sign of meaning to whisper, but her nasal voice was still sharp enough to carry. "There been other things. JoAnna—Ms. Pearson's daughter—she been asking after her mother, ever since I told her about the furniture. I didn't like to tell her nothin' else, after how much it worried her when I told her about the first time the furniture was moved around."

"But what else has been happening?"

Nedra glanced at the archway again, then leaned a little closer. "I find things. I find things where they're not supposed to be."

Emily elevated her shoulders slightly. "After all, it's not unusual to misplace things."

"Not like that," Nedra said, making a concerted effort to lower her voice. "It's things like, I found Ms. Pearson's hairbrush in the refrigerator one time. 'Nother time, I found one of her nightgowns stuffed halfway down the drain in the kitchen sink. It's not like she just been forgetful, Miss Charters. It's like my Aunt Sarah when her mind started to go. She used to walk out of the house in the middle of the night, middle of winter, with nothing on but a nightie and a smile. I try..." Nedra's voice broke. Tears welled and hung like two soggy crescents atop her lower lids. "I try not to let Ms. Pearson know I found nothing. I been with her a lot of years, and I don't want to see nothing happen to her. But I'm afraid for her. I don't know that she should be on her own. Lord knows what happens during the week when I'm not here."

Emily looked up suddenly at the woman's face, then her gaze traveled off into the distance. "Yes, yes...that's an interesting question."

"What, miss?" Nedra dabbed her eyes with her wrists.

"Oh, I'm sorry," Emily replied, coming back to herself.

"You shouldn't distress yourself. You've been very good to Ms. Pearson, and I'm sure she appreciates it. It's possible you've been a greater help to her than you know." Emily paused for a moment, then said, "Now, Nedra, tell me, do you have a key to this house?"

She drew back slightly. "'Course I do."

"I understand that you work Wednesday mornings. Have you ever had to come here at any other time?"

"What are you sayin'?"

"Forgive me, I put things so badly." Emily looked properly regretful. "It's just that Mrs. Pearson woke the other night and thought someone was in the house. I thought, perhaps, you'd needed to come here for something."

"If something's gone missing, I'm not the one that took it. More than likely Ms. Pearson just put it somewhere she forgot."

"Oh, no, no, no, my dear. I'm not accusing you of anything. Nothing would be more natural if you'd forgotten something than for you to slip in to retrieve it. No, I'm only trying to account for the unexpected presence of someone here late at night."

"I wouldn't know about that," Nedra replied, not completely mollified. But from the look on her face, it was apparent she realized there might be more problems with her employer than she feared. "But if you ask me, there never was anyone here. Poor Ms. Pearson just ain't right anymore. Much as I hate to say it."

"Nedra?"

Abigail stood in the archway, her right hand lightly touching the wall for balance. Nedra was startled at the sound of her voice, but didn't cry out. She gave a worried glance to Emily, then said, "Good morning, Ms. Pearson."

Abigail's eyes did a quick, anxious scan of the room. "Is everything…in order?"

"Yes, it is."

"Good, good," Abigail replied, her body visibly relaxing. "Good morning, Emily."

"Good morning," said Emily, crossing the room to her. "It's good to see you up and about, but you really didn't need to do it. I would've been glad to bring your breakfast up to your room."

"I'm not an invalid," Abigail said crossly.

"Of course you're not. But that doesn't mean that you shouldn't rest after what you've been through."

Abigail hesitated, then smiled. "You're right. I'm still tired." She glanced back into the living room, where Nedra had started dusting. "I just wanted to make sure everything was all right."

Emily looked her squarely in the eyes and said firmly, "Everything is exactly as it should be."

As on their first meeting, Abigail seemed to take a great deal of comfort from Emily's reassurance. "All right. But I've been in bed enough. I'm going to go upstairs and get myself dressed and done up, then I'll come down to breakfast."

"Very good," said Emily. "Would scrambled eggs be all right?"

"That would be fine."

Abigail went up the stairs.

"See what I mean?" said Nedra, thumping her temple with her index finger. Without waiting for a response, she continued moving the furniture back into place.

Emily resumed her interrupted investigation of the house. Just past the living room, on the left side of the hallway, was the dining room. It was large and might have been quite sunny were it not for the thick bushes that had overgrown the windows. The far wall was comprised of a huge built-in sideboard, the center of which was a sliding panel about a foot and a half high and three feet wide that opened into the kitchen.

On the opposite side of the hallway, through a door beneath the staircase, was a den, or what Emily thought might have been called a TV room by the family. An easy chair and small table were set at an angle in one corner of the room, facing a very old console television set. A brocade settee was placed under the window.

Having satisfied herself that she was now more familiar with her surroundings, Emily went into the kitchen to start breakfast. She was pulling a carton of eggs from the refrigerator when she saw something she hadn't noticed the night before. In the corner, just past the refrigerator, there was another door. She set the eggs on the counter, went to the door, and turned the knob.

"Nedra?" she called out.

"Yes, miss?" Nedra's voice reached the kitchen before she did. She followed soon after carrying a well-used dust rag.

"Do you know where this door leads?"

"Down the basement." She wiped her free hand on her dress.

"It seems to be locked."

"Never been opened that I know of. Never had to go down there myself. All my cleaning things are kept in the closet over there." There was a pause, then she added, "You need something down there? I could try and find a key if you like, but I don't know where it would be."

"No, that's all right, I was just curious."

"All right, then," Nedra said with a shrug as she left the room.

There were three hinges on the right side of the door. Emily reached out and ran her finger along the middle hinge. It had recently been oiled.

BY THE TIME Abigail reappeared, Emily had prepared a large plate of scrambled eggs, a few slices of toast, and a pot of tea. The kitchen table was set with the only china she'd been able to locate: cream-colored plates with vines printed around the perimeter.

Abigail looked rested, though the anxiety in her eyes showed that she was still ill at ease. Emily suspected that, like anyone who has suffered an unexplained illness or event, Abigail was acting as if she was unsure how to proceed with her everyday activities for fear of accidently triggering the event again.

She wore a loose-fitting gray dress with a thin, ropelike belt around the waist, and had tied her hair at the back of her neck with a black ribbon.

"Did you sleep well?" Emily asked casually.

"Yes, I did," Abigail replied with a guarded glance. "Did you?"

"As well as I normally do. I've found as I've gotten older that I can be a bit restive in the night. I usually wake up several times." She mentally crossed her fingers. She didn't like to lie, but felt this harmless deception acceptable under the circumstances. Unfortunately, it didn't succeed.

"I usually sleep like a top," Abigail said with forced heartiness.

"Really?" Emily looked perplexed. "I only wondered because one time when I woke last night I came down for a glass of water, and I looked in on you to make sure you were all right, and you weren't there."

Abigail's eyes widened for a second, then contracted. "I must've been in the bathroom."

"Of course, that's just what I thought," Emily replied. "Well, breakfast is all ready."

Abigail gave her a uneasy smile as she took a seat. "I really should be ashamed of myself, letting you cook the breakfast. You're my guest."

"Nonsense," Emily said as she sat across from her. "You haven't been well, and I'm pleased to help out. But whenever you feel up to it, you just let me know and you can do everything yourself."

Abigail looked up at her apprehensively. "You mean you'll leave?"

"I didn't mean that at all," Emily replied. "From what you've told me, your children treat you as if you are an invalid. I merely wanted you to understand that I know you're not." Her tone implied a slight disapproval at the children's presumption.

For the first time, Abigail laughed. "Do any of your children live in town?"

Emily raised her brows. "My children? Oh, no. Only my grandson, Jeremy."

Abigail swallowed a forkful of eggs. "They're amazing things, children. I guess mine are like everybody else's. When they were younger, they doted on me; when they got older, they all but ignored me; and now they act like I'm the child."

Emily nodded. "It's always seemed to me that parents need to content themselves to gracefully fade out of the picture if they don't want to be heartbroken."

"My children—especially JoAnna—they've always kept in touch. Drop in from time to time. But more in the past couple of years."

"Really?" Emily said, her interested tone meant to draw Abigail out further.

She laughed again. "Guess it's age. Who knows? Maybe they're afraid they'll lose me. JoAnna stops by every day, and calls, and Gregory comes over when he's not too busy." Her voice was curiously flat when she mentioned her son.

"I imagine he's very busy," Emily said, sounding as if she were sympathizing.

"Yes." Abigail took another bite of eggs and washed it down with some tea.

Emily found this reaction very interesting. She thought it likely that Abigail's reticence on the subject of her son could be attributed to hurt feelings over the infrequency of his visits. But if that were the case, she would have expected Abigail to simply say so. The fact that she didn't left Emily feeling that there was a deeper reason for the rift.

"Anyway," Abigail said, heaving a sigh, "I don't know

why they've gotten so fiddly about me these past few years. It's not like I'm leaving them anything. I'm not a rich woman, you know.''

"Perhaps they love you," Emily said simply.

Abigail glanced at her over the rim of the cup that was poised to her lips. She lowered it slightly and smiled. "They do love me. They're good kids."

"Do you have any grandchildren?" Emily asked.

"Oh, yes!" Abigail brightened. "Cassie—that's Jo-Anna's girl—she's out in Seattle. I don't see her or hear from her much. And Robert! He's Gregory's son." She added with obvious affection, "Robert's a pistol!"

"Is he?" Emily raised her eyebrows inquiringly.

"I'm at that age, I guess, where I think young people—the good ones, at least—are a lot of fun. Don't you think so?"

"Yes, I do," Emily replied with gusto. "There's something about the young that makes one feel as if everything will be all right with the world—that the generations will carry on."

A cloud seemed to darken Abigail's face again. It was the same uncertainty that Emily had noticed the night before when they were talking about the house.

"But tell me about your grandson. Why do you say he's a pistol?"

The cloud passed as quickly as it had come. "He just is! I don't know how to explain it. I guess because he's just starting out, really. He's had some knocks already. He hasn't found a suitable job, for one. But he's working. Do you notice how most young people nowadays always expect everything right away? Well, Robert isn't like that. I guess there's something old-fashioned about him. He married his sweetheart, you know. Nice girl, way too thin, named Leslie. While they were in college. Now doesn't that sound like something we did when we were their age?"

Emily nodded readily. She couldn't help noticing that Abigail spoke of her grandson with more affection than she had of her own son. "Did you get married when you were in school?"

The happiness drained from Abigail's face almost as if someone had pulled the plug on it. She stared down at what was left of her eggs. "No. Not while I was in school. But right after. It was a mistake. It wasn't a happy time."

"I'm so sorry."

"I was… You see, I was raised with a very firm hand."

"Well, we all were in those days," Emily said lightly.

Abigail glanced at her, then lowered her eyes again. "I don't mean that. I mean with a *firm hand*. I was happy to get married, but my husband, as it turned out, he wasn't very good to me, and he carried on."

"Carried on?"

"With other women, all the time. Though how he could find anyone else but me to put up with him is beyond me." A smile stole across her face. "I never would've admitted it at the time, but the day he left me, that was the happiest day of my life." She looked up suddenly, her eyes wide, and said, "You don't think that's what Robert did, do you?"

Emily cocked her head; her eyes grew more intense. "I'm afraid I don't know what you mean."

"You don't think he married too young, do you?"

"I would have no way of knowing," Emily replied.

"He wouldn't turn out like his grandfather, would he?"

Emily was quite puzzled by the turn the conversation had taken. "Did he even know his grandfather?"

"No…no…" Abigail said vacantly. "I just don't want to think I made a mistake…."

"A mistake?"

Abigail looked up and smiled. "You're right. Robert is a fine boy. There's nothing to worry about."

Good heavens, Emily thought. She was beginning to wonder if she might have been a bit precipitous in her defense of this woman.

AFTER BREAKFAST, Abigail chatted a while longer while Emily did the dishes. By now, Abigail seemed much more comfortable neglecting her hostess duties. She didn't offer to help. It didn't matter to Emily, who was just as happy to keep busy. When the work was done, Abigail expressed her fatigue and retired to her bedroom.

Once Abigail had gone, Emily poured herself another cup of tea and sat at the kitchen table ruminating over what she'd learned so far, which was precious little. It seemed clear to her that if Abigail Pearson was in her right mind, the recent events could only mean one thing: Somebody was trying to scare her. But to what end? She had angina, but would it be possible to *frighten* her into her grave? And who would do such a thing?

Emily's forehead creased with perplexity. She took a sip of tea, then set the cup back in its saucer. She was bothered by the thought that she really couldn't be sure at this point that Abigail *was* in her right mind. Her peculiar reaction to some of the subjects Emily had brought up was certainly worrisome, but there could be many reasons for that. The one that presented itself most readily was that there were some family skeletons at play here that troubled Abigail. Then there was the matter of the moving furniture. Abigail hadn't been in bed when Emily heard the noise below, though her explanation for her absence had been logical, if a bit convenient. But if Abigail had been the one moving the furniture, how could she have gotten back upstairs without being heard? In her inspection of the house, Emily hadn't found another staircase to the second floor.

She sighed heavily. Even if it was Abigail who moved the furniture in the night, to the despair of Nedra, there was no reason to believe there was a sinister or psychological reason for it. It could be nothing more than the odd form of somnambulism.

Emily shook her head and went back to her original thought: If someone was trying to scare Abigail, who could it be? Setting aside for the moment any thought of the er-

rant husband, there were Abigail's children, Gregory and
JoAnna. She hadn't met the son yet, but the daughter
seemed perfectly sincere in her distress over her mother's
health. Abigail also said that both children had expressed
concern over her mental state, but that was natural, too,
under the circumstances. The only other relations she had
mentioned were a granddaughter who lived out of state, and
Robert, the grandson she seemed to love more than her own
children. Presumably these were the only four people who
could benefit from anything happening to Abigail.

I suppose, thought Emily, *I should try to find out who
would gain from Abigail's death. But it would be difficult
to ask about her beneficiaries without sounding overly in-
quisitive.*

Emily's mind made the natural progression from "Who
would benefit?" to "What would he or she gain?" Abigail
had said she wasn't a rich woman, and that was reflected
in the condition of the house. But Emily was all too aware
of the tendency of some people to value frugality to the
point of squalor. She smiled to herself. If Jeremy had been
there, he would surely have cited the example of Ebenezer
Scrooge.

But insisting on taking things at face value—at least for
the moment—Emily chose to assume that Abigail had been
telling the truth about her financial status. Still, what might
not be riches to the old woman might seem like a fortune
to her children. And then there was the house. It must be
worth something.

"Miss Charters?" Nedra stood in the doorway holding
a bucket from which protruded a variety of rags.

"Yes, Nedra?"

"I'm ready to do the kitchen, if you don't mind." She
wiped the back of her wrist across her temple, pushing the
kerchief askew.

"Certainly," Emily replied with a smile. She was
tempted to mention that the stove needed a good cleaning
and the walls could use a wash-down, but she restrained

herself. After all, it wasn't her place to instruct a worker in a house in which she was a guest. She contented herself to thank the powers that be for her good fortune in having Lynn Francis working for her. And she reminded herself that while Nedra might not be very efficient, she suspected the cleaning woman of having a very kind heart.

With some time to herself, Emily retrieved her shopworn copy of *Macbeth* and settled herself in an armchair in the living room. *All this speculating has left me feeling as if my head were full of dust, and Shakespeare is just the thing to sweep it away,* she thought.

The creaking, looming old house provided the perfect backdrop in which to read the story of treachery, deceit, witchcraft, and murder. Though she never thought herself given to flights of fancy, Emily felt as if the room was darkening around her as the witches spouted their unholy prophecies. It was comforting to hear Nedra softly singing in the distance as she did her chores.

She read through Act One, pausing here and there, as was her custom, to savor the poetry, and stopped when she reached the end of the act, the last line of which struck a chord with her.

"False face must hide what the false heart doth know...." she read aloud. Her mind went to JoAnna. "I wonder."

Emily continued to read until just before noon, when she was interrupted by the arrival of JoAnna, who came noisily through the front door carrying two shopping bags full of groceries. She was dressed in a navy blue business suit and a white blouse with a small black bow at the neck.

"Oh! Hello," she said breathlessly, spotting Emily through the doorway. "I noticed that the refrigerator wasn't very well stocked yesterday, so I took an early lunch and did some shopping."

"That was very nice of you."

JoAnna set the bags down and came into the room. "And

I wanted to see how... Is everything all right? I mean, how's Mother doing?''

"She's doing just fine. She came down for breakfast this morning, we talked for quite some time, and now she's having a nap.''

"Good,'' JoAnna said with a definite lack of confidence. She sounded like someone who didn't believe what she was hearing but would dearly have liked to. "I'll just go and put these away.''

"Miss Pearson?''

The firmness of Emily's tone stopped JoAnna in the act of picking up the bags.

"May I have a word with you?''

The color drained from the younger woman's face. "What is it?''

She laid her book aside and folded her hands in her lap. "I don't think you told me everything when I came to stay here.''

"What do you mean?'' JoAnna asked anxiously. "Has something happened?''

"You said that your mother's collapse was the first incident. But there have been others, have there not?''

"No! She's never collapsed before—at least, not that I know of. Has something...?''

"No, my dear,'' Emily continued. "I didn't mean that in particular. But Nedra told me something about an incident involving the furniture in this room.''

JoAnna shook her head. "That was a mistake. It had to be. I'm sure Nedra moved things around and forgot she'd done it. Or maybe she just forgot where things were to begin with. It was just...a lot of fuss over nothing.''

Emily hated to distress JoAnna, but she believed that if she was going to get to the bottom of what was happening in that house, she had to try to satisfy herself that Abigail Pearson was, indeed, of sound mind and body.

"Miss Pearson, *has* your mother been acting differently lately? Have you noticed any changes in her?''

"Why?" She sounded more uneasy than before. "You told me she was fine! Has she been acting strangely?"

"My dear child, I only met your mother yesterday. I wouldn't know what was strange for her and what was not."

"Then why do you ask?" JoAnna looked completely lost.

Emily smiled. "Unlike yourself, I have a great deal of experience with being an aged person. I suppose that's given me a measure of empathy for anyone of my generation who is so readily written off as being unwell."

JoAnna lowered her eyes. She looked faintly shocked, but was blushing at the same time. "I wouldn't do that."

"You wouldn't *mean* to do that," Emily corrected, "but it's an easy mistake for even the best of us to make. Now, I was inquiring about your mother's state only because I would like to make up my mind for myself what her condition is."

JoAnna looked up. "How does she seem to you?"

She gave a little shrug. "To me she seems like a perfectly healthy older woman who, at the moment, is a bit confused."

Like her mother, JoAnna appeared to gain confidence from Emily's self-assuredness. "Miss Charters, I stop by to see Mother every day. And I swear... I swear, she doesn't seem any different to me. I know what Nedra says happened and I know...it was a shock to find her on the landing like that. But she doesn't seem any different to me."

"I see," Emily said quietly. "Have you always visited your mother so regularly?"

"No, not always," JoAnna said, a faint blush creeping back into her cheeks. "When I was married, I couldn't visit as much...."

"Of course not. And you were a mother as well, so I'm sure you didn't have as much time."

"About three years ago I was divorced. I've spent more

time with Mother since then.'' She paused for a few seconds, during which time she appeared to be mentally cas-
tigating herself. She frowned deeply, looked at Emily, and
said, ''I guess it's twenty-twenty hindsight.''

''I beg your pardon?'' Emily's eyes glistened with interest.

''When you're young, you don't think... Well, you think
your parents are the world, no matter how things really are.
I guess I thought Mother was to blame when Daddy left.
But then...my own marriage was terrible. When I finally
got up the courage to leave, I guess it finally got through
to me that it wasn't necessarily Mother's fault—I mean the
split between her and Daddy—and that divorce isn't necessarily a bad thing.''

''Did it have to be someone's fault?'' Emily asked softly.

JoAnna shook her head. ''When I looked back at it, I
could see that Daddy was awful to her. I don't know why
it was so hard to see it at the time.''

''It's as you said. Children tend to overlook the faults of
their parents.'' She paused, then added carefully, ''Even if
they're afraid of them.''

''I guess I neglected Mother for a time. I've tried to make
up for it since.''

''That's most understandable.''

JoAnna started to say something else, then checked herself and looked at her watch. ''I'll be late soon. I'd better
get these things put away. I've got to get back to work.''

She grabbed the shopping bags and scurried out of the
room. Emily sat back in her chair and said, ''Hmm.''

JoAnna LEFT a few minutes later, after a quick look in on
her mother, who was still sleeping, and a hurried good-bye
to Emily. Nedra left not long after, and Emily couldn't help
but perform a cursory inspection of the kitchen. Just as she
had feared, the walls were still unwashed, and the stove
looked as if it had been gone over lightly with a sponge,

leaving a clean layer of grime. Emily spared a single "Tsk" for the state of service in the country today.

The rest of the day was spent in relative peace. Abigail was up in time for a late lunch, and was content to spend most of the afternoon in the den in front of the television set. Emily kept her company for a while, but later set out to make up for some of Nedra's deficiencies. She didn't feel equal to tackling the walls, but thought the least she could do was take care of the stove.

Both Jeremy and Lynn would have my hide for this, she thought as she scrubbed the top of the appliance into a virtual rebirth. Despite the concern it might have caused her loved ones, she was enjoying herself. When she finished, the stove practically gleamed in the dark kitchen.

Later that evening they were just finishing dinner when they heard the front door open. A male voice called out, "Mother?"

"We're in the kitchen," Abigail responded loudly. Then she said to Emily, "It's my son." She didn't sound very pleased. In fact, she sounded rather dull, as if she were speaking from behind a newly erected invisible wall.

When Gregory entered the kitchen, Emily was struck at once by his confident bearing and his resemblance to his mother. He stood straight and tall, and his suit and tie, though standard issue, lent him an air of authority. When he spoke he sounded commanding and detached at the same time, like someone leading a group of schoolchildren with whom he had only a passing acquaintance. Clearly he expected no challenge from two old ladies.

"Hello, Mother. How are you feeling?"

"I'm fine."

He looked at Emily. "And this is...?"

"This is Miss Charters," Abigail said, unnecessarily extending a hand in Emily's direction.

"Miss Charters," he said with a slight nod, "I'm Gregory Pearson."

Emily half expected him to click his heels. "I'm pleased to meet you."

He turned back to his mother. "I'd like a word with you."

"I have a guest, Gregory, and if it's about—"

"In private, Mother." He cut her off and shot a sidelong glance at Emily.

"I can go in the other room," Emily offered.

Abigail heaved a world-weary sigh. "No. We'll go. All right, Gregory." She pushed back her chair and got up, then mother and son went down the hall and into the den. Gregory closed the door behind them.

Emily sat nursing a cup of tea and regretting her scruples. Interested as she was in what was transpiring, she couldn't bring herself to listen at the keyhole. *Besides,* she thought with an inward smile, *I'm a few years beyond beating a hasty retreat at the sound of approaching footsteps.*

The idea of eavesdropping soon became a moot point, though. Within moments the voices were raised, and although Emily couldn't discern exactly what was being said, she could tell that the bulk of the angry words were coming from Gregory. Two more minutes had passed when the door to the den suddenly flew open, banging against the wall.

Abigail marched out the door and down the hallway to the staircase. For someone who had been found in a heap on the landing two days earlier, the only indication of weakness was a hesitation as she reached the bottom of the stairs.

"I'm not finished," Gregory called after her retreating frame.

"Yes, you are!" Abigail took a firm hold on the balustrade and went up the stairs.

Gregory leaned against the doorjamb for a moment, lost in thought, then pushed off and came into the kitchen.

"I'm sorry you had to hear that." He retrieved a glass from the cabinet and filled it with water from the tap.

"I didn't hear what was said," Emily said, watching him closely. "Only raised voices."

He glanced over his shoulder at her as he drank the water.

She continued. "I was just thinking that in light of her recent illness, it might be best if she wasn't upset."

"Might be best?" he said with a laugh, thumping the glass down on the counter. "It might be best if she got round-the-clock care."

Emily's thin eyebrows arched. "Do you think so? She seems quite well to me."

"To you? You don't know her, do you?"

"That's true," Emily said, contriving to look put in her place. "But from what I've been able to observe so far, she seems perfectly all right."

"Does she? I suppose to someone who doesn't know her she does. It's nice of you to stay with her, at any rate. Saves us some trouble." His unwelcoming tone belied his words.

"She was in need, and I was available."

"There is *one* thing you could do." He sounded as if he really believed that one thing was all she could manage. "You can keep an eye on Mother for me."

"That's what I am doing."

"No, that's not what I mean. I mean for signs of anything being wrong, for any signs of deterioration. I think she's been failing for some time now, and I don't think she should be on her own."

Emily widened her eyes and said breathily, "Do you really believe she's so badly off?"

Her performance had the desired effect. Gregory's face relaxed. Apparently he thought he had gained the upper hand. Not that he ever doubted himself.

"Yes, I think it's that bad," he replied with a superior smile.

Emily placed a hand over her heart—a hand that looked decidedly more frail than it really was. "I thought that she...I thought when she collapsed, that had been the first..."

"Oh, no. There've been a lot of other things."

"*Really?*" Emily said with Victorian interest. "What else has happened?"

"I don't need to go into that. What I need for you to do is help if you can. I'm sure you don't want my mother to hurt herself or anyone else."

Emily recoiled daintily. "Do you think there's a chance of that?"

He nodded. "So if you really want to help her, keep an eye on her, and report any odd behavior. With you as a witness, I may be able to get her the help she needs. Do you think you can do that?"

"Oh, yes, yes," Emily replied eagerly. "I'll try. I've been told that I'm rather observant. I truly will try to keep my eyes open."

There was a split second of uncertainty in Gregory's eyes before he muttered "Thank you," and left. When Emily heard the front door close, she went upstairs.

She knocked on the door to Abigail's bedroom and was answered with a lethargic "Yes?"

Emily found her lying against the pillows as before, but her eyes were red and her face pale. She had obviously been crying. The energy she had exhibited earlier had been depleted.

Emily went over to her and sat on the side of the bed. "I'm sorry, I couldn't help but hear that the two of you were having an argument."

"You heard?"

Emily shook her head. "Not what was said, only raised voices. Are you all right?"

"Oh, Emily!" Abigail suddenly raised her palms to her eyes and emitted a series of abbreviated hiccoughs. This was what passed for sobbing for her.

"There, now," Emily said, giving a gentle pat to Abigail's leg. "Why don't you tell me what's wrong?"

She sniffed loudly and grabbed a tissue from the box on

the nightstand. She dabbed it against her eyes, then wiped her nose.

"I didn't realize he could be so cruel. I suppose…"

"Yes?"

Abigail took a deep breath. When she exhaled, her body trembled. "It's about the house. I've decided to leave the house to Robert instead of to Gregory."

Emily nodded her understanding. "And Gregory believes that as your son, the house should come to him."

"Yes, but Robert…Robert doesn't have anything. He and Leslie *need* the house. Gregory doesn't. He has enough as it is."

"For some people, enough is never enough."

"That's not it at all," Abigail said, letting her arms drop to her sides as if they were weighted with lead and she couldn't hold them up any longer. "I want the house to stay in the family. It's the only thing I own of any importance. I worked hard to keep it up. Gregory says he wants the same thing. He says he doesn't want the house to go to Robert because he's afraid—no, not even afraid—he says he's sure Robert will sell it. But he won't do that! I'm sure of it!"

Emily looked at her in silence, then said, "I imagine Gregory has some emotional attachment to the house."

Abigail shot her a wary glance. "Of course he does. He was born here."

Emily noted the reaction. She shrugged nonchalantly. "He hasn't lived here for several years, has he? Still, I believe that it's normal to be possessive about a home that holds one's childhood memories."

There was dead silence, then Abigail looked at her and said, "Emily, can I tell you something?"

"If you wish."

"My husband—Gregory and JoAnna's father—was not nice to them. Especially to Gregory. He was very heavy-handed with them…."

There was a slight pause before Emily said, "Do you mean he beat them?"

Abigail's expression became uncertain. "I don't think it would've been called that back then. It would've been called discipline."

Emily cocked her head slightly, her china-blue eyes narrowed. "And what form did this discipline take?"

She looked away. "He hit them...." She amended quickly, "He spanked them. Nowadays they say you shouldn't do that, but look at the kind of kids that are around nowadays. I can't say that disciplining them was wrong."

Emily knit her eyebrows and said, "And you think their childhoods were unhappy because they were spanked?"

There was a long pause, then Abigail said, "He may...he may have gone overboard. I'm not saying he didn't go...overboard. Phillip was a very unhappy man, and unhappy people sometimes...don't think about what they're doing and how it will affect other people. He once told me that he'd been unwanted. That must've been... Can you imagine how it is for a little boy to know that he wasn't wanted?"

Emily said gently, "But he wasn't a little boy when you were married."

Abigail shook her head. "It doesn't matter now. All I meant to say is that I don't think there are a lot of pleasant childhood memories for either of my children."

"How very odd, then, that Gregory would want the place. You say he doesn't want Robert to have it because he'll sell it?"

Abigail nodded.

"And what about Robert?" Emily asked.

Abigail looked momentarily confused. "He never knew his grandfather."

"No, I mean, does he have any reason to feel attached to the house?"

Abigail unexpectedly smiled. "No. But he won't sell it."

The smile quickly disappeared, and she looked at Emily anxiously. "Do you think I'm wrong?"

"About what?"

"To leave the house to Robert?"

"It's not a matter of right or wrong, it's yours to leave as you wish. But it's not something you should worry about right now. Perhaps by the time it becomes time to leave the house to someone, the whole matter will have sorted itself out."

Abigail's smile returned. "Thank you."

Emily squeezed her hand, but inwardly she thought, *If only I didn't feel someone was trying to hurry the matter along.*

A LIGHT DRIZZLE had started later in the evening, and by eleven o'clock, when Emily was preparing for bed, it had built into a full-fledged thunderstorm. She had already checked on Abigail to make sure she was settled for the night, then donned her nightgown and the powder-blue dressing gown that made the color of her eyes deepen. She now sat on the edge of her bed brushing out her hair. The hairpins were laid out on the dresser in an orderly fashion. The windows were open just a crack, which did little more than allow a thin stream of hot, wet air to filter into the room. An occasional gust of wind lashed the rain against the windows, and the dim light afforded by the tiny lamp on her bedside table was supplemented by sudden flashes of lightning.

Far from finding the electrical storm ominous or unsettling, Emily, as usual, found the unleashing of the elements to be rather exciting, and a fitting accompaniment to her continued reading. Once she was done with her hair, she laid the brush beside the pins, settled back in the bed, and flipped *Macbeth* open to where she had stopped earlier. After a few minutes, the air was rocked by a particularly sudden and ear-splitting clap of thunder, which made her jump despite herself.

"'But screw your courage to the sticking-place,'" she muttered to herself sardonically as she went back to her book.

Almost an hour went by without any abatement in the storm. In fact, if anything, its violence seemed to increase. The sporadic buffet of rain against the windows became a steady torrent, and the ratio of lightning and thunder to peace seemed to double.

The bedside lamp flickered, dimmed, then regained its strength for a moment before finally extinguishing itself.

"Oh, dear!" Emily said aloud. She let her eyes adapt to the darkness, then laid the book on the table and reached up and switched off the lamp. She didn't want to be startled by the light when the power came back on. She slid down in the bed, pulled the top sheet up to her neck, and turned on her side. Despite the storm, before long she was drifting off to sleep.

But her sleep was not untroubled. She was vaguely aware of a dream in which she was unsuccessfully listening for sounds above the noise of a storm outside. In the middle of the cacophony, she thought she heard someone calling Abigail's name. In her dream she strained to hear where the voice was coming from, but couldn't quite make it out. Her limbs felt heavy and her mind fuzzy.

All at once a shriek cut into her sleep. She roused herself and for a moment was unsure whether or not the cry had come from within her dream. Then she heard it again, and this time its source was unmistakable: Abigail was screaming.

Emily was out of bed quickly and drew on her dressing gown as she hurried to the door. She stepped out into the hallway and looked toward the stairs. A flash of lightning revealed Abigail on her knees by the banister, desperately clinging to the railings. She screamed again as Emily approached her.

"Abigail," Emily said authoritatively, "what's the matter?"

Abigail swung around. Her eyes were wide with terror and her hair shot out wildly in all directions.

"My husband!" Her voice dropped to a horrified whisper. "My husband! Phillip! He's here! But he was dead!" She grabbed handfuls of Emily's dressing gown and hung on for dear life. "He's here, but he was dead! He's down there!"

She pointed with a trembling finger toward the hall below, but refused to turn her head to look.

Emily dislodged herself gently, drew closer to the banister and looked over. The hall was empty.

"There's nobody there," she said soothingly.

"But there was!" Abigail screamed. "There was! He was there!"

SEVEN

"JEREMY!" EMILY SAID as she opened the front door.

"Emily, I don't know how you can sound surprised to see me, since you called and asked me to come over."

"I'm so grateful to you for coming here at this ungodly hour!"

"You have me very well trained." He said this affectionately as he stepped onto the mat just inside the door and stomped his feet in a futile attempt to dry himself somewhat. Water streamed off his now closed umbrella. From the look of him the umbrella had not afforded much protection in his brief trip from the car to the house.

"Good heavens! You're soaking!"

"It's raining," he intoned.

"I'm so sorry to call you out like this," she said as she took his trench coat and hung it on a peg by the door. He propped his umbrella on the floor beneath it. "I didn't know who else to call. I thought of calling the police and reporting an intruder, but that would've caused no end of fuss."

"I *am* the police, Emily." Clearly he didn't relish being wet.

"I know," she replied with a smile. "But I mean, if I reported it officially, there would be a great to-do. Most likely they wouldn't find any proof of anything, if they even believed me to begin with."

"A detective would only disbelieve you at his own peril."

"Thank you," she said, sparing a blush, "but I've a feeling that the end result would only be to provide Abigail's children with more ammunition."

"Ammunition?"

Emily nodded. "To use in regard to whether or not she should be put in a nursing home." She shepherded him into the living room. The lights had restored themselves soon after the latest incident on the landing. "Abigail's children seem to believe that she may be unbalanced."

"She may be."

"Granted. But if she is, we would need more evidence than we have now to prove it...or disprove it, for that matter." She took a seat in the armchair.

"We?" Ransom replied as he dropped onto the nearby couch. "You forget, I'm not involved in this case, if there even is one."

Emily raised her eyebrows. "You're here."

There was a beat, then Ransom said, "You have me there. So, where is Mrs. Pearson now?"

"Up in her room. I managed to get her quieted down. I had to give her one of her nitroglycerin pills, which restored her fairly quickly. As least, as much as that is possible. I wanted to call for an ambulance, but she wouldn't hear of it. She insisted she was all right. I don't know if she was more afraid because of what happened, or because her children might find out about it. Personally, I don't blame her for being worried about that. Her children are very...solicitous about her!"

"You say that as if it's a bad thing."

"It may very well be."

"Was she able to tell you what happened?"

Emily shifted in her seat and folded her hands in her lap as if preparing to recite. "Apparently it was much like the first incident. She was in bed but not asleep. She heard a noise and tried to turn on the lights but found they didn't work. I can verify that, by the way. I was reading *Macbeth* when the lights went out."

"How appropriate."

"She lay there in the darkness for a while, then she heard someone call her name. She thinks it was a man's voice.

She went out to the landing, looked over the banister and saw—or thinks she saw—her husband. She called to him and, unlike the last time, this time he stopped, turned, and looked up at her. It was then, I believe, that she screamed. I heard her and came out to the landing.''

''And what did you find?'' Ransom asked.

Emily shrugged. ''I found Abigail, clutching the railing and screaming in terror.''

''But you didn't see her husband.''

''I saw no one else. She told me she'd seen her husband again, but he was dead.''

''Dead?'' said Ransom. ''He ran off with another woman some thirty years ago, didn't he? How would she know that he'd died? Have they had any news of him since he left?''

''I don't know.''

They sat in silence for a few moments while Ransom let all of this sink in. His expression became very grave as he said, ''Emily, excuse me for saying this, but this woman *does* sound unbalanced.''

''Perhaps,'' Emily admitted reluctantly.

''Have you learned anything else while you've been here?''

''Yes, I have. All of it seems damning.'' She filled him in about the moving furniture and the items that Nedra had found in odd places.

''I'll amend what I said before,'' Ransom said when she had finished. ''Maybe she's not unbalanced. She may just be developing Alzheimer's disease or some other degenerative disorder. It would be a perfectly natural thing to happen.''

''Yes it would....'' Emily said slowly, her face a mask of bewilderment.

Ransom smiled. ''All right, Emily, what is it?''

''Well,'' she said after taking a deep breath, ''this business of the furniture being moved about and the hairbrush in the refrigerator and such. It seems odd to me that so *little* of it has happened.''

Ransom raised his right eyebrow. "You wanted more?"

"I would think if she were developing Alzheimer's disease she would be doing these strange things more often. Doesn't it seem odd that Nedra is always the one who discovers them?"

"You think Nedra's up to something?"

"I don't know why she would be. As far as I know she has absolutely nothing to gain. But the rearranging of things seems to happen just before Nedra is here. Nobody else has said anything about discovering anything out of place, although they may have hinted at it. I can't be sure."

"So you think Nedra's meant to be, what? A witness?"

"She was very quick to tell me about it, although she swears she never says anything to the family because the first time she told JoAnna it caused too much of an upset. I asked JoAnna about it, and she truly seemed to only know about the first instance."

"She could have been lying."

"Yes, but why?" Emily replied. "If the children want their mother put away, then surely they wouldn't want to cover up the bizarre goings-on, they would want to use them as further proof of Abigail's condition."

Ransom thought about this, then said, "Unless the daughter is a lot more clever than you think she is."

"I suppose that's possible."

"Are you sure that the children want her to be put away?"

Emily nodded sadly. "JoAnna, I think, believes there's something wrong with Abigail but doesn't *want* to believe it. Gregory, the son, is much more forceful. He believes there's something wrong with her and thinks she needs to be put away. And he's in rather a hurry to get it over with."

"Too much of a hurry?"

"I don't know about that," Emily said with a cluck of her tongue. Apparently she was disgusted with her own lack of insight. "It may be merely a matter of him thinking it inevitable and wanting to get the whole matter over with. He's rather abrupt.''

Ransom searched her face and was surprised by what he found there. This was one of the few occasions in the time he'd known her that she looked really distressed. "Emily," he said, trying to put it as kindly as possible, "although I'll agree that the business of things moving around *may* be odd, you really haven't told me anything so far that would make me believe there's anything *sinister* going on here. What's happened may be strange, but the most obvious explanation is senile dementia.''

She further surprised him with a wry smile. "Yes, that would be the obvious answer.''

He laughed. "I can see I'm to be hoisted on my own petard!''

"You would be the last one to accept the obvious answer, if it seemed suspect to you.''

"Do you have any other reason to believe that something is being done to Mrs. Pearson?''

She stared at his face for a moment, then looked away. It was an action so uncharacteristic for the straightforward elderly woman that it amazed the detective.

"Emily?''

She turned back to him and started to speak, but stopped herself. She looked down at her folded hands, raised them a few inches, then tapped her lap with them three times. "You'll think I've been imagining things.''

"Only a fool would do that.''

She straightened her back and faced him head-on. "I heard whoever it was.''

"What?''

"I heard someone call Abigail's name. At least, I believe I did.''

"You *believe* you did?''

"There is no need to check me back as if I were stumbling through a catechism. Yes, I believe I heard it. It's just so difficult to be sure....''

"I don't understand," said Ransom.

"I thought I was dreaming, you see. I was dozing off and thought I was dreaming that someone was calling her name. And then I heard her scream. At first I even thought the scream was just another part of my dream, but it wasn't. So you see, most likely I wasn't completely asleep. I must've been hearing what was actually happening." She gave her lap another frustrated tap. "But I simply can't be sure, can I?"

"Emily," Ransom said after a lengthy pause, "I would accept your dreams over anyone else's reality anytime."

"Thank you," she replied primly.

"So we are going to proceed under the assumption that more is going on here than meets the eye." He rose from the couch, "I suppose I should start by having a look around."

"Yes...."

He smiled. "I take it you have a little idea about where I should look."

"Yes, well, I noticed something a bit strange earlier today," she said as he helped her up. "There's a door in the kitchen that leads to the cellar. Nedra told me she didn't think anyone ever used it, but the hinges have been freshly oiled."

"Nedra could be wrong."

"Possibly," she said with an impish smile.

Ransom laughed. "You can infuse more meaning into one word than anyone I know."

Emily took his arm and steered him down the hallway to the kitchen. "Whatever her deficiencies as a cleaning woman, I believe Nedra is a gem. And she very well may prove to be a key player in this business."

"What do you mean?"

She looked at him pointedly. "I mean, she hasn't been doing her job."

Ransom's eyes narrowed as he looked down at his friend.

"I don't suppose you're going to explain what you mean by that."

"Not just now."

"All right, keep your secrets. I'm sure you'll let me know what you're talking about when the proper time comes."

"I'm not purposely being cryptic," she said with a light laugh. "Let's just say I've put what little reputation I have far enough out on a limb that I'm not willing to push it any further. If it should turn out that Abigail is simply becoming senile, I'd like to survive with a little bit of my dignity still intact."

"This really is a gloomy old place, isn't it?" he said as they reached the kitchen. "I thought this room might be a bit less gothic, but it's as bad as the rest of the place."

"Yes. Here it is."

She gestured to the door beside the refrigerator as she released his arm. He examined the hinges.

"You're right," he said.

"Nedra said she didn't have a key and she didn't know where any were. I suppose I could ask Abigail...."

"No," he said. He pulled something out of his pocket and crouched down in front of the keyhole. As he went to work on the lock, he said, "I think I can handle this. If Mrs. Pearson is frightened now, we don't want to make things worse by telling her we think there's something going on in her cellar before we're sure." He worked at it for another minute, then there was a soft click. "There. That did it."

He pulled the door open. The smell of dank earth flooded the room. There was a long string dangling just inside the door, and he reached up and gave it a tug. A bare bulb on the ceiling sprang to life, revealing a long, steep wooden staircase hemmed in so closely by walls and ceiling that it looked more like a chute than a flight of stairs.

"Not exactly inviting, is it?" said Ransom. "I'm going down and have a look. You stay here."

Emily didn't protest. Ransom descended the stairs slowly, testing the first couple of steps before giving them his full weight. The ceiling was so low that he had to stoop as he went down.

The bulb at the top of the stairs didn't provide much more than a square of light on the floor of the basement proper, but it was enough that he could find a second string dangling from another bulb in the center of the room. He turned on the light and took in the surroundings.

Like most basements, there was a conglomeration of objects piled up around the walls: cardboard boxes that had been wetted and dried so many times it was a wonder they didn't disintegrate altogether, a few unmarked crates that probably hadn't been opened since they'd been placed there, and bits and pieces of furniture in various states of disrepair. All of these things were covered with a thick layer of dust and interconnected by an endless expanse of cobwebs. The floor was cement and so uneven that the dips and ridges were visible to the naked eye. It looked as if it had been painted gray right after being laid and hadn't been touched since.

On the far side of the room was a door leading to the outside. Ransom tried to look through the small window in the top section of the door, but it was so begrimed that he couldn't see anything. He carefully put his fingers around the edges of the doorknob and turned it. It rotated easily but didn't open, not that he expected it to. He crouched down for a closer look. Though the outer part of the knob was rusted, the inner part, as well as the lock, had been oiled. Still crouching, he pivoted and examined the floor. There were faint wet marks at regular intervals leading away from the door. They faded away completely about halfway across the room.

Ransom pursed his lips and said, "Hmm," then stood and crossed the floor, turning off the light on his way. Emily was waiting at the top of the stairs for him. He took a moment to check the backside of the door before switching off the second bulb and closing the door behind him.

"Did you find anything?" she asked eagerly.

"You'll be glad to know—or not, as the case may be—that there really *has* been somebody here. There're traces of footprints—just traces, not enough to make anything out of—so whoever it was must have gotten down there before the rain got really bad."

"That would've been before eleven o'clock."

"There's only one bulb down there, and it doesn't give off a lot of light. For a closer examination I'll have to come back during daylight, and I'll still need to use a flashlight."

Emily frowned. "I don't know that that would do any good. If someone's terrorizing that poor woman, then it's most likely someone in her family, and I'm sure they could give any number of reasons for their fingerprints being in the cellar."

"Unless it was her ex-husband," Ransom said significantly.

"Oh, dear," Emily said after a pause.

"And Emily, it's much more than likely that it's a member of the family."

"Why do you say that?"

"Because there's no sign of a break-in. No signs of the locks being picked. And the doors were relocked. Burglars don't usually lock the doors on their way out."

"So whoever's coming in here must be using a key." She stopped, her expression completely perplexed. "She was most emphatic that it was her ex-husband she saw. Would he still have a key after all this time?"

Ransom shrugged. "They're very old locks. It might be possible. I think I'd better have a talk with Mrs. Pearson."

Emily smiled. "In your official capacity?"

"No, as a concerned grandson, but I'll make it official if necessary. Do you think she's still awake?"

"It's most likely. She was very upset, of course, and I did tell her I was calling you, so she's probably waiting up.

Do you really want to do this tonight? Should we wait until morning?''

"No. From what you've told me I think she'd rather know that she may be in real danger than go on thinking that she's losing her mind.''

Emily nodded in agreement. They went up the stairs to the second floor and she lightly tapped on Abigail's door. She didn't want to wake Abigail if she'd been able to get to sleep. The knock was answered by a quiet "Come in" from within the room.

Emily opened the door slightly and peeked around it. "Abigail, I have my grandson here to see you. Would that be all right?''

"Yes.''

They found her sitting on the chair by the window, staring out at the storm and nervously plucking the collar of her pink robe.

"Abigail, this is Jeremy.''

"Hello," said Ransom.

She responded with a weak wave of her hand.

"You haven't even tried to go to bed," Emily said in a mildly disapproving tone.

"How can I? How can I after what I've seen?''

"That's something I'd like to talk to you about," said Ransom. He gestured toward the end of the bed. "Would you mind?''

Abigail shook her head, and Emily and Ransom sat side by side on the edge of the bed.

"Em—my grandmother tells me that there's been another upset here tonight.''

She glanced at Emily, then looked back out the window and whispered, "Yes.''

"You saw someone in the downstairs hallway and you thought it was your husband?''

"He called to me," she said softly. "And I went out there...and there he was!''

"He called to you?" said Ransom. "Did you recognize his voice?"

"I... It sounded like his. But I haven't heard him for so long...."

"Are you sure it was a man's voice?"

"It was so faint and...I don't know what word you would use...wispy. But yes, I think it was a man's voice. My husband's!"

"How can you be sure?"

"I saw him.... I saw him...." Her voice trailed off. She sounded like she was tired of repeating the same thing and knowing that she wouldn't be believed.

Ransom scrutinized the woman for a few moments, then took a deep breath. "Mrs. Pearson, there're a couple of things you should know. First is that—" He glanced at Emily and she nodded. "Aside from being Emily's grandson, I'm a detective. I'm with the Chicago Police Department."

Abigail looked almost horrified. "A detective? But—"

"No, I'm not here in my position as a detective. I'm here because Emily called me. There's nothing official about my being here, unless you want there to be."

"I don't know what to say." She looked as if she didn't believe what was happening.

"The second thing is, I don't know exactly who it was you saw, but I do know one thing: You are not imagining things."

She slewed her head around suddenly. Her eyes were wide and her expression uncertain, as if she was afraid to hope for fear the rug would be pulled out from under her.

"I've looked around a bit, and I found evidence that someone has been in this house."

She reached out and touched his arm. "Someone *has* been here!" Her relief was palpable but brief. It was quickly replaced by fear. "But how? Why?"

"Well, the 'how' I can explain. Whoever it was came in through the basement."

She drew back slowly. "The basement?"

Ransom nodded.

"You've been down there? But it's locked!"

He glanced at Emily. "I was able to open it."

"He's very good with his hands," Emily chimed in, manufacturing grandmotherly pride.

"He came up from the basement," Abigail repeated in an anxious whisper. She looked as if the thought of someone sneaking in from under the house was truly frightening to her.

"As to the 'why,' that's something probably only you can answer."

"What do you mean?"

"Well, first of all, I understand that your husband left somewhere around thirty years ago. Have you heard from him since then?"

Abigail looked almost scandalized. "No! Of course not! I wouldn't...I wouldn't have wanted to!"

"I'm sorry," said Ransom, "somehow I got the idea that you had heard he was dead."

"What?"

"When I went out to the landing," Emily explained, "you said you saw your husband, but he was dead."

Abigail looked confused for a moment, then shook her head. "No, no, I meant when I saw him here *tonight,* he was dead! It was his face! When he looked up at me...his face was white and blotched. His skin looked decayed...and his eyes were black.... He looked...he looked—"

"Mrs. Pearson," Ransom said firmly, cutting her off for fear that she would work herself into a frenzy, "the thing is, you weren't seeing a ghost. What you were seeing was a real person, so we have to take into account the possibility that your husband has come back and is pulling this nonsense on you for some reason."

Abigail stared at him blankly, then her face ran through a series of changes, from fear to anger, with several more indistinguishable emotions in between. "No. No, that's too fantastic. I can't believe it's him."

"But before you were so sure it *was* him," Ransom said after a beat.

"I know, but I thought I was seeing…some sort of ghost or something. It was horrible. But if it's a real person, then I just can't believe… How could he do such a thing?"

"That's what we need to find out," said Ransom, looking none too pleased. "But I assure you that what you've been seeing is a real person. Now when your husband left, did you report his disappearance?"

"No," she replied irritably. "He didn't disappear. He told me he was leaving." She sucked in her lips, looking very much as if she didn't want to go on. She was silent for so long that both Ransom and Emily were beginning to wonder if she would continue. Finally, she exhaled and said, "There was a scene—just like there'd been a thousand times before. Only this one ended with him telling me he was leaving. He said he found someone he loved more, which wasn't hard to believe because he couldn't have loved me less! He went up and threw his things in his suitcase and went out the front door, and I haven't seen him since."

"You never tried to find him?"

She rolled her eyes broadly. "Lord, no! The last thing I wanted was for him to come back! And I can't believe… I can't believe that all these years later he really *has* come back!"

"If it's not your former husband, then it was someone made up to look like him." Ransom paused to let this sink in, then said, "Apparently, someone is trying to frighten you. Who, we don't know. Which brings us back to why?"

"Why?" Abigail echoed vacantly. "But…I don't know."

"Abigail," said Emily, "who would benefit if something were to happen to you?"

"Benefit?" For a few seconds, Abigail looked as if she

didn't know what the word meant. Then slowly the worried creases across her forehead smoothed away and her mouth formed a hard frown. "Benefit!" She turned to Ransom. "You really think someone's trying to frighten me?"

"Yes."

"I'm not a wealthy woman. Nobody would really benefit. The only one who gets anything substantial is Robert, my grandson. He gets the house. That's all I have. I barely get enough money from Social Security for upkeep. Gregory does the rest, and JoAnna does what she can."

"Did you tell Robert about this?" Emily asked.

She nodded. "He knows he'll get the house. He also knows he won't get it until I die." She looked from Emily to Ransom, her jaw set and her eyes defiant. "But nothing in this world would get me to believe that Robert would hurt me."

"Do you know of anyone else who would?" asked Ransom.

"No. Nobody."

She said this with such finality that neither Ransom nor Emily thought there was any point in pressing her further.

Ransom sighed. "Mrs. Pearson, how many people have keys to this house? Particularly the basement?"

"Who? Well, my children, JoAnna and Gregory. Robert does, I believe. He used to store some things down there."

"What about your ex-husband?"

"I don't understand."

"Have you changed the locks since he left?"

"I..." She looked confused for a moment, then said, "No. No, I don't believe I did."

"Hmm." He couldn't think of anything more to ask her, and he was rather puzzled by her attitude. For someone who had just learned that her house was being broken into, she didn't seem to be very forthcoming. He rose and said, "Well, it might be a good idea to change them now."

He headed for the door, accompanied by Emily, but they were stopped by Abigail just before they reached it.

"Mr. Ransom? Are you *sure* that someone…that a real person has been coming into this house?

"Yes, I am."

She stared at him for a second, then said, "Thank you," and lay back down.

"Well, you've won me over," Ransom said as he and Emily went down the stairs. "There is something very strange going on in this house."

Emily was much too proper to say "I told you so," but there was a playful glint in her eye that said it for her.

He continued. "This elaborate business of trying to scare her to death just doesn't make sense."

"Do you really think someone is trying to scare her to *death*?"

"Don't you? She's already ended up in the hospital."

"Yes, I know," Emily said hesitantly. "It just strikes me that if you were trying to kill someone, attempting to scare them to death is a very inefficient way of doing it—even someone with a heart condition. Although, I'm sure there are many people who mistakenly believe that it's quite easy to scare an old woman to death."

"Even if someone did believe that, it doesn't make sense anyway," said Ransom as they reached the front door. "Someone's been sneaking in and out of this house pretty freely, it seems, and until now Abigail's been on her own. Whoever it was could easily have killed her. Why try to scare her to death?"

Emily cleared her throat. "I don't think the object has been to kill Abigail. I think it much more likely that our culprit may be trying to unhinge her mind. Or at least, convince other people that her mind is unhinged."

"But why? Nobody would inherit from her if she's still alive. What's the point of trying to get her put away?"

"I wonder…" Emily said absently.

"What?"

"Abigail believes that Robert would live in the house when it comes to him. Why she's so convinced of that, I don't know. I also doubt if she's right about it. The house is very old, and young people do tend to want a newer place. Certainly a place nicer than this. And I get the impression that he doesn't have a lot of money. He may need to sell the house.''

Ransom shook his head. ''If she really doesn't have any money, she'd probably go into a nursing home on Medicare, and if that's the case her assets would be seized, including the house.''

Emily's eyebrows formed two small points. ''Unless she signed it over to someone else first.''

''Ah,'' said Ransom. ''Perhaps you can find out if someone's been pressing her to do that.''

Emily thought for a moment. ''She had an argument with Gregory earlier this evening. An argument that she walked out of. She told me it was about the house. Gregory very firmly believes it should come to him.'' She pursed her lips with displeasure. ''I must say I find this whole thing very unseemly, squabbling over an inheritance while a person is still alive.'' She paused, lost in thought. ''Jeremy, now that you've investigated and you believe that something really is wrong, isn't there something you can do in your *official* capacity?''

''Other than report the break-in, I don't know what it would be. She hasn't been directly threatened and we don't even know who's responsible for what *has* happened. I suppose I could let her children and grandson know that the police are aware that something's not right here, but even that would have to be unofficial.''

''If you could talk to Gregory and Robert, I can speak with JoAnna. She stops in every day to check on Abigail.''

''Emily! You are not going to confront a potential—'' He broke off, finding himself at a loss for a description.

''A potential what?'' Emily said with a twinkle in her eye. Ransom blushed. ''I shall be perfectly safe talking to JoAnna about what happened here tonight.'' Suddenly, her eyes widened. "Oh! I hadn't thought of that. Yes, that's a possibility."

"What is it?"

"I just thought of something. The way Abigail described the voice: 'wispy.' She's quite right, you know. Now that I've given it some thought, I really couldn't tell whether it was a man's or woman's voice. We assume it was a man because of what Abigail saw, but could it have been a woman? Would it be difficult for a woman to make herself look like an elderly man—especially when she'd only be seen in the dark in the middle of the night by a frightened old woman?"

"I wonder if Abigail's thought of that," said Ransom. "You know, she didn't exactly act like she wanted any help."

"That's true. She seemed satisfied just knowing that there was a corporeal explanation for what's been happening to her. But that may change once she's had time to think about it."

Ransom looked at Emily pointedly. "I know one thing, though. I want you to get out of this."

"What?"

"Tomorrow morning I'd like you to pack up and go home."

"I can't leave Abigail here alone."

"She knows she's not crazy now, and they'll be getting someone else to look after her anyway."

"Someone hired for her by one of the very people you think may be trying to harm her."

"Right now I'm not worried about her, I'm thinking of *your* safety," Ransom said. "Whatever these people are mixed up in, I don't want you getting hurt because of it."

She eyed him for a moment. "I'm going to stay until we have this matter settled. I can't leave her here like this."

"You're awfully ornery for a grandmother, aren't you?"

"I'm sure you mean that as a compliment," Emily said with a playful gleam in her eye.

Ransom released an exasperated sigh. "Well, as long as you're staying, there's another thing I can do: I can try to find out if her ex-husband is alive or dead. At least we can eliminate that possibility."

"Do you really think it could be him?" Emily asked, her eyebrows arching once again. "What would be the point?"

"Who knows? Emily, if it weren't a normal part of my job to determine motive, I would most likely spend most of my time throwing my hands up in despair of ever figuring out why anybody does anything."

EIGHT

THE NEXT MORNING found Ransom and his partner, Gerald White, making an unscheduled trip to Rosemont. Gerald was about an inch shorter than Ransom's six feet, with straight, mousy brown hair and skin that made his surname seem like a label. He had been partnered with Ransom for over five years, and had grown accustomed to most of his eccentricities: the long silences when Ransom's wheels and gears churned for answers, the constant cigar smoke that left Gerald smelling like he had spent the day in a bar, and Ransom's tendency to treat him as his own personal Watson. One of the reasons their partnership had been so successful was that Gerald had a fond respect for his partner's abilities (and, to a lesser extent, his uniqueness); another reason was that he didn't have a great deal of ambition. Like Ransom, Gerald enjoyed being a detective and didn't want to move up in the ranks of the department to a position where he would no longer be able to do the work he loved. He was content to play second banana to Ransom, as long as he was still able to do his bit.

Despite his familiarity with Ransom's peculiarities, Gerald was surprised when he announced that he needed to make two stops that morning, both to question people not involved in the case on which they were working. Emily had provided him with the names of the businesses at which the male members of the Pearson family worked, information that Abigail had shared during one of their lengthy talks. As Gerald drove northwest on the always crowded Kennedy Expressway, Ransom related the scenario in which Emily had become involved.

"So you think that the son or the grandson is trying to

scare the old lady," Gerald said, glancing at the sideview mirror.

"Or the daughter is doing it."

"But from what you've said, the grandson is the one that inherits. Wouldn't that make him more likely? Why are we talking to the son first?"

"Because Emily believes—and I agree with her—that the object may not be to kill Abigail Pearson, but to convince people that she's losing her mind."

"So?" said Gerald as he changed lanes.

Ransom unwrapped one of his plastic-tipped cigars. "The grandson only inherits if she dies. Now, why would you want to prove someone mentally incompetent?"

Gerald shrugged. "So you could contest the will when it comes up, I suppose. But Jer, doesn't that sound farfetched to you?"

"In what way?" He lit the cigar.

Despite the heat outside and the air-conditioning inside, Gerald rolled his window down a few inches and Ransom followed suit. "I know we see the dregs of humanity, but do you really think Pearson would drive his mother nuts to cheat his own son out of an inheritance? Especially for some crummy house?"

Ransom blew a stream of smoke out the window. "Not exactly great expectations, I know, but that crummy house is probably worth over seventy thousand dollars. People have killed for far less. What's a little insanity in the family?"

"I guess you're right," Gerald said doubtfully.

"It's amazing the amount of unpleasantness that can be caused by the thought of an inheritance, no matter how it's given, even if it's while the donor is still alive. Look what happened to Pip."

"Pip?"

Ransom heaved a dramatic sigh. "*Great Expectations*. Dickens. You really should read the classics sometime, Gerald."

"Agatha Christie is classic enough for me," Gerald needled, and Ransom shot him an amused glance. "Why did you want me along, anyway? You know we can't do anything official about this."

"But we can *look* official," Ransom replied with a wry smile. "I thought if I saw him alone I would look like a grandson who's trying to throw his weight around. With you along, I'm hoping I appear to be on an official visit—without—exactly—saying that."

Gerald laughed as he steered the car onto the River Road exit. They headed south and turned onto Sixty-fourth Place, which ran for only three blocks before being cut off by O'Hare Airport. The street was lined on either side with identical buildings of faceless brick. The monotony was broken up by a small diner on the north side of the street, and a hot dog stand on the south.

They found a parking space a third of a block down from Gorden Chemicals, the plant at which Gregory Pearson worked. The entrance was through double doors in the southeast corner of the building. Over the doors was an arched sign with a dark green background on which the name of the company was painted in gold.

The reception area was barely decorated at all, which Ransom took to mean that visitors were not exactly welcome. It was a nine-foot square with walls of exposed drywall. A sliding-glass panel in the wall on the right revealed a receptionist who couldn't have been over twenty. She was wearing very heavy eye makeup, jeans, and a blouse that was tied loosely beneath her breasts, amply displaying what the detectives took to be the most likely reason she had been hired. Her hair was long and blond, with dark roots, and was tied at an awkward angle at the back of her head in a design that seemed to start as a bun and end as a ponytail.

"Yeah?" she said, with a snap of her gum.

Ransom smiled, then suddenly slapped his badge against the window. "We're here to see Gregory Pearson."

"What?" Her eyes bugged at the badge. "What did Greg—wait." She grabbed the phone and punched a four-digit number. After a short wait, she spoke into the receiver. "Greg? Greg? There's two guys here to see you. They're police!" There was a pause, then she added, "Yeah..." She drew out the word as if her disbelief had deepened. She replaced the receiver, looked up at Ransom and said, "He'll be right out."

She looked down at her magazine and pretended to read.

After a wait of about three minutes the inner door popped open and Gregory Pearson came out. He was dressed in a brown suit and red-striped tie that was loosened at the collar.

"Mr. Pearson? I'm Detective Ransom, this is Detective White."

"Detectives," Pearson said blankly, "I know. Reception told me." Apparently the receptionist wasn't referred to by name, even in her presence. "What is this? Is something wrong? Has something happened to Mother?"

Ransom raised his right eyebrow. "Should something have happened to your mother?"

"No. Of course not! But she's old and if anyone—well, what are you here about, then?"

"Could we speak to you in private?" Ransom said with a sidelong glance at the receptionist, who was doing all she could to look as if she wasn't listening.

"Sure, sure," Pearson replied after a brief hesitation. "Come back this way."

They followed him through the door and up six metal steps to a catwalk that ran along the side of the right wall. Beneath them was a host of machinery that had gauges and hoses sprouting off them like obscene, cancerous growths. It was an analogy that Ransom quickly regretted calling to mind. He wondered just how unhealthy it was to be in a chemical plant.

The catwalk was lined with glass-fronted offices, the last of which belonged to Pearson. He showed them in and offered them the two uncomfortable metal chairs on the opposite side of his desk. The desk was a sea of papers of all kinds including memos, invoices, letters, and one sheet that looked like some sort of formula. All of the papers were jumbled together in an indistinguishable mess. The only relatively clear spot was the far edge on which rested a framed picture of Abigail.

Pearson closed the door and crossed to his seat behind the desk.

"Do you want these closed?" said Ransom, reaching for the cord that operated the venetian blinds over the glass wall.

"What? No," Pearson said quickly. "That's all right. Now, what's happened?" He folded his hands on top of the papers. "It *is* Mother, isn't it?"

Ransom scrutinized the man for a split second before answering. "Something very strange happened at her house last night. It seems that someone broke in."

"What? Is she all right?"

"Yes. As far as we can determine the intention was to frighten her. Whoever it was just walked through the house and left."

There was a pause during which Pearson stared at him in disbelief. Then he sat back in his chair and rolled his eyes. "Oh, you've got to be kidding! You mean she called the police? I can't believe it!"

"Why? Wouldn't you expect her to under the circumstances?"

"My mother is very old, detective, and she's not what she used to be, to put it nicely. For a while now I've been afraid that we're going to have to do something about her, and it looks like I was right. Honestly! I can't believe this!" He let out a derisive laugh.

Ransom crossed his legs smoothly. "I think you've misunderstood, Mr. Pearson. Your mother didn't call the police. My grandmother is staying with her for a while. I believe you've met her. Her name is Emily Charters."

"You're kidding! That old lady is your grandmother?" He seemed unaware or unconcerned that his tone might be considered offensive.

"She's the one who called me in."

"Well, excuse me, Mr. Ransom, but she probably isn't exactly on the ball, either."

Ransom shook his head and smiled. "I must be expressing myself very poorly today. She called me because she was worried. She found your mother screaming on the landing. It seems your mother woke up in the middle of the night and saw an intruder in the first floor hallway."

"But that's just what—"

"I went over there and looked around," Ransom cut him off calmly, "and I found evidence that there actually *had* been an intruder."

"What?" Pearson looked as if he'd just been struck over the head with a heavy object.

"The intruder came in through the basement."

He stared at Ransom for a moment, then said, "There really *was* an intruder? You sure Mother—was she hurt or anything?"

"No. Just frightened. Seeing as how nobody was hurt and nothing was taken, that apparently was the point."

He shook his head slowly. "Why would anyone do such a thing?"

"That's what brings us here."

"What do you mean?" Pearson said, looking up sharply.

"When your mother saw the intruder, she said it was her husband, only he was dead."

"What?" Pearson exclaimed. His face paled and his jaw dropped. Much to Ransom's surprise, he looked angry rather than shocked.

Ransom looked at him quizzically. "Forgive me, Mr. Pearson, but you seem surprised."

"Why...of course. Of course I'm surprised."

"But surely you knew that this had happened once before?"

"I did know that," Pearson said, bringing himself under control. "But it never occurred to me that it might be true. I thought she was just...I don't know. Of course, it just goes to prove that I've been right all along."

"About?"

"If somebody's breaking into her house, it's just another sign that Mother shouldn't be on her own. I just...I never imagined..." Unable to find the right words, he let his voice trail off, accompanied by a helpless shake of his head. He lifted his eyes to Ransom and said, "What do you think it means?"

"Either that your father has come back and is trying to frighten your mother, or somebody else is impersonating him for the same purpose."

"Who would do that?"

"You would be able to answer that better than I could."

Pearson stared at him blankly. "Me? How would I know?"

Ransom recrossed his legs. "I understand you had a quarrel with your mother yesterday."

Pearson snorted. "Your grandmother has big ears, doesn't she!"

"What was the argument about?"

"None of your damn business!"

"Was it about the house?"

Pearson slapped his palms against the desktop. "I said it's none of your damn business!" He paused for emphasis, leaning forward slightly. Ransom took the posture as an unconscious warning that if provoked, he was likely to spring. Pearson then added, "What goes on between me and my mother is private."

Ransom remained singularly unfazed. "The only people I can think of that would want some kind of harm to come to your mother are the people who have something to gain."

"Oh, I get it now!" Pearson said, relaxing back against his chair. "Let me set you straight on that one. I don't get anything. I'm Mother's executor, and that's all. That means I get all the responsibility and nothing to show for it. JoAnna, my sister, gets some trinkets. Junk. Sentimental value, like they say. The house goes to my son, Robert. He loves his grandmother. He wouldn't do anything to hurt her, and anybody that thinks he would is an idiot!''

Ransom gazed at Pearson for several seconds with a slight smile on his face. Then he said, ''Do you have any idea where your father is?''

''What? No! Of course not! We haven't heard from him since he left us!'' He grabbed the knot of his tie and loosened it more. ''What does *he* have to do with anything?''

''Well,'' said Ransom with a nonchalant shrug, ''if the three of you haven't been trying to scare your mother, then there are only two possibilities left: Either a complete stranger has been impersonating your father for reasons I can't even begin to fathom, or your father really has come back. After all, renegade fathers have been known to return after a long absence, in hopes of reuniting with their families...although they don't usually do it by popping up in the middle of the night and frightening their former loved ones half to death.''

He stopped. Pearson looked like he would have liked to say something, but didn't.

''I think we'll have to locate your father.''

''You've got to be kidding! If... Even if he's still alive, he'd have to be in his seventies! You believe he'd be doing something like this?''

''It's a very cruel trick, whatever its purpose,'' Ransom said lightly. ''Would that be out of character for your father?''

Pearson's visage hardened. He got up suddenly and walked to the window, where he stood looking out into the plant. ''No. It wouldn't. I was young when he left, but even then I knew he was a bastard. He hit my mother, you know. Did she tell you that?''

''No.''

"He did. All the time. For anything. Have her show you her upper arm, here." He pointed to a spot on the outer part of his arm about three inches below his shoulder. "He took a strap to her once when she got in the way."

"In the way of what?"

Pearson pressed his fingers against the glass. "In *his* way."

"Did he treat you the same way?"

"Oh, yeah. He would whip me, and if I cried, he'd take me up to the attic and lock me in the closet. No, it wasn't really a closet, it was this storage thing, about four feet wide. No light." He flexed his fingers. "One night he locked me in there and left me for hours. I was...I panicked. I started screaming. And he still didn't let me out. It wasn't until the neighbors called the police that I got let out. And you know what? He told the police he'd been punishing me because I was so hard to handle, and they just shrugged it off and told him they understood and had a good laugh over it. A good laugh. When they were gone, he twisted my arm until he dislocated it."

"I'm sorry," said Ransom. "That would've been back in the sixties?"

"Uh-huh." Pearson went back behind his desk and resumed his seat.

"Things were a lot different then," Ransom said, sincerely apologetic. "People were just learning about abuse. Hopefully the police would react differently now."

"Hopefully," Pearson said mockingly. "I'm not telling you this for sympathy. I'm telling you so you'll know none of us was sorry when he left. None of us were any too interested in keeping track of him."

"Well, it sounds like the scare tactics being used on your mother wouldn't be out of character for your father."

"It does, huh? I don't believe it! He'd be a lot more direct. Why would he scare her? He'd probably just slap her around."

"That may be true, but the fact remains that your mother said that she saw your father...."

Pearson turned up his nose. "An old woman? In the dark? In the middle of the night?"

"Be that as it may," Ransom said with a show of patience, "I think it really is important that we find him."

Pearson's eyes widened slightly, and he seemed to withdraw inside himself. It was as if the mere thought of having to face his father again returned him to the narrow closet in which he'd been locked many years ago, and the terror it had caused. "As much as I hate him, I can't believe... That's crazy. Like I said, he'd be too old, wouldn't he?"

"You should never underestimate the abilities of older people," said Ransom.

Gerald smiled. He knew his partner was speaking from personal experience.

"Mr. Pearson, I understand that when your father left, he went off with another woman. Do you know who that was?"

"I was fourteen years old when he left. Do you think anyone would've told me something like that?"

"It's been my experience," said Ransom, "that children usually know what their parents are trying to keep from them."

"Well, your experience is wrong," Pearson snapped. "Mother told me he left, and that he went away with someone else, but I have no idea who it was. I didn't want to know. I didn't care. I was just glad he was gone! We all were!"

"IT'S UNBELIEVABLE the kind of scars abuse like that leaves, isn't it?" Gerald said as they climbed back into the car.

"It's a crime," Ransom replied wryly as he pulled another cigar from his inner pocket. Gerald rolled his eyes. "And as usual, it seems to have been handed down to the next generation. Did it strike you that Mr. Pearson is a bit on the volatile side?''

"Yeah. But I can see why. I mean, if your father is beating you up all the time, you probably end up not feeling safe at all.'' He started the car and switched on the air-conditioning. "Did you see how he acted, though, when you talked about locating his father? God, he's still afraid of him!''

Ransom sighed and pushed in the dashboard lighter. "I'm sure his feelings about his father are very compli-cated.''

"Yeah, sure,'' said Gerald as he executed a three-point turn. "But he's a grown man now, not a kid. And he's not exactly a small man, either. You'd think he'd grow out of thinking his father could still hurt him. Heck, it's like he said, his father would have to be in his seventies.''

The lighter popped out and Ransom lit the cigar in sev-eral puffs. He then stuck the lighter back into its socket, leaned back in his seat, and took a deep drag. "I don't think he's physically afraid of his father. That wouldn't make sense. It probably goes deeper than that. Have you noticed how your parents can always make you feel like a child? I imagine it's the same for Pearson, only worse.'' He took another drag, then blew the smoke out the window. "There's usually some sort of psychological attachment formed with the abuser. Gregory Pearson's father left him a lot more frightened and insecure than the average per-son.''

Gerald steered the car onto River Road and headed back toward the expressway. "Yeah, but I don't see what any of that has to do with what's being done to his mother now.''

"I'm sure I don't know, either.''

"I was surprised you didn't press him more about why he argued with his mother yesterday.''

"I didn't need to. I already knew. It was about the house. He's not happy that his mother isn't leaving it to him.''

"Oh."

"That was a very odd tone, Gerald."

"Well," Gerald said with a shrug, "I don't really think that children should expect an inheritance."

"And you with two little girls," said Ransom as he flicked an ash out the window

Gerald ignored him. "But still, if it was me, I would probably be hurt and angry if my mother decided to pass me over."

Ransom slowly turned to face his partner. "Gerald, you're amazing."

"Of course I am," he replied with a smile, "You just don't usually let me show it. What did I do?"

"You came up with a reason why Gregory Pearson might want to harm his mother. Perhaps this inheritance business has made him angry enough to act out. After all he suffered at the hands of his father, who knows? Maybe if he thought his mother had turned on him, he would snap."

"I still think it's strange that Mrs. Pearson would do it to begin with, don't you?"

Ransom shrugged. "Maybe the chief inheritor can explain that."

Gerald sighed broadly. "I'm sure glad we're not on this case."

Ransom squinted at him. "Just drive, Gerald!"

THEIR NEXT STOP was Merchandise Mart. They left the car in the vast unloading area on the river side of the building. Gerald flashed his badge at the attendant who ran up to tell them they would have to move. It stopped him in his tracks. He turned on his heels and scurried away in the opposite direction, as if he believed the mere presence of the police meant that shooting would start at any moment.

They did a quick check for Marlac Fixtures on the building's massive directory.

"The thirteenth floor," Ransom said, underlining the

name through the glass with his index finger. "How fitting."

After a quick, quiet ride up in the elevator, they stepped off into the rabbit warren that made up the thirteenth floor. Like the rest of the floors, this one was a maze of showroom windows facing into long aisles, secluded cubby holes, and confusing byways. It wasn't unusual for the most seasoned buyer to suddenly find himself bereft of his sense of direction after simply turning a corner in this building.

The detectives considered themselves fortunate that Marlac Fixtures was located just to the left of the elevators. A double-toned chime rang as they walked through the entrance, and a young man materialized in answer to it. He wore a navy blue suit, white shirt, and plain blue tie, and despite the comfortable air-conditioning he looked hot. Both detectives noticed his striking resemblance to Gregory Pearson. "Good morning, gentlemen," he said with professional polish. "Can I help you?"

"Are you Robert Pearson?" Ransom asked.

"Yes...?" he replied, with the look of someone amazed that anyone would know his name.

Ransom introduced himself and Gerald, then said, "Is there someplace where we can talk to you privately?"

"Uh...yeah...." He turned toward the back of the showroom and called out, "Janine?"

After a brief pause a fortyish woman in a tight knit dress appeared. "Yes?"

"Could you watch up here for a minute? I've got to talk to these guys in the back."

She pulled off her black-rimmed glasses, which were secured around her neck with a chain, and let them drop onto her chest. She gave an appraising look at the detectives that made Ransom feel as if he had just been nipped by a small dog. Then she turned to Robert and said, "Sure."

Ransom and Gerald followed Robert through a variety of displays of sinks, toilets, and bathtubs to a cramped office at the rear of the showroom. There was only one chair, jutting out from beneath a narrow, black-lacquer desk, so the three of them stood together while Ransom explained the reason for their visit. Robert's eyes widened as the story was related, and when Ransom finished, the young man sank into the chair, his face a mask of disbelief.

"You're kidding!" he said, unconsciously echoing his father.

"So," said Ransom, "we're left to determine who could be doing this. We've been told that you're the only one who would benefit from your grandmother's death."

Robert blinked. "What? You mean because of the house? You've got to be kidding! I love my grandma! I wouldn't do anything to hurt her!"

"Well, you have to understand how it looks. An old woman is being terrorized and you're the only one who stands to gain. Naturally we would come to you."

"But that's nuts! I wouldn't do anything like that! And you know Grandma doesn't have any money! All she has is that house, and I don't even want that! I wouldn't live in it if you paid me!"

"Exactly. You would sell it."

Robert's eyes widened even more. He was looking more dumbfounded by the minute. "But I didn't want the house! I didn't even ask her for that!"

There was a pause, then Ransom said, "What *did* you ask her for?"

"What?"

He repeated the question.

"I didn't—we didn't ask her for anything."

"We? That would be you and your wife?"

"Leslie. Yeah."

Ransom looked at the young man, who immediately averted his eyes. "Mr. Pearson, the decision to leave you the house, that was a fairly recent change, wasn't it?"

"Yeah. She did it a couple of months ago."

"A couple of months...hmm...." Ransom tilted his

head, moving his lips to one side. "The timing is really extraordinary."

"What are you talking about?"

"Just that that was about the time these strange things started happening to your grandmother. Isn't it a remarkable coincidence that she changed her will in your favor and then someone started this little campaign of terror?"

Robert was off his chair in a shot. He stood almost nose to nose with the detective when he yelled, "I told you I would never hurt her! What kind of man do you think I am?"

"Let's back off a little," said Gerald, lightly pressing his palm against Robert's chest. He didn't usually interrupt Ransom's interrogations, but it was very close in the room and the proximity of the three of them was making him uneasy. Robert took two steps back, but his expression remained unchanged and his eyes were fixed on Ransom's.

"I think," Ransom said quietly, "that you may be the type of man who hasn't fallen far from the tree."

Robert's face melted in despair. "Are you saying that I'm like my father?" He dropped back down into the chair. "Christ, I try not to be."

"Why's that?"

"He's just... He's got a bad temper. If I catch myself acting like him, I try really hard to stop myself. I'm sorry. I guess I lost mine just now."

"Is that why your grandmother decided to leave the house to you instead of your father? Because of his temper?"

"No."

"What was the reason, then?"

"That's personal," Robert snapped, forgetting himself again.

"I was under the impression that you loved your grandmother."

Robert looked up. "I do," he said with a defensive whine.

"Then shouldn't you want to do everything you can to help her? Someone's been trying to scare her. They may mean to kill her, we don't know. But we need to find out everything we can to sort it out."

"I don't see what my getting the house has to do with it."

Ransom shrugged. "Neither do I, if you're not involved."

There was a long pause, then Robert sighed. "Well, you've got to promise me that you won't tell anyone."

"Not if it can be helped."

He looked as if he wasn't quite pleased with this response, but he went ahead anyway. "We aren't very well off, me and Les. And we're...well, we're going to have a baby."

"Congratulations," Ransom said automatically. "I wonder why your father didn't tell us that. He seems quite unhappy about you getting the house, but this is a pretty good explanation of why it's happening."

"Because he doesn't know! And I don't want him to know!" Robert said quickly. He looked almost scared.

"Why is that?"

"Because... Oh, jeez!" He sighed heavily. "Because he already thinks I'm irresponsible. Nothing I ever do is right. He thought it before I 'married too young'—which is what he always says about my marriage—and it would be even worse if he knew we were going to have a baby. God! I can just hear him! 'How can you take care of a family when you can't even take care of yourself?' and all that. And even that would be preferable to the cold stares and the stifling silence he'd treat us to when he wasn't berating me for being so stupid. Between you and me..." He glanced at Gerald as if he wasn't sure how to include him. "I don't think my father even *likes* children. I know he didn't like me when I was a kid."

"What about your mother?" Ransom asked.

"What about her?"

"Does she offer you any support—emotional or otherwise?"

Robert looked away from him. "My mother died a long time ago, so she's out of it." There was a long silence, then Robert picked up as if there hadn't been an interruption.

"Anyway, me and Les, we're planning to keep the fact that we're having a baby from him as long as we can, just so we don't have to put up with him before we have to. We hardly ever see him, so it's not that hard. I mean, things are tough enough already. Les is sick half the time and the other half she's miserable, and pretty soon she's not going to be able to work, and I don't know how we're going to be able to afford to live then." He stopped and looked from Gerald to Ransom. "Wait! That probably makes me look like I'm desperate for money, but I wouldn't kill Grandma for it, for Christ's sake! But we *are* hard up. I admit it. That's why we went to see her."

"You went to ask her for money?"

"No! That's not it at all! We talked about it—me and Les—before we went over there. We made it up between ourselves that we weren't going to ask her for money. We were just going to tell her we were going to have a baby. And then we hoped…maybe…" His voice trailed off and he spread his hands helplessly. To this he added a sheepish smile.

"You hoped she'd see fit to give you some sort of endowment, perhaps?"

"Yeah. It's not like we were begging or anything, but she knows our situation."

"And that was when she decided to leave you the house?" Ransom asked.

Robert nodded. "It was…I don't want to sound ungrateful, but it was disappointing. Dad always said she didn't have any money. I don't think I ever really believed him, but it must be true because she told us that herself when she heard the news about the baby. She said she wished she had something to give us, to help us out. But she didn't really have any money. That's when she decided about the house. She told us that if she couldn't help us financially, then the one thing she *could* do was see that we had a place to bring up our child.''

Ransom raised an eyebrow. ''But that couldn't help you now.''

''I know,'' Robert replied. ''But she said she's an old woman and she won't last forever, so it wouldn't be all that long before it would come to us. She's got a dicey heart, but she's had that for years. I mean, she could live for another ten years, you know? I think she was doing it just to have something to give us. She loves me, and I love her, too.''

''So you've said. Weren't you afraid that your grandmother would tell your father about the baby?''

''No. We asked her not to. She would never give him anything to use against us.''

''You know, your grandmother insists that you won't sell the house, and yet you admit you will.''

Robert's face flushed. ''I wouldn't admit it to her. Please, please don't tell her that. I guess she's sentimental about the place. I don't know why, because her marriage was rotten and everything, but she wants me to hold onto it, and I promised I would.''

''But you would still sell it?''

''Please don't tell her,'' he said again. ''I know I promised, but what the hell difference will it make after she's gone?''

There was a long silence while Ransom considered this. At last, he said, ''Do you know anything about your grandfather?''

''What?'' Robert exclaimed, his eyes almost popping from his head. ''No, I don't. Nobody ever talked about him. I mean, of course, when I was little I asked a couple of times why I didn't have a grandpa like everybody else, but it made my dad so angry that I never asked again. Why would you ask about that?''

"Because your grandmother said that that was who the intruder was. Or at least, that's who it looked like. I must say, though, you all have a very strong family resemblance."

The inference was lost on Robert.

"So you don't have any idea where he might be?" Ransom concluded. "Uh-uh. You don't think it really *was* him that Grandma saw, do you?"

"I have to check out all the possibilities."

"But he'd be really old now, wouldn't he? He's probably dead."

"He'd be around the age of your grandmother, and she's still doing fine. It could've been him."

"But that's crazy!" Robert replied.

Ransom smiled. "Yes. Crazy is exactly what it is."

He started for the door with Gerald close behind him. Ransom stepped aside and let his partner pass through, then paused and looked back at Robert.

"By the way, do you know what your grandfather looked like?"

Robert thought for a second, then said, "I've seen pictures of him, a long time ago. Grandma has some, up in the attic, I think."

"WELL, THAT WAS interesting," said Ransom as they rode the elevator back down to the lobby.

"What?"

"That Robert knows about Abigail's heart condition."

"Why shouldn't he?" Gerald asked.

"No reason. I just thought it was interesting that he mentioned it. It made it sound as if he's been contemplating the possibilities, doesn't it?"

"Well…" Gerald said slowly. "He's young and he only recently learned that he's going to get an inheritance. Isn't it kind of natural he'd think about it?"

Ransom smiled. "Always my little devil's advocate, Gerald. I didn't say it wasn't natural, just that it was interesting. It also seems that Robert has a bit of a temper, though he's not as bad as his father.''

"Why did you ask him if he knew what his grandfather looked like?"

"It stands to reason if somebody is impersonating Phillip Pearson, they have to know what he looked like. Robert is the only one who wasn't alive yet when his grandfather took off.''

"There's something I don't get about that. This business of Abigail Pearson saying that the man she saw—all right, her ex-husband—that he looked dead and decaying. She doesn't know if he's dead or alive. What was the point of that?"

"Probably just to terrorize her further. And to disguise whoever it was better. The circumstances under which she saw him—or her—weren't optimum, but I have to believe that without a lot of work she still would've been able to tell her children or grandson from her husband.''

They got off the elevator and went to the exit in the middle of the building. As they stepped out into the bright sunlight, Ransom pulled out one of his plastic-tipped cigars and withdrew a lighter from his pants pocket.

Gerald stopped in his tracks. "A lighter? You bought a lighter?"

"Yes, Gerald," he intoned in reply as he lit up.

"I've never seen you use a lighter outside of the car.''

"I've refrained from buying one in the past because I thought it would make me look like a smoker.''

"You *are* a smoker.''

"I know that," Ransom replied. "I'm trying to stop fooling myself, not you!''

Gerald laughed and they got back into the car. "So, where to now?"

Ransom pulled his cell phone from his breast pocket. "I'm going to call Emily and let her know what we found out. My aim in talking to these two men was to let them know that the police are interested in what's going on with

Abigail Pearson. Hopefully that will put an end to any more nocturnal visits.''

''What do you want to do now?''

''We should do some of our *paid* work.'' He dialed the phone.

NINE

WHILE RANSOM and Gerald were pursuing their unofficial investigation that morning, a change had come over the Pearson household. Or rather, a change had come over the lady of the house herself. When Abigail came down to breakfast her entire bearing had altered: Her back was very straight, her jaw firmly set, and her hair was pulled back and wrapped in a tight bun. This made her look more severe than Emily had yet seen her. There was none of the confusion or uncertainty about her that had been so evident over the past few days. Instead, she had about her the stern serenity of a woman who has gone through a lifetime of ordeals and has triumphed. She looked as if she knew exactly what she was doing.

"I'm just making tea," Emily said as Abigail came into the kitchen. "What would you like for breakfast?"

"I'll take care of that," Abigail replied peremptorily. Emily began a polite protest, but Abigail cut her off. "Emily, I really appreciate you taking care of me. And God knows I'm glad for your company. But now that I know there's nothing wrong with me, there's no reason I shouldn't start behaving like you're my guest, instead of the other way around." Emily smiled and graciously accepted the hospitality. She had half expected a change, but hadn't expected it to happen so quickly. When she had first come to stay with Abigail, she had noticed right away how her confusion had abated merely by finding someone who would give her story some consideration. Now that Abigail knew her mind was sound, her self-confidence had come flowing back with a vengeance. Emily did find it a little worrisome, though, that Abigail seemed so unconcerned with the identity of the person who had been playing the cruel tricks on her, and why. If anything, Abigail seemed to be angry, but controlling it with effort. Several times over the course of the morning Emily tried to introduce the subject of the recent events, but Abigail resolutely refused to talk about it, fobbing it off as "somebody's idea of a sick joke," and saying that she was sure now that whoever it was had been found out, there wouldn't be any more trouble.

"But that's just the point. They haven't been found out," Emily said as they finished their tea. "And without knowing who it was, there's no way of knowing whether or not you're still in danger." Abigail smiled knowingly. "I was never in any real danger. Nobody's going to kill me." She spoke these words over the rim of her cup, which made her look as if she was pronouncing some sort of spell.

Emily eyed her quizzically. "But someone has tried to do you harm already. You must realize that."

"My children wouldn't hurt me."

"But it may not have been your children, Abigail. It was your husband you believed you saw. Now, as Jeremy said, it's possible that it was someone made up to look like him, but you have to acknowledge the possibility that it may actually have been your husband."

Abigail shook her head. "Nobody's going to hurt me now."

Emily tried as subtly as possible to get her to elaborate, but Abigail remained tight-lipped. After a while, Emily gave up.

It was mid-morning when she received the call from Ransom. He related what had transpired in his interviews with the two men, and their apparent shock at finding that the intruder had been real.

"Gregory seemed quite dismayed by it. By the way, you were right. He acted as if he'd already made up his mind that his mother was slipping, and wasn't too happy to be proven wrong."

"I shouldn't think he would enjoy that," Emily replied.

"He also seemed to think that proof of an intruder is just further proof that Abigail shouldn't be alone. I got the feeling he's leaning toward a nursing home."

Emily let out a gentle "Tsk," then said, "What about Robert?"

"A paler version of his father. He seemed shocked that anybody would try to hurt his grandmother, and protested a bit too much that it wasn't him."

"Oh, dear," said Emily.

"Don't be too concerned," he said lightly. "Both father and son have tempers, and I'm afraid it may make them look more suspicious than they really are."

"Hmm," said Emily. "Now, what will you do next?"

"Next? I'm hoping there isn't any need to do anything next. I think if one of these men was playing this game, they'll give it up now that they think the police are involved. I am going to make some calls this afternoon, though, and see if I can find out where the father disappeared to."

"Very good, Jeremy."

"And I assume you still plan to tackle the daughter when you see her?"

"Somehow I think she'll still feel she's been tackled." said Ransom with amusement in his voice.

At a little after noon JoAnna stopped in during her lunch hour to check on the two old ladies. She found them finishing their lunch. "How are you?" she said as she gave Abigail a peck on the forehead.

"I'm perfectly fine," Abigail replied tersely. "There's nothing at all wrong with me."

"Of course you're fine. Is there anything you need today? You still have enough food in the house, right?"

"Yes, there's enough food," Abigail said impatiently. "Honestly, JoAnna, you just brought some yesterday."

"Well...is there anything else you need?" the daughter asked tentatively.

"Don't fuss over me!" Abigail said sharply. "I've been fussed over too long and I'm sick of it! It's time for it to stop! I'm not going to be treated like an invalid anymore."

There was a surprised pause. "Please don't upset yourself, Mother."

"I know you don't mean to sound patronizing, JoAnna, but you do. I'm not upsetting myself. I don't need to. I have my children to do that for me." She sounded so bitter that Emily wondered if Abigail believed that JoAnna might have had a hand in what had been tried on her. "All I want is to be left alone!" With this Abigail pushed back her chair, got up, and walked out of the room. When they heard her going up the stairs, JoAnna turned and braced herself on the edge of the sink and began to cry.

Emily remained in her seat at the kitchen table. She felt sorry for JoAnna but by no means would she allow that to cloud her judgment. She couldn't dismiss the fact that if some crime was afoot, JoAnna was one of the suspects. Had the younger woman turned around, she would have been surprised to find Emily peering at her with searching eyes.

"I'm sorry," she said as she tore a paper towel from the roll under the cabinet. "It's just these past few days have been so hard. I don't know how Mother can..." She sniffed and dabbed her eyes with the towel. "I don't know how she can be so mean. I do everything I can for her. I always have. I'm here every day. I try to take care of her as best I can. She's just...I don't know why she would treat me this way." She stopped and turned to Emily, but kept her eyes lowered. "I guess it's just another sign that...I've heard that when older people start...I mean, that sometimes things like senility can make an older person more irritable, can't they?"

"So I've been told," said Emily, her expression unreadable.

"Do you think it's true? Do you think that's what's happening to Mother? Is there really something wrong with her?''

''Oh, there's much more to it than that, my dear.''

JoAnna looked up. Her eyes were puffy and she hadn't exactly been successful at drying her cheeks. ''What do you mean?''

''Please sit down and I'll tell you what happened here last night.''

JoAnna obeyed and listened with increasing astonishment as Emily related the events of the previous night, including the fact that she had called in her ''grandson,'' who happened to be a detective. When she was finished, JoAnna sat back in her chair, her eyes wide and her mouth slightly open.

''So you see,'' Emily said by way of summary, ''Your mother's behavior this morning was not from having lost her senses, it was from finding that she *hadn't* lost them.''

JoAnna looked as if she couldn't quite take it all in. ''You mean someone actually *has* been breaking in here and doing these things?''

''Yes.''

''Your grandson—the detective—he's sure of this? Somebody's been trying to scare Mother? Why?''

''Presumably either to hurt her or to convince everyone that she was losing her mind.''

JoAnna shook her head in disbelief. ''But why?''

''Well, we must assume it's not for sport,'' said Emily without a hint of sarcasm. ''So the most logical explanation is that someone has something to gain by it.''

''Gain? You mean by hurting her?''

''Yes…in one way or another.''

JoAnna stared blankly at Emily for several seconds, then her gaze traveled off into the distance. Apparently she was having a difficult time assimilating this information.

Emily decided to take the lead. ''I understand that if your mother dies, the house would go to your nephew, Robert.''

''What? Yes,'' said JoAnna blankly. Then the full import

of what was being said hit her. "No! No, Robert adores Mother! He wouldn't hurt anyone." Emily wondered if it was mainly due to JoAnna's astonishment that she didn't sound very sure of what she was saying.

"I also understand that your brother wasn't happy about that arrangement."

JoAnna stiffened. "That's true."

"Do you have any idea why that is?"

"No. Probably just... Knowing Gregory, he's probably upset that he's not getting the house himself just because he thinks he should. That would be like him."

"Well," Emily said with a slight shrug, "Your mother is what we used to call 'land poor.' That could account for the great store she sets about keeping the house in the family. And you could be right. Perhaps, since it's the only thing of value she has to leave to her heirs, Gregory simply feels it should come to him."

JoAnna nodded. "And originally Mother was going to leave it to him, before she changed her will. But I still don't understand why he would mind it going to his own son."

"Apparently he's afraid that Robert will sell the house, and he wants it kept in the family."

JoAnna looked genuinely surprised by this. "I can't imagine! We didn't...I can't imagine why Greg would want to keep the house."

There was a slight pause, then Emily said, "You are also one of your mother's beneficiaries."

"Me? But that's not... She's just leaving me some of her things. Things she thought I might like to have, like her silver brush and a few other personal items, like her jewelry. But it's all costume."

"Are you sure of that?" Emily probed. "Are you sure there isn't something in her belongings that might be valuable?"

JoAnna looked horrified. "Do you think I'd actually *hurt* Mother for something like that? Or for any other reason?"

"No, no, no," Emily said placatingly. "I'm just searching for something that would account for *someone* wanting to hurt her.''

"There's nothing," JoAnna replied, only somewhat mollified.

Emily watched her for a moment. "JoAnna, did it ever bother you that you were never considered to receive the house?"

"What?"

"Well, it seems it was always going to go to either Gregory or Robert, never you. Does that upset you at all?"

"Oh, God, no!" She sat back in her chair. "She was doing me a favor!"

"In what way?"

JoAnna frowned and intertwined her fingers. "You know how Mother feels about the house. I couldn't possibly live in it." She was overcome by an involuntary shudder. "But I...I would find it hard to go against Mother's wishes. I would end up saddled with it, because I couldn't sell it. I'd probably end up giving it to Gregory or Robert, so what would be the point of leaving it to me?"

"Why wouldn't you want to live here? It's true it might not be in the best condition right now, but it's a good, solid house. It could be brought up to repair and put in order."

JoAnna looked down at her hands. "It's just that we weren't...I wasn't happy here."

"You mean, because of the way your father treated you?"

"Mother has told you an awful lot," JoAnna said, her face turning a deep crimson. "Not me so much as... He was awful to Gregory, and to Mother. He was unpredictable. You never knew what would set him off. I was young when he left. I must've been about eleven or twelve. But I do remember that you'd be talking to him, and then suddenly you'd feel everything going wrong, and you wouldn't know how...or what caused it. Suddenly it would be like there was anger in the air—the air would almost tingle with it—and one wrong move would bring it crashing down on you. And it could be anything. Especially with Mother—if he thought she wasn't paying enough attention to him, or too much, if she bought anything for herself...or even if he just thought she was looking at him funny.''

"That must've been very, very difficult for you," Emily said sympathetically. "Especially at a young age."

"It wasn't as hard as..." JoAnna looked up, her eyes tearing, then dropped her chin to her breast and wept openly. To Emily she suddenly seemed to be that little girl who has just learned that, for better or worse, she'll never see her father again. Emily reached over and laid a delicate hand on JoAnna's, offering silent compassion rather than bromides. After a few moments, when JoAnna had calmed down a bit, she looked up.

"How could I feel so deserted by someone who was so awful?"

"Why, my dear, you were a little girl at the time. Most children adore their parents, whether they deserve it or not. Children depend on their parents for their security. You were brought up in a household where your sense of security must have been shaky at best, but it was the only thing you knew." JoAnna's hand tightened around Emily's, then released it. Emily straightened herself in her chair and folded her hands on the table. "JoAnna, there's one other thing I need to ask you about. If neither you, nor Gregory, nor Robert are responsible for breaking in here and scaring your mother, we have to take into account one other possibility."

"What?"

"That your father may actually be back, and has been doing these things for reasons of his own."

JoAnna's eyes widened. "I don't... That can't be."

"It may not be probable, but it is indeed possible. Now, do you have any idea where your father is?"

"No. How could I?"

Emily pursed her lips. "Jeremy feels that it's imperative that we find him, if we're going to be sure that he isn't involved. You have no idea where he went when he left here?''

JoAnna shook her head sadly. Tears welled up in her eyes. ''No.''

''Your mother said that he left with another woman. Did you know who that was?''

''Not at the time. Mother and Gregory never told me anything. I asked a couple of times, but it made Mother cry and it made Gregory furious. But I couldn't help it. I didn't understand why he left. I wanted my daddy back.''

''Of course you did.''

''I didn't find out until later, at school. One of Gregory's friends told me. It seemed everybody at school knew except me.''

Emily leaned in, her eyes burning with interest. ''Who was it?''

''There was a family that lived about three blocks away from us. The Loughlins. I didn't know them, because their kids went to a Catholic school and we went to public school. I was surprised to find out that my parents even knew them at all. Or at least, my father did. That's what Greg's friend, Dave, told me when he found me crying in the alley. I told him I was sad because I didn't know where my father was, and he told me what he had heard. The Loughlins moved away when my father left. Dave said that the Loughlins moved because the mother, Marjorie, ran off with my father, and Mr. Loughlin was too ashamed to stay around and face the neighbors.''

''I see,'' said Emily.

ABIGAIL DIDN'T COME BACK downstairs until JoAnna had gone. She found Emily peacefully reading in the living room.

''I'm sorry about making that scene earlier,'' Abigail said. ''I must be more tired than I thought.''

"I think your reaction is perfectly natural, given the circumstances," Emily said. "You're like someone who has been the victim of a very nasty practical joke. If you don't know who did it, you're likely to be angry with everyone."

"A practical joke!" Abigail replied, adding a "humph!" "Perhaps not a very good analogy, but an accurate one. That's why I think it's so important that we find out who was behind this."

A sardonic smile played about Abigail's mouth. "No. I don't need to know." The look in her eyes made clear to Emily the reason: Abigail believed she already knew.

Abigail left the room without another word, and Emily heard her busying herself in the kitchen.

That evening, after dinner, the two of them returned to the den for one of Abigail's favorite pastimes, watching television. It was an activity in which Emily rarely indulged, other than to watch the news, but she felt that since her role had changed to that of a guest, she might as well be a good one and keep her hostess company.

They had not been occupied very long at this when they heard the front door being flung open.

"Mother!" Gregory yelled. "Mother! Where are you?"

"We're in the den."

Unlike the first time Emily had heard Abigail call to her son, this time there was no weariness in her voice at all. If anything, she sounded ready to meet him. They heard the front door slam loudly, then heavy footsteps approaching at high speed. When Gregory appeared in the doorway, he was already flushed with rage. It had been several hours since the surprise visit from Ransom, and the fact that he'd had so much time before being able to confront his mother about it hadn't improved him. "What the hell do you think you're doing?" he demanded.

"Watching television," Abigail replied, fixing her now steely eyes on his own. Seeing the two of them staring each other down like this, Emily was even more struck by the resemblance between them.

"Don't even try to be funny, Mother. You know what I'm talking about!" He suddenly noticed Emily sitting by the window. "You! Get out of here! Leave us!"

"Gregory!" Abigail said in her most commanding voice. "Don't you dare talk to my guest that way!"

"Your *guest?* She's not your guest! She's supposed to be taking care of you! And she's doing a pretty piss-poor job of it!"

Abigail's eyes narrowed. "Maybe that's because I don't need as much looking after as people thought I did."

"Oh, I don't think that's true at all, Mother," he said as he slowly crossed behind her. "I think you need even more looking after than any of us ever imagined. If this place is so *vulnerable* that anyone can come waltzing in here in the middle of the night, then maybe it's time for us to finish that talk about your living arrangements."

With this he placed his tensed hands on her shoulders. Abigail almost leapt with fright. She fought to control a shudder, then turned in her chair and looked up at him. "The hell it is," she said. "I'm fine right where I am. And I'm staying right where I am."

They glared at each other, then Gregory reluctantly removed his hands from her and moved back to the door.

Emily cleared her throat and said, "Perhaps I *should* leave the two of you alone."

"You don't have to do that," Abigail said, still looking at her son.

"I know, but I think it would be best." She crossed the room and paused at the doorway while Gregory made a show of stepping out of her way. Emily shook her head sadly and left the room. He seemed so determined to make himself appear to be a danger to anyone who crossed him, he failed to realize that exercising this "power" over two elderly women only made him look ridiculous.

Gregory would have felt even more ridiculous had he known that Emily was not removing herself from the scene through any sense of delicacy or fear. She believed that by leaving, Abigail and Gregory would feel more free to speak without reservation. And as she hoped, Gregory was so furious that he resumed his heated words immediately after she had left the room, unmindful of the fact that she hadn't completely closed the door. Scruples notwithstanding, Emily felt that things were coming to a head within this troubled family, and information was now vital, perhaps to the survival of her beleaguered hostess. Besides, she felt perfectly justified in believing that eavesdropping on this occasion could be excused by her concern for Abigail's safety in the face of her furious son. She stayed by the archway to the living room as their argument continued.

"You called the police?" Gregory yelled once Emily was out of sight. "I can't believe it! You called the police! You really *must* be going insane!"

"I didn't call the police. When I saw someone in this house last night, Emily called her grandson. As it turns out, he is a detective." She stopped and raised her eyebrows significantly. "Fortunate for me that he is, and that he knows his business, don't you think?"

"Do you know what it looks like when I have a cop coming to question me at work?"

"Makes you look suspicious, doesn't it?" There was a wicked smile in Abigail's voice. "Even if Emily's grandson hadn't been a policeman, I would've called them in after what he found."

There was a slight pause, then Gregory said, "Look, you still shouldn't have anything to do with the police. Don't you see that? Even if that cop really did find evidence that somebody broke in here and tried something, we didn't need the police. We could've handled it inside the family."

"Inside the family," Abigail repeated, drawing back with distaste. "What do you mean?"

"If somebody's trying to scare you to death, I think we know who it is, don't we!"

"You mean Robert? I'll never believe that!"

"Then you're blind as a goddamn bat! You don't know

what he's capable of. You've always been blind where he's concerned! You were never willing to look at his faults.''

''That's because you were always so willing to look for nothing else!'' Abigail exclaimed with a vehemence that surprised Emily. ''Of course I doted on him! After his mother died he needed *somebody* to do it for him! He needed somebody to tell him he was worthwhile. I watched year after year as you beat that boy down. You might not have used your fists the way your father did—maybe at least that much of the chain has been broken—but you beat him down just the same! He's fought as hard as he could to not be like you—to be a decent human being—and for the most part, he's succeeded. And if just a little part of that success is because I tried to give him the love he couldn't get from you, then I'm happy I did it!''

The strain in Gregory's voice was obvious. ''I raised him the best I knew how!''

''You raised him the way you couldn't help raising him. Not after having a father like yours.'' There was a relenting in Abigail's tone. ''Gregory, in your own way, you're not a bad boy. In fact, you're very good. You tried to protect JoAnna and you tried to protect me, but you took too much of the burden on yourself. And then when you had your own son, you thought you were protecting him by never telling him about his grandfather. The only thing is, you couldn't help being the product of your own father, hard as you tried. So Robert's always thought you were angry and he didn't know why. You should've told him about his grandfather. He would've understood.''

''He was too young,'' Gregory said—so softly that Emily almost didn't catch the words, but she caught the tone: He sounded as if he resented the idea that he might've done something wrong.

Abigail continued. ''He's tried so hard not to be like you, and he never knew what he was fighting against or why you were the way you were. He's older now. And he *needs* to know. That should be obvious to you. Tell him about his grandfather. It will help him understand everything.''

There was a very long silence. When Gregory spoke again, he sounded less fierce and more resigned. ''You're wrong about Robert, you know. There's more of me in him than you know. He won't respect your wishes, no matter what you think. He'll sell this house and you know what that means. I'm not going to let that happen.''

''Gregory!'' Her voice once again became commanding. Emily thought she must have been stopping him as he started to leave the room. ''I can see to it that you have no part of my estate.''

''Your estate?'' he replied contemptuously. ''You don't have any estate. I'm the one that pays for everything around here. Are you so senile that you think this is about money?''

''I know exactly what it's about. And I know exactly what you've been trying to do. I'm here to tell you that it won't work. The police are looking out for me now. I think I'll be perfectly safe.''

''Safe!'' he spat back. ''The only person who's jeopardized your safety is you!''

This sounded so final that Emily thought it best to disappear. She went into the living room and took up her seat and her book before Gregory passed the archway. She needn't have bothered to rush. He went out the front door without so much as a glance in her direction. As the door slammed behind him, Emily laid the book on the side table and placed a calming hand over her heart. ''Goodness! I was right. I am beyond beating a hasty retreat.''

After giving herself a few moments in which to relax, and Abigail some time to calm down, she got up and went to the den. She found Abigail seated on the settee, her elbow poised on its back and her hand propping up her head. She didn't look upset or even sad, she just looked disillusioned.

''Are you all right?'' Emily asked.

"Oh, Emily, how do you break the chain of abuse?"

Emily thought for a moment. "I must admit that I couldn't help hearing some of what was said. It sounds to me as if you've done all you can."

"I worry…"

"That's perfectly understandable," Emily said kindly. "Even though it doesn't help anything."

"I don't mean about the past, I mean about the future. Robert and Leslie… Nobody's supposed to know this, but they're going to have a baby."

"Why, that's wonderful," said Emily, feigning surprise to cover the fact that Ransom had already told her about this when he phoned.

Abigail looked up at her. "Is it? I thought so when they told me. Now I don't know. How long does it take before you finally break the chain? I tried with Gregory, but it was too late, and I tried again with Robert, and he still has to fight against it himself. I guess that's a good sign. I guess with each generation, there's a little less than there was before…but how long does it take until there's none at all?"

"I don't know," Emily replied quietly.

"Robert and Leslie, they love each other, and they seem happy together, in spite of… They just seem happy together. This…" She waved her arms broadly to take in the whole house. "This has always been such an unhappy place. I thought maybe Robert and Leslie, when they come to live here, they might finally dispel some of that unhappiness. But now I don't know…. I don't know…."

TEN

"WELL, WE HAD quite a little excitement around here today," said Emily as she led Ransom into the living room of the Pearsons' house.

Despite Abigail's newly recovered strength, she had found the day emotionally exhausting and had retired for the night. Ransom stopped by after he finished his work, which he'd stayed late to do because of that morning's excursion on Emily's behalf.

"It seems you lit quite a fire under Mr. Pearson with your visit. He stormed in here right after dinner and there was a scene between the two of them. Threats were exchanged by both parties."

"You listened?" Ransom said with one raised eyebrow.

Emily gave a gentle cough and adjusted her skirt. "Well, the door was left open, and I could hardly help overhearing, the way they were yelling at one another."

"I see." He tried not to look amused. Emily's cheeks turned pink.

She gave him the gist of the argument. When she was finished, she sat back in her chair and a slightly troubled look came over her.

"What's the matter?" asked Ransom.

She shook her head slowly. "I do wish I didn't feel so sorry for Gregory Pearson. He's a very unpleasant person, but I don't think he can help himself. He was treated atrociously by his father, and now he doesn't know how to behave. It's really very sad. Abigail asked me how one can finally break a cycle of abuse, and I didn't know what to tell her."

Ransom sighed. "He's passed a bit of it on to his son,

although Robert is wound a bit less tightly than Gregory. I suppose either of them could be the one that was trying to scare Mrs. Pearson. You've met Gregory and JoAnna. What do you think of them?''

She folded her hands in her lap. ''It's very difficult to say. I suppose you could say that both of them are intent on convincing me that their mother is mentally unfit. Gregory was most insistent that there was something wrong with his mother, and pressed me to keep an eye on her so that I could bear witness. But in her own way, JoAnna did exactly the same thing yesterday. She wanted to know if I thought her mother was behaving strangely. And apparently she has asked Nedra repeatedly for reports of her mother. She *seemed* completely sincere in her concern to me, but after all, I don't really know any of these people. She could just be a very good actress.''

''She'd have to be to get by you. Does JoAnna have any motive that you know of for wanting to hurt her mother?''

''A rather weak one. She blamed Abigail for the fact that her father left. She says that she has come to understand that it wasn't her mother's fault, but who knows? Obviously *someone* is lying to us about what's going on here.''

''Unless it's the father,'' Ransom added of necessity.

Emily nodded. ''Unless it's the father.''

''You know, the only trouble with what you're telling me about Gregory and JoAnna is that after the things that Abigail has said and done, her children's concern would have been justified.''

''Perhaps, but there's another problem: Once the idea has been planted in one's head that someone is acting strangely, there is a tendency for anything that that person does to seem strange to one, from the way they eat to the way they put their brush back down on the counter.''

''Especially if you're putting it in the refrigerator,'' Ransom said wryly.

''The point is,'' Emily continued patiently, ''if you're looking for peculiar behavior, you're likely to find it.''

"So you think one or the other of them may have been planting seeds of doubt in your mind so that you would back them up if they wanted to have Abigail put away."

"I'm saying it's a possibility. But it's just as possible that Robert is responsible. He's still the only one to gain. What was he like?"

Ransom shrugged. "Average, I guess. He didn't like being compared to his father."

"I shouldn't think he would."

"He was very upset when it was suggested he might have something to do with this. But guilty or not, the reaction I would expect. I did ask him if he knew what his grandfather looked like, since the intruder looked like his grandfather. He said he'd seen pictures of him."

Emily gave him a appreciative nod. "Robert is fortunate that he wasn't subjected to his grandfather. Apparently he was the *real* tyrant of the family, and Gregory is just a shadow in comparison."

"Yes," said Ransom, shifting in his seat, "from what we've heard of Phillip Pearson, I'm surprised he would find a second woman who would have anything to do with him."

Emily pursed her lips for several seconds. "Sometimes women can be their own worst enemies. As can men. I have no doubt he was able to attract another woman, heaven help her. The men in this family have been fighting against Phillip Pearson's influence all their lives. To think that he went somewhere else and started another family! Were you able to find out anything about his whereabouts?"

"Nothing positive," Ransom replied. "Peterson in Missing Persons talked to a contact at the Social Security Administration for me. There hasn't been any activity on his account since 1966, but that's not surprising. If he didn't want his family to track him down, all he had to do was move away, change his name, and get a new Social Security number."

"I don't know why he would've bothered. Nobody in this family was interested in where he went—they were all too happy that he left."

"They could've had reason to find him. Alimony, for one. But then again, Abigail didn't divorce him, did she?"

Emily looked up, her eyebrows rising. "I never thought to ask her. She didn't mention it. But she probably never needed a divorce. I can't imagine she ever contemplated marriage again."

"But she might have wanted child support."

Emily shook her head. "I don't think she wanted anything from him. She struggled to make ends meet. That's one of the reasons she's so attached to this house, because she worked so hard to keep it up."

"Well," said Ransom, heaving another sigh, "Peterson thinks as far as locating Phillip Pearson, we're probably at a dead end. If nobody tried to find him thirty years ago, the chances of doing it now are almost nil."

"I wonder what the chances would be of finding the woman he ran away with?"

"We don't know who she is."

"I do," Emily replied with a smile. She pulled a small piece of paper from her pocket and handed it to him. He unfolded it and read it.

"James and Marjorie Loughlin? How did you manage this?"

"JoAnna knew the name of the woman her father supposedly went away with. Of course, just as you would expect, there was talk at the time. It was a woman who lived three blocks away from here. I called Lynn this afternoon and asked her to go down to the Chicago Historical Society and check the old telephone directories for the name, and this was the result."

"You have Lynn doing your legwork?" Ransom said with an amused smile.

"She was more than happy to do it."

He looked down at the paper for a moment, then refolded

it and stuck it in his pocket. "Well, I'll hold onto this in case it's needed sometime. But there isn't any point in pursuing it any further at the moment."

"Really?" She looked surprised.

"Emily, we still have the fact that no real crime has been committed here. One of Abigail's relatives breaking into the house, especially since whoever it is is using a key, isn't exactly...well, breaking in."

"But surely since he's trying to frighten her..."

"We can't prove who it is, and even if we could, I doubt very much that Abigail would press charges."

"That's true," Emily said, sounding none too happy. "As you said before, Abigail doesn't seem to even care who it was. And I can vouch for that from what she's said to me today." She stopped and clucked her tongue. It was clear she was finding the situation quite frustrating. "I suppose I'll go back to my own house tomorrow. Abigail appears to be fine now. There doesn't seem to be a reason for me to stay."

"You sound disappointed."

"Not disappointed," she said, looking him directly in the eye. "Worried. I can't help thinking that something monumental is about to happen. But for the life of me, I don't know what it is!"

GREGORY CLIMBED the stairs to his son's apartment rather slowly. He had never been to the home Robert had made with his wife, nor had he ever been invited. It wasn't that they weren't on speaking terms, but both had found their stalemated relationship less problematic if they simply steered clear of each other. But there was no avoiding talking to him now.

The building was worse than he expected. He knew Robert wasn't flourishing financially, but hadn't realized that he was doing this poorly. All this knowledge did was reinforce Gregory's fears of what was going to happen. He reached the apartment and rapped on the door with his knuckles with a deliberation he wasn't feeling.

Robert's voice called from within, "Who is it?"

"It's your father."

There was a lengthy pause, during which Gregory assumed Robert was trying to get over his shock. Then the door opened.

"Hi," Robert said flatly. "What are you doing here?"

"Can I come in?" Gregory's tone was haughty, designed to let him know he was forgetting his manners.

"Sure, sure."

Robert stepped aside and his father crossed the threshold. He stopped for a moment and took in the surroundings. He didn't say anything, but he didn't appear to be pleased with what he saw.

"It's not what you're used to, I know," Robert said, barely masking his own irritation. "I assume you want something."

"Where's your wife?"

"*Leslie* is lying down. She doesn't feel well. Now, what do you want?"

"I want to talk to you."

Realizing that he wasn't going to be rid of his father quickly, Robert dropped onto the secondhand couch. Gregory looked down at him, waiting to be offered a seat. When that wasn't forthcoming, he sighed and sat in the chair across from his son.

"The police came to see me today," he said.

"I know. They saw me, too."

"They told me about your grandmother. They said they know somebody's trying to scare her."

"I know that, too."

There was a tense pause, then Gregory said, "I want to know what you've been up to."

"What?" Robert exclaimed, his jaw dropping. "You know damn well I wouldn't hurt Grandma. She was...she was..." He was so angry he had trouble finding the words he wanted. He shook his head brusquely. "She practically raised me! I'd kill *myself* before I'd hurt her!"

Gregory stared at him silently. This evening his mother had flinched at his touch, and now his own son was expressing his filial devotion to someone else. It didn't escape Gregory's notice that his son had bypassed him. Abigail had been right. She had offered Robert the love that Gregory himself wasn't capable of, and in the process Gregory had gotten lost.

"Tell me the truth," he said at last, "When you get your hands on that house you're going to sell it, aren't you?"

"That's none of your business," Robert replied as civilly as he could.

"Admit it. You'll sell it in a split second, won't you?"

Robert let out an exasperated sigh.

"What do you think? Look around you! We're not exactly rich, are we? But I'm going to tell you again, when that house comes to me, what I do with it is up to me...and to Leslie. It doesn't have anything to do with you or anybody else."

"What about your grandmother?"

"Whatever I do isn't going to matter to her once she's gone."

Gregory stared down at the floor, then looked back up at Robert. "What did you do to your grandmother?"

"I just told you—"

"I'm not talking about that! What did you do... What did you tell her to get her to give you the house? It must have really been something!"

Robert was silent for a few moments while he collected his thoughts. A confrontation about this was one of the things he'd been trying to avoid, but with the craziness that had taken place over the past few days, along with the bitter feelings that obviously existed within his father over the disposition of the family home, Robert knew he couldn't sidestep the issue any longer. He took a deep breath.

"I told Grandma...some news." He stopped to gather his courage. "I told her that we're going to have a baby."

There was a beat, then Gregory said, "Is that true?"

"Is it true?" Robert said loudly. "Of course it's true! Do you think I'd lie about something like that?"

"A baby," Gregory said softly. Far from the explosion Robert had anticipated, his father seemed on the verge of imploding. "You're going to have a baby."

"Look, I'm sorry I didn't tell you about it before, but you know how you are. I already know what you're going to say, and I might even agree with half of it. So why don't you spare us both the trouble and just don't say anything at all? There's really no point."

"You're going to have a baby...." Gregory emitted a wet, choking noise that cut off abruptly, as if he was desperately trying to hold it in.

"Dad?" Robert said. But almost before the one syllable had passed his lips, Gregory erupted into uncontrolled sobs. Even though Robert was far from a child anymore, he was horrified and somewhat appalled at the sight of his father falling apart. And with no frame of reference for such an event, he didn't know how to react. The bedroom door opened, and Leslie peeked out. She and Robert looked at each other in disbelief before he motioned to her to go back in the bedroom. He then got up and went to his father. Not knowing what else to do, he very gingerly placed a hand on Gregory's shoulder.

Gregory was sitting with his legs apart and his hands on his knees. His body trembled and he leaned forward, rocking slightly. "I'm sorry," he cried, "I'm so sorry.... I'm so sorry...."

"What?" Robert didn't know what to do.

Gregory made an effort to calm himself down. He looked up at his son. His eyes were puffy and bloodshot, and he looked as if desperation had overtaken him.

"I have to talk to you, Robert. I have to tell you...so that you know it wasn't your fault...."

AFTER LOOKING OUT the door when she had been woken by the disturbance in the next room, Leslie had gone back to the bed and lain there, saucer-eyed, wondering what on earth could be going on. She knew that her father-in-law didn't approve of her—or even like her, for that matter—and from what little Robert had told her about the past, she was pretty sure that Gregory didn't care for Robert, either. But truth to tell, Leslie didn't much care for her father-in-law. She was no less desirous of the approval of her in-laws than everyone else is, but once withheld she could live without it.

The few times since marrying Robert that she had come into contact with his father, she had found him cold and distant. *You wouldn't stop him on the street to ask him directions,* she thought to herself. *You'd be too intimidated.*

All of that was what made the scene in the living room so disturbing and baffling. She didn't think that Gregory was capable of tears, let alone the completely unbridled spectacle she had seen.

It was only a few minutes before Leslie heard the front door open and close. Apparently Gregory had gone. She sat up in the bed and was eagerly awaiting Robert when he came through the door.

He looked distracted. "I'm going out for a while."

"What?" Leslie exclaimed. "Not until you tell me what happened! I've never seen your father like that! Don't tell me it's your grandma!"

"No. Everything's all right. Nothing's wrong. I'll tell you about it when I get back. But I've got to go for a walk now. I've got to get some air and clear my head. I'll be back in a little while."

"All right," she said, a bit disconsolately. "But you be careful and you hurry back and tell me, okay?"

He glanced at her curiously for just a second, then acquiesced. "Okay."

She listened as Robert went out the front door, then she lay back in bed. She tried for a while to stay awake, but the day had been long and her stomach was queasy, and there was a slight pulsing sensation over her left eye that she feared would soon become a full-blown headache. She wanted to wait up for Robert, but if he was as upset as he looked, he could walk for hours before he calmed down. It wouldn't have been the first time.

It wasn't long before Leslie turned on her side and went to sleep.

ELEVEN

"READY TO GO for a ride?" Gerald made it sound as if they were going on a pleasure trip rather than on an investigation.

Ransom looked up from behind the mound of accumulated paperwork on his desk. "What have you got?"

"Call just came in on a body found in an alley up by Foster and Winthrop, and it's ours."

Ransom's eyes went heavenward at the prospect of the long drive through the hot city streets. "You know, we really should ask to be reassigned to the other side of the river. Not that that would happen."

"You're not serious!" said Gerald as they headed down to the car.

"No, I'm not. But I wonder sometimes what it would be like to hop on the expressway when a call comes in."

"You mean like our trip to Rosemont yesterday?" said Gerald.

Ransom grimaced. "Touché, Gerald."

Gerald was gratified that the ride up Western and then over to Winthrop was devoid of one of the monologues on the idiosyncrasies of Chicago geography that his partner was apt to deliver whenever their job took them to a neighborhood near the lake—not that he ordinarily minded, but it was hot and they had to have the windows down, at least partway, to accommodate Ransom's smoke. Instead, Ransom filled him in on the remainder of the gratis moonlighting he had done on Emily's behalf, which he seemed to find much more interesting than any geographical peculiarities.

"So Mrs. Pearson doesn't want it to go any further?" Gerald said when Ransom paused to puff on his cigar.

"I think we've already taken it farther than she wanted. She was satisfied just to know she wasn't going crazy."

"I can understand that."

"So can I, but I think I agree with Emily. Once Mrs. Pearson has had time to think about it, she may want to know who was doing it."

"What then?"

"Probably nothing. What is there to do about it? Prosecute one of her own children for trying to scare her? And how would we determine which one it was?"

It took them over half an hour to reach their destination. Gerald steered the car into the alley just beyond Winthrop, and about halfway down they found a squad car pulled up behind a rather rickety-looking garage. Two uniformed policemen were leaning against the front of the car and chatting. The taller of the two was the first to notice the detectives' approach. He drew it to the attention of his partner with a nod.

"I'm Flaherty, this is Baker," the tall cop said as Ransom and Gerald climbed out of their car.

"Who found the body?" Ransom said after reciprocating the introductions.

"A Mrs. Fulton. She lives on the first floor of that building there," said Flaherty, jutting his thumb in the direction of the small, dilapidated apartment building to which the garage belonged. "First floor. I told her she could go in and wait, as long as she didn't call anybody or go anywhere."

"Did she recognize him?"

"Says she didn't," Baker chimed in before his partner could answer. He did this with the zealousness of someone who wants to remind everyone that he's there. "She says she's never seen him. She seemed really shook up. Found the body about half an hour ago when she brought out the trash. Says she's gonna let her husband have it when he

gets home, because he's the one supposed to take out the
trash, and if he'd done it like he was supposed to, then she
wouldn't have had to see what she seen.''

"I see," said Ransom with an opaque smile.

Gerald had wandered over to where a pair of legs protruded from between two rusted garbage cans. He craned
his neck to see behind the cans without moving them, then
said, "Oh, God! Jer, you'll want to have a look at this.''

Ransom was struck by his partner's tone and went over
to him. He looked down at the legs and then, like Gerald,
peered over the tops of the cans to see the rest.

"It looks like your unofficial investigation just became
official," said Gerald.

The body was that of Robert Pearson.

They waited for the crew from the crime lab before leaving. Once pictures had been taken, Ransom very gingerly
checked the dead man's pockets.

"No money," he said. "His wallet's gone.''

A QUICK CHECK with directory assistance gave them Robert
Pearson's home address. It was less than four blocks from
where his body had been found. They managed to find a
parking space directly around the corner from the front door
of the building. Neither Ransom nor Gerald was surprised
by the condition of the entrance. The lock on the front door
was broken, and the tiny vestibule into which it opened
looked like it hadn't been cleaned in years. A great number
of the buildings in the area were owned by people who
didn't care to or couldn't afford to keep them up. The ten-
ant-landlord relationship was purely adversarial, with both
sides worrying solely about the rent: The tenants with paying it and the landlords with collecting it.

A sliver of paper on which was written "Pearson-303"
was taped under one of the mailboxes in the vestibule. The
detectives silently went up the dingy, winding staircase to
the third floor, located the apartment, and Ransom stood
back while Gerald knocked.

"Who is it?" The thin voice from behind the door sounded choked with tension.

"Mrs. Pearson? We're from the police. Can we talk to you?" said Gerald.

There was a pause before the door opened a crack. Leslie was in an old shirt and a pair of jeans. She somehow managed to seem startled and downcast at the same time. Her face was streaked with tears and her eyes were red. She looked pale and ill. For a moment, Ransom wondered if someone had already told her of her husband's death.

Before he could say anything, Leslie said, "I didn't think... When I called they said it was too soon to report it. Did they send you out anyway?"

"I beg your pardon?" said Ransom.

"My husband. I called the police when I woke up. I don't know why he hasn't come home. Something must've happened to him." She turned her watery eyes back and forth between the detectives in bewilderment. "Didn't you come because of my husband?"

"Yes, we did," Ransom replied quietly.

The gravity of his tone was enough to tell Leslie what had happened. She shook her head, slowly at first then faster and faster. "Oh, no, oh, no, oh no!" Her hand flew up to her mouth and she began to sob. "My God! Not Robert!"

She threw open the door and braced her back against the wall. Her tears flowed freely and coursed down her cheeks and over her fingers. After a while, she pushed herself away from the wall and wavered back into the living room. Afraid that she was going to collapse, Ransom reached out to hold her elbow, but she pulled away and dropped down onto the couch, burying her face in her hands.

Gerald closed the door behind them and followed them in. He and Ransom sat on two of the cheap table chairs and quietly watched her, allowing her to exhaust some of the first flood of grief. This was one of the hardest parts of their job, and at times one of the most necessary. The reaction to news of a death could be one of the most telling aspects of an investigation. It is so difficult for the average person to manufacture a genuine show of grief that often first suspicions are formed just from viewing the response. In this case Ransom, who was known for his snap judgments of people anyway, was sure that Leslie Pearson had had nothing to do with her husband's murder.

After a few minutes had passed, Leslie's sobs began to ebb. She lowered her hands, and wrapped her arms tightly around herself. "When I saw that he hadn't come home last night, I knew something was wrong. I called the police, but they wouldn't listen. They said it was too early to report it yet." She looked up at Ransom. "What happened?"

"It looks like he was killed while being robbed. His wallet was taken."

She stared at him, confused. "How did you...how did you know who he was? They didn't let me..."

"Mrs. Pearson, I met your husband just yesterday, so I knew who he was when I saw him."

"You did?" She slid her fingers across her cheeks, smearing the tears sideways.

"Yes. About a break-in at his grandmother's house."

"Yes...yes, he told me. It's just...crazy. I couldn't believe it. But..." Again her eyes moved from Ransom to Gerald, then back again. "You don't think that has anything to do with his murder, do you?"

"I don't know," said Ransom. "It may be just a coincidence. May I ask you a few questions? I know what a terrible, terrible time this is for you right now, but the sooner we can get some answers, the sooner we may be able to find out what happened to your husband."

"Robert..." Leslie said weakly. Her eyes welled with tears again, and her hand went back up to her mouth for a moment. But she made a great effort to control herself. She lowered her hand and nodded to Ransom to proceed.

"What time did you last see him?"

"It was eleven…after eleven…" she answered vacantly. "I was in bed."

"Why did he go out so late?"

"He was so upset. He always went out for a long walk when he was upset. If he had things on his mind, he felt cooped up inside and he had to go out. That's what he said last night."

"What was he upset about?"

She brushed the blond hair out of her eyes. "His father. His father was here. Oh, God, it was just…I don't even know how to describe it."

"Did they argue?"

"No…I mean, I'm not sure. I was lying down in the bedroom when he got here. And they were noisy but…" Her voice trailed off and her face showed her disbelief, as if even the memory of the scene was puzzling.

"But?" Ransom prompted gently.

She looked at him. "He cried. His father cried. I'd never seen him do anything like that before. I mean, he *really* cried. I looked out the door of the bedroom when I heard him. And Robert signaled me to leave them alone for a while. But…I never saw anything like it."

"Didn't Robert tell you what had happened?"

"No…" She shook her head slowly and her tears resumed their flow. "After his father left, he came in and told me he had to go for a walk, he was so upset…and he would tell me about it when he got back. And after he left I fell asleep. I tried not to, but I did! And now I'll never see him again!" She sounded almost as if she thought her husband's murder might have been the direct result of her inability to stay awake.

"Mrs. Pearson," said Ransom, after allowing her some time to cry, "was last night the first night your husband has gone out this week?"

"What do you mean?" she asked with a sniff.

"Did he, for instance, go out for any reason in the middle

of the night, say, the night before last? Or maybe Monday or Tuesday night?''

"No. Why? Why do you ask that?''

"Those were the nights that someone went into his grandmother's home.''

"No!'' Leslie sounded indignant at the inference. "He would never have done anything like that! How can you even think that?''

"I assure you I don't think anything,'' Ransom said apologetically. "But we have these strange happenings at Abigail Pearson's house, and now the death of your husband. The two may not be related at all, but I have to look into all of the possibilities, as unpleasant as that may be. That includes the possibility that Robert was going over there and scaring his grandmother for some reason.''

"But why would he do such a thing? He wouldn't!''

"There is one reason,'' Ransom said after a lengthy pause. "It was brought to my attention that Robert would be the only one to benefit from Abigail Pearson's death.''

Leslie sputtered, "That's a...that's a terrible thing to say!· Robert wouldn't—'' She suddenly broke off and her pale skin seemed to droop. She had flashed back to the conversation she and Robert had had when she told him that his grandmother was in the hospital. What was it he had said? That he was disappointed when he learned that she was going to be all right? Because they needed the house? But they had laughed about it then. At the time it had seemed like a perfectly innocent, human emotion on Robert's part. Why did it suddenly seem so sinister to her? Leslie found herself with the uncomfortable feeling that she hadn't really known her husband at all. She gathered herself together and tried to infuse conviction into her tone when she said, "Robert would not have done that. He wouldn't have done anything to hurt his grandma.''

Ransom had elevated one eyebrow during the spectacle of Leslie's shifting emotions. After a beat he said, "Mrs. Pearson, if Robert was the one trying to scare Abigail, that might be the reason he was killed. It may even be possible that he was killed because he *wasn't* the one doing it. I have to look at all sides. Do you understand that?'' She nodded warily, then he continued. ''So please tell me, did your husband go out any night this week?''

''No...no, he didn't...except...'' She looked up suddenly, her eyes full of confusion. She shook her head emphatically. ''No, I'm sure he didn't go out.''

''Except what, Mrs. Pearson?''

She raised a trembling palm to her forehead and didn't answer. Ransom offered an explanation. ''Except that you didn't know until this morning that he hadn't come home last night?''

She nodded without looking at him. ''I've just been so tired. I might have slept through it. He might have gone out without me knowing....''

EMILY OPENED THE DOOR and rather than registering the surprise she normally showed at Ransom's arrival, which might have been understandable on this occasion, she looked concerned.

''Jeremy? And Detective White, how nice to see you again.''

''Nice to see you, ma'am.''

She turned to Ransom. ''Is something the matter?''

''I'm afraid you were right when you said you thought something monumental was going to happen. May we come in?''

''Oh! Where are my manners?'' she said, stepping aside. They went into the living room but didn't sit down.

''Where's Mrs. Pearson?'' Ransom asked.

''She's in the kitchen. Jeremy, what's happened?''

''Robert Pearson has been murdered.''

''What?'' She exhaled the word.

''Sometime last night. It looks like a mugging gone wrong.''

''Surely you don't believe that.''

"It's exactly what I would have thought given the circumstances of the murder if I hadn't known about the craziness going on in this family, but the timing of his death is a little too coincidental for my taste," Ransom said.

"Oh, dear." Emily's gaze traveled off into the distance. "I expected something to happen, but not this. Being with these people has been rather like waiting for a fever to break. I thought perhaps there would be a big blowup, or a final confrontation of some sort. But murder? And Robert? Why?"

"That's what we have to find out. And by 'we' I mean Gerald and me. It's time for you to go home."

She looked at him as if he had lost his mind. "I can't do that now. Not when you're about to give this news to Abigail."

"Emily, you started out helping a sick old woman—"

She began to protest, but he corrected himself.

"—a woman who was thought to be sick, and found that it was just some nasty prank, that may or may not have serious intent, that was being played on her. But now there's been a murder. I don't want you to stay here."

Emily's expression softened. She might disagree with him, but she appreciated his concern for her and told him so. "But I can't leave her alone," she added. "She's going to be devastated by this."

"She has her family."

"No, she doesn't. She has relatives, but she doesn't have a family. And I think right now she may need a friend more than she needs relations. Even a new friend."

"Emily," Ransom said resignedly, "I know I can't force you to leave, but I want you to understand that I think it's dangerous."

"I'm aware of that," Emily replied with affection.

With nothing more to be said, Ransom and Gerald followed Emily to the kitchen. Abigail met the news of her grandson's death without tears or any other outward demonstration of grief. Instead she immediately descended into an almost catatonic state through which she answered Ransom's questions with a trancelike absence of emotion.

After offering his apologies to her, Ransom said, "Mrs. Pearson, the person you saw here those two times in the night, the man you thought was your husband, could it possibly have been Robert?"

"What does it matter?" she answered soullessly.

"It matters because it may have something to do with why he was murdered. Please, try to picture it in your mind. Could it have been him?"

"I don't know. I don't know."

He tried a few more questions, but it was no use. Abigail became even less forthcoming. When he finally gave up, Emily helped Abigail up to her bed, then rejoined the detectives by the front door.

"You realize, of course, what a mess this makes of everything. Robert was the only one with any tangible reason to harm Abigail, and now he's dead."

"Yes, I know," Ransom said with a heavy sigh. He raised his eyes toward the second floor. "Do you think she'll be all right?"

"Not anytime soon."

"We're going to see Gregory. Leslie Pearson will probably have called him and told him by now, but we need to see him. There was some kind of argument at Robert's apartment last night that ended with Gregory in tears, and we have to find out what that was about."

"*Gregory* was in tears?" said Emily, her voice sliding upward.

Ransom nodded. "Exactly. It was an unusual thing to happen, and it was followed by his son's death."

Emily looked skeptical. "The only real point of contention we know of between the two of them is about this house. Would he kill his own son over a house?"

BEFORE SETTING OFF for Rosemont, Ransom called Gorden Chemicals to make sure Gregory Pearson was there. The

gum-twanging receptionist informed him that Pearson had
gone home for the day, and provided his home address
when Ransom identified himself.

"What time did he leave?" Ransom asked.

"About ten," the receptionist answered with a crackle
of her gum.

Ransom disconnected, then looked over at Gerald and
said, "Lincoln Park."

As Gerald drove down to Lake Shore Drive, Ransom
made a second call to his friend Peterson in Missing Persons. When he'd finished, he stuck the cell phone in his
pocket and pulled out a cigar, which he lit with the deliberation he tended toward when he was on the scent of
something. The only difference this time was that he didn't
know what it was he was on the scent of. But he found
himself feeling as if he had been freed from a sense of
frustration that he hadn't known was there before. Perhaps,
like Emily, he had thought the bizarre goings-on in the
Pearson household would culminate in something big, and
now that it had happened it was a relief just to know what
the events had been leading up to. But it was more likely
he was simply relieved to be operating in the more familiar
arena of his official capacity.

They drove down Lake Shore Drive to North Avenue,
then over to Lincoln Avenue, one of Chicago's few diag-
onal streets. They turned right and drove about three blocks
north before parking illegally in front of a fire hydrant a
couple of doors down from Gregory Pearson's home.

"He lives here?" said Gerald. "He must have some
money."

"One would think." Pearson lived in the middle of a row
of tall, slender town houses in various shades of brick that
stood shoulder to shoulder for a full city block. His was of
brown brick and like the rest appeared to be three stories
tall, although Ransom thought it was probably two stories
with an attic. With windows in the front and back of the

building only, the inside Ransom knew, would be pretty dark.

They mounted the staircase and, once they reached the front door, Gerald rang the bell and they waited. There was no response.

"Maybe he didn't get home yet," Gerald said. "Or maybe he's not coming home. He might go to his mother's house."

"He left work an hour and a half ago. If he was going to his mother's house, he would've been there before we left."

Gerald rang the bell again, then leaned over the railing in an attempt to see in the front window. "There's a light on in there." He knocked on the door, then called out, "Mr. Pearson? It's the police. We'd like to talk with you."

There was silence for so long that both detectives were beginning to think there would never be an answer—then they heard the door move, then open slightly.

Pearson stood in the opening. "I already know about my son, if that's why you're here. Leslie called me."

"I thought perhaps she would," said Ransom, "but we still need to talk to you."

Pearson didn't move for several seconds then, without a word, he opened the door the rest of the way and walked back into his home. The detectives followed.

As Ransom had thought, the interior was quite dark. The congestion of buildings, trees, and the angle at which Lincoln Avenue was built kept any direct sunlight from filtering in through the large front windows, which was the reason for the lights being on.

A dark blue couch was along the north wall, and was fronted by a maple coffee table on which magazines were scattered much in the manner of the mass of papers on the desk in his office.

Pearson sat in the center of the couch. The collar and cuffs of his white shirt were unbuttoned, and his tie lay like a badly coiled snake on one corner of the right cushion.

His hair was mussed, as if he'd run his fingers through it several times, and his eyes held the vacant look of someone who has received a shock and hasn't had enough time for it to sink in.

"We're very sorry about your son," said Ransom. Without invitation, he sat in a ladder-back chair at the right end of the couch. Gerald took a seat by the window and extracted his small spiral notebook from the inner pocket of his sports coat.

"Are you?" Pearson replied with quiet intensity.

"Yes. And I assure you we'll do everything in our power to find whoever killed him."

Pearson looked up. "You mean, instead of looking for my mother's phantoms?"

"Possibly both," Ransom said after a slight pause. "It wouldn't surprise me if the two things were connected."

Pearson shook his head with disgust. "You must be out of your mind! My son was killed by a mugger! Leslie told me that much!"

"His wallet was stolen. There was no money on him. That would indicate a mugging that got out of hand. But there are other possibilities to consider. Someone might have discovered him after he was killed and taken the wallet…or it might have been taken by his killer to make us believe it was a mugging."

"He was mugged, for Christ's sake!" Pearson bellowed. "It happens a thousand times a day! Only this time it happened to my son. Why the hell can't you just leave me and my family alone? Let us grieve in peace!"

"I'd like nothing better than to do that, Mr. Pearson. But my job is to find out who killed your son."

"Then do it! Go out and find the bastard and put him in jail! Just leave us alone!"

"First I need to ask you some questions."

"Me?" Pearson shot back blankly. *"Me?"*

"You were one of the last people to see him alive, weren't you?"

Pearson looked thoroughly confused. "I was?"

Ransom nodded. "At his apartment. You went to talk to him, didn't you?"

"Yes. Yes, I did," Pearson replied after a pause. He seemed relieved to have finally understood what Ransom was talking about. He sat back against the couch wearily. "Yes, I saw him."

"Can you tell me what time that was?"

"Some time after ten. I don't know."

"And how long were you there?"

"About twenty minutes...." Pearson said more slowly.

"Can you tell me where you went after that?"

"I went home!" Pearson said, his face red with anger. "I'd had enough emotional scenes for one night. I went home! What the hell are you getting at?"

"Nothing at all," Ransom replied, his calm tone meant to convey that there was nothing to get excited about. "These are just routine questions." He paused to let this sink in, then said, "That seems a bit late for a visit."

"It was important."

"Would you mind telling me what you talked about?"

"Yes, I would," Pearson said sharply, regaining some of his energy. "It was personal. It was *very* personal."

"Nothing is very personal in a murder investigation," Ransom countered. "Especially important things that happened just before the victim was killed."

"Well, this *was* personal. And it doesn't have anything to do with some piece of street crap killing my son!"

Ransom studied the man for a few moments. Like anyone who had just learned of the death of a loved one, Pearson seemed to be a mass of conflicting emotions. Ransom knew that this was common in someone experiencing a tragedy, but normally he could put his finger on one emotion underlying all the rest. With the loved ones of a victim, there may be a complex mixture of sadness, anger, anxiety, and confusion (among other things), but underlying it all is an intense grief. He sometimes believed that the more evident emotions were an unconscious attempt to keep that grief at bay for a time. But he found Pearson impenetrable. While the father appeared to be experiencing many things, anger being the most prominent, Ransom found himself unable to determine what the base emotion was, and this troubled him.

While the detectives watched him, Pearson stared at the floor with a sharp-eyed scowl. Gerald rested his notebook on his knee and kept the stub of a pencil poised in his fingers.

"Mr. Pearson," Ransom said at last, "I understand that you argued with your son last night."

Pearson's head snapped up. "Who told you that? That idiot Leslie? As if she ever knows what's going on! She calls to tell me that my own son is dead, and then says, 'What am I gonna do? What am I gonna do?'" He mimicked her unattractively. "As if the only thing she's worried about is herself, instead of my boy."

"Maybe she understands that your son is beyond worry now. And her situation is not without complications. Even with Robert alive, their financial situation was precarious...and now she's alone and poor, with a baby on the way."

Ransom was looking for a reaction in divulging this news—which he felt justified in doing now that Robert was dead—but he didn't get the one he expected.

"It was just like him," Pearson said bitterly. "A crummy job, no prospects, can't even support a wife, and then he goes and gets her pregnant."

There was a beat before Ransom said, "You knew about the baby?"

"He told me. Last night."

"Is that why you argued?"

"We didn't argue!" Pearson said loudly. "We just...oh, hell, I don't know what difference it makes now! I just needed to talk to him about some things."

He stopped and looked back down at the floor. When he didn't continue, Ransom prompted him.

"Yes?"

"It's because of my mother—because of all this stuff that's been going on. I talked to her yesterday, and she just...she wanted me to tell Robert about his grandfather, my father."

"What about him?"

Some of the wildness faded from Pearson's eyes. When he answered, he sounded truly regretful.

"I wasn't...I wasn't a very good father. I tried to be, but I wasn't. I tried not to be like my own father, but it's hard. You find yourself reacting the way your parents did despite anything you might want to do, and you hate yourself for it at the same time. I was hard on Robert. I didn't want to be. Mother knew how I felt, and what caused it. Just like any mother, she probably knows her children better than they know themselves. She said I should tell Robert about his grandfather, that that was why I had been so hard on him all the time...why I've given him such a hard time all his life. She thought it might help him understand that it wasn't his fault." He stopped again, then added, "I suppose I should be grateful that I told him about that before this...before this awful thing happened."

There was a long pause, then Ransom said, "Mr. Pearson, why do you want your mother's house?"

Pearson looked at him, the anger returning to his eyes. He didn't answer immediately. He appeared to be struggling against himself. "It doesn't matter now."

"It does if we're going to cover all the bases."

Pearson still looked like he would rather vent his fury at the detective than answer the question, but after a while he relented. "The house *should* come to me. I'm her son."

"You seem to be doing quite well for yourself. A Lincoln Avenue town house doesn't come cheap. And Robert needed a house. He was starting a family."

"Yes, well, I didn't know that until last night." He

looked down as his face flushed. "I guess that's another example of... You see, I thought he should make his own way in the world, just like I did."

"Hmm," Ransom replied enigmatically. "There's one other thing I don't understand. I'm told that your childhood in that house was very unpleasant. Why don't you want the house to be sold?"

"*Mother* doesn't want it sold," Pearson corrected forcefully. "I'm just respecting her wishes. Robert wouldn't have done that. He would've sold it."

Ransom couldn't argue with that, since Robert had told him as much the day before.

"One last thing," he said after a short silence. "I told you that I found evidence at your mother's house that someone really was breaking in, presumably with the intent to scare her. Do you think it's possible that Robert was the one doing that?"

An unpleasant smirk formed on Pearson's face. "What? You mean you're giving up on the idea that my elderly ex-father was doing it?"

Ransom flashed an unreadable smile. "Oh, I haven't ruled anyone out yet."

The implication was not lost on Pearson. He blinked once, then said, "No, detective, I don't believe for a minute that Robert was doing it."

"Do you really think Pearson murdered his son?" Gerald asked as they walked back to the car.

"What makes you say that?"

"You gave that impression."

"Did I?" Ransom said with a sly smile.

"Come on, Jer, you always know what you're doing."

"Not in this case. I have absolutely no idea what I'm doing."

"What did you think of Pearson?"

Ransom sighed. "I think that as a child he probably amused himself by pulling the wings off of small bugs."

They got into the car, and as Gerald started the engine, Ransom pushed in the dashboard lighter.

"I suppose Gregory Pearson isn't the type of person one would be inclined to like," said Ransom. "I wish I knew what he was like under normal circumstances. The two times we've talked to him he seemed very angry, and he also seems to be trying very hard to restrain himself."

Gerald shrugged. "That could be just what he said. He could be trying hard not to be like his father."

"Perhaps." The lighter popped out and he extracted it and lit the plastic-tipped cigar he had stuck between his teeth.

"Did you believe him?" Gerald asked.

"About what?"

"That they didn't argue last night."

Ransom blew a cloud of smoke out the window. "Yes. It's in line with what Leslie told us, that he was crying. Given the nature of what he was supposedly telling his son, especially after holding it in for so long, I wouldn't be surprised if he couldn't control himself."

Gerald rested his wrists on the bottom of the steering wheel. "But I don't get that. Why keep it all a secret to begin with?"

Ransom shrugged. "Out of some misguided notion that he was protecting the boy."

"You don't sound too sure."

"It never ceases to amaze me how often people feel they're protecting someone by withholding the truth, when the truth is the one thing that *will* protect them. Ach!" A thick ash dropped off the end of the cigar and onto the right leg of Ransom's pants. He quickly brushed it away. "Everything we've been told so far sounds so damned plausible, and yet I get the feeling that nobody is really telling us the truth. Who knows? The way this family is set up, maybe nobody really *knows* the truth." He stopped and sighed again, this time more heavily. "The more we learn, the muddier the waters seem to get. It's this business of

Phillip Pearson appearing in the night. I don't see the point of it at all. If it was really him, I don't see the point. And if it was someone else pretending to be him, I *still* don't see the point! And yet it seems to be the catalyst for what's happened.''

They fell silent for a moment.

"Where to now?" Gerald said as he put the car in gear.

"Back up to Abigail Pearson's. If that blasted house of hers is so important, I think we'd better find out who it goes to next.''

Neither of the detectives spoke much on their way back up to Rogers Park. Gerald divided his concentration between the road and their case, and Ransom smoked absently while staring at the windshield as if a particularly baffling logic problem was written on it. About halfway to their destination, the silence was interrupted by the chirping of Ransom's cell phone. The call was from Peterson, who gave him the information he had requested. After snapping the phone shut and sticking it back in his pocket, he went back to his cigar without relating whatever news there was to Gerald. Instead he narrowed his eyes even further, propped his elbow on the armrest and continued his study of the windshield. Gerald didn't bother to ask what the call had been about, preferring to allow his partner to mull over his own thoughts.

"HOW DID YOUR TALK with Gregory go?" Emily asked as she let them into the house.

"Pretty much the way the rest of this case has gone," Ransom said with a frustrated huff. "Apparently what happened last night between Gregory and his son wasn't an argument at all, it was a confession.''

"Really?" Emily said with interest. The three of them stood at the bottom of the stairs.

"Yes. It seems he chose last night to tell Robert why he'd been such a terrible father.''

"Oh!" said Emily, drawing back in surprise.

"Oh...why...yes, so he *did* take Abigail's advice after all."

"Hmm?"

"The confrontation here that I...overheard...yesterday. Remember? I told you about it. Abigail said that Gregory should tell Robert about his grandfather."

Ransom pursed his lips and shook his head slowly. "This is the most damnable case I've ever been on. We have these midnight visits to scare an old woman, the only person with a discernable motive for doing it is the one that everyone involved agrees couldn't have done it, and then he's murdered after an argument that didn't happen. And apparently all of this is over a house that nobody likes, but everybody wants. None of it makes any sense."

"Oh, but not everybody wants it," said Emily. "JoAnna is most emphatic that if the house came to her, she would give it to Robert or Gregory, and he's the only one left now."

"That's very interesting," Ransom said. "I think, before we question anybody else, I need to ask Abigail a little more about her will. Specifically, who will get the house now that Robert is dead."

"Mother's asleep right now," JoAnna said from the top of the stairs. She had appeared there without anyone hearing her. As she descended, she added, "I'm not sure she could answer you at the moment, even if she was awake. She's barely said a word since she heard about Robert."

"JoAnna," said Emily when the younger woman had joined them, "this is Detective Ransom and Detective White."

"You're Emily's grandson," she said to Ransom.

"Yes." He didn't see any reason to correct this now, since it would only cause more confusion.

JoAnna's once-worried expression seemed to have hardened to stone, and a coldness had crept in about her eyes, intensifying the resemblance to her mother. "I guess I should be glad you were on hand, but look what's happened.'' She made it sound as if she thought his being called in by Emily initially had created their dilemma rather than being necessitated by it.

''I understand how you feel,'' Ransom said with no particular expression. ''Could we have a word with you?''

''All right,'' JoAnna said reluctantly. ''We can go in the kitchen.''

''If you need me I'll be in the living room,'' Emily said with her usual discretion.

The detectives followed JoAnna into the kitchen. She sat at the table and Ransom sat across from her. Gerald was used to staying in the background, but the lack of any other seating arrangement left him with no choice but to sit at the table with them. When he laid his notebook out, JoAnna gave it a surreptitious glance.

''Do *you* have any idea who the house goes to now?'' Ransom asked.

''No. I thought it would go to Leslie, wouldn't it?''

''Only if your mother had died first or has specified that in her will. Otherwise it would most likely go to a member of the immediate family.''

JoAnna shrugged. ''Then you'll have to ask her about it. I don't know and I don't care. I'm sure it won't come to me, and I don't want it.''

''Just as a matter of form, I need to ask where you were last night, from about ten o'clock on.''

The hardness in JoAnna's expression was replaced with complete surprise. ''I don't understand....'' she said tentatively, looking from one detective to the other. ''Emily said it looked like Robert was killed when someone tried to rob him.''

''That's the way it looks. But it's very easy to make a murder look that way. Even under ordinary circumstances, we'd be obligated to investigate those close to a murder victim, no matter how it appeared he was murdered. But these are hardly ordinary circumstances, are they?''

''What do you mean?''

"Well, there've been some rather odd things happening in your family lately, haven't there?"

"So you think that one of us might have killed Robert? No...no, that can't be!"

"That's what we mean to find out. Could you tell me where you were?"

"I was at home. Asleep. You don't think I..." She glanced at Gerald and appeared to be pained that he was jotting something down.

"I don't think anything yet. Were you on good terms with Robert?"

"Was I...?" She looked positively shocked, but after a moment her face relaxed and she almost smiled. "Robert was probably the best of the lot when it comes to the men in our family." She paused, then added quietly, "He loved his wife."

Ransom cocked his head slightly. "I beg your pardon?"

She looked down at her intertwined fingers. "I'm sorry. We haven't exactly made good marriages in our family. But Robert was trying hard to be different."

"You mean he was trying to make his marriage work?"

"No. I meant he was trying to be different from his father."

"There's a lot of that going on in your family. I understand that Gregory also tried not to be like *your* father."

"He wasn't very successful. But you're right. He tried. I don't think he beat Robert, but...you know how it is. He couldn't help acting like... He always picked at Robert. Robert couldn't do anything right."

"But you don't think that Gregory beat him."

"No, I..." she looked back down at her fingers and started to click her thumbnails together.

"Miss Pearson?"

She looked up at him from beneath her brow, like a guilty child who was afraid of what the reaction would be to her confession. "I don't think so, but...I know that he hit his wife."

"Gregory, you mean."

"Yes. At least once. But she said it was more. That's why she divorced him."

Ransom raised an eyebrow. "Robert told us that his mother is dead."

"She is. She died a couple of years after they split up. That was a long time ago."

She was silent for a moment, then added somewhat wistfully, "I liked Grace. She was strong. Stronger than I could ever be. I would've liked to have stayed friends with her, but she wouldn't have anything to do with any of us after the divorce."

Ransom said, "We've been told that there was a very emotional scene between Gregory and Robert last night."

"It doesn't surprise me," JoAnna replied, thinking he meant an argument. "That's pretty much all there's been since Robert was old enough to stand up on his own two feet."

"Do you think that was the cause of the unpleasantness between them, Robert standing up for himself?"

She gave a muffled laugh. "No. It's just that Greg is so mad all the time. I think he's mad at the world. Not that he doesn't have a reason to be. When we were young, he took care of Mother and me, because Daddy didn't do it. He tried to protect us—especially me—and as a result he got the brunt of Daddy's wrath. He didn't have much of a childhood, and I don't think he's had much of a life since."

"Exactly how angry do you think he is? Angry enough to kill?"

"No!" JoAnna replied, shaking her head vigorously. She looked aghast at the thought. "He would never kill Robert! His own son! You can't think that!"

"I don't know of any reason he would," Ransom said simply. "Do you?"

"No, I don't!" her cheeks reddened. She looked as if she were angry on her brother's behalf. "Why would he do it?"

"Because he wanted this house," Ransom said.

"That's insane! Who would kill over a thing like that? Greg might have resented Mother leaving the house to Robert, but he wouldn't *kill* him. Knowing Greg, he would just bear a grudge against him for the rest of his life. Greg isn't the nicest person on the face of the earth, I'll admit that. But murder? I *know* he wouldn't do that!"

"How can you be so sure?"

For a moment, JoAnna looked stumped, and embarrassed for not being able to think of an answer more quickly. Then suddenly her face brightened a bit and she said, "Well, if for no other reason than he would never do anything that would possibly get him put in jail. He's very, very claustrophobic—another byproduct of our dad. He'd go insane if he was locked up!"

JoAnna looked so worried that Ransom might not believe her that he felt moved to say, "We're not focusing exclusively on Gregory. Nor are we ruling out the fact that Robert's murder might be exactly what it appears to be, a mugging gone bad. But we also have to take everyone else into consideration: you, your brother, Robert's wife. Even your father."

JoAnna shook her head brusquely, as if she couldn't believe they had come back to that. "Daddy must be dead by now."

"There's no reason to believe that," said Ransom.

She screwed up her face. "Why would Daddy kill Robert? He didn't even know him."

"Why would anyone?" Ransom countered. "He seems to be the one member of your family that everyone loved. Your father probably *is* a long shot, but answer me this: Do you think your father was capable of killing someone?"

JoAnna wasn't looking at Ransom. Instead she seemed to be peering into the past. And something like fear marred her lovely face at what she saw there. Suddenly she snapped back to the present and looked Ransom in the eye.

"Yes," she said, her voice trembling. "Yes, I think my father could commit murder!"

WHEN THEY HAD FINISHED with JoAnna she went back upstairs to sit with her mother. Ransom and Gerald stopped in the living room to have a word with Emily before leaving and found her sitting in an armchair reading *Macbeth*.

"You haven't finished that yet?" said Ransom with some surprise.

"I'm going through it again. What you said earlier about nothing making sense brought me back to it. The three witches, you know. 'Double, double, toil and trouble' and all that. I wish I could get beyond the feeling of all of this being purposely stirred up by someone."

"Well, it may be getting a little clearer. On my way up here I got a call from Peterson. According to Social Security, Marjorie Loughlin is here."

"In Chicago?" Emily said, arching her eyebrows in surprise. "So that brings us a step closer to finding Phillip Pearson."

"Not necessarily. The address they have for her is the Oak Tree Nursing home in Niles."

Emily seemed not to hear this for a moment. Her face had gone blank, and she appeared to be lost in thought. Suddenly she looked up at Ransom. "Did you say you found Marjorie Loughlin?"

Ransom glanced at Gerald. "Yes."

"That's very curious, isn't it?"

"What is?" Gerald asked.

"Why, that her name is the same, of course." She looked at the two of them as if this should explain it all.

"The same as what?" Ransom asked.

"The same as it was. Wouldn't you think her name would have changed?"

"Oh," said Ransom. "Well, we don't know that she ever married Pearson, or even that she stayed with him for very long."

"I suppose that's true," Emily said absently. "After all, it was a strange situation. It probably means nothing." She adjusted herself in her chair, and shook her head as if to clear it. "Now, what do you intend to do?"

"It's getting late. We're going to go back to area headquarters and check in. I'll report what we have to Newman. In the morning I guess we'll be going to Niles to talk to Loughlin and see if she has any idea where Pearson is."

Emily smiled coyly. "By 'we,' I assume you mean Detective White and yourself?"

Gerald had to struggle to keep himself from laughing.

"Yes," said Ransom. "Why?"

"I was just thinking, if she's in a nursing home, don't you think it might be better if I went with you and talked to her? There's no telling what condition she may be in, and it would probably be less intimidating for her."

"Emily…"

She raised her index finger, signaling for him to wait until she had finished. "*And*, it would cause much less of a stir if you brought me there in the guise of…say…a visiting old friend, rather than having two police detectives showing up and asking after her."

One corner of Ransom's mouth curved upward. "She might like that kind of stir."

"I doubt it," Emily said primly.

"Emily, I can't take you along on an official investigation."

"Why not? You were kind enough to help me in an unpaid capacity while I looked into what was going on here. Now that it's official, I see no reason that I shouldn't help you in *my* unpaid capacity." She folded her hands in her lap. "Any concerned citizen would be willing to do as much."

"I have the distinct feeling that in the politest possible way you've just accused me of horning in on your case."

She made a sound that came out something like "Tut,"

and looked at him in a way that made him feel like a naughty child. He glanced at his partner.

"Don't look at me," said Gerald. "She's probably right. The Loughlin woman probably would find it easier to talk to her than to us together. And besides, we need to check into the finances of everybody connected with this to see if anyone besides Robert Pearson needed money. I can do that in the morning while you run up to Niles."

Ransom looked from Gerald down to Emily, who smiled up at him sweetly.

"I feel like I'm being conspired against," he said. Then he sighed. "Well, after all, we're only going to see if she can help us locate Phillip Pearson. I guess it'll be all right as long as we're not after anything that could get thrown out of court."

"I'm sure you've made the right decision," Emily said without a hint of irony.

THE HOUSE GREW QUIET around Emily as she continued her reading after the detectives had gone, the air of solemnity deepening as afternoon passed into evening. The silence was only broken by the insistent ticking of the grandfather clock in the hallway, the steady and unyielding nature of which made it seem as if time was somehow passing quickly and slowly at the same time.

Emily sighed to herself as she reached the scene in *Macbeth* where the ghost of Banquo enters during the banquet, much to the dismay of Macbeth, who can see him, and to the general puzzlement of the diners, who cannot.

So much like poor Abigail when I came into this business, Emily thought. *Only the apparition she was seeing turned out to be real.*

Her ruminations were interrupted by the sound of Jo-Anna coming down the stairs. She paused at the bottom of the staircase, lost in thought. Then she saw Emily and came into the living room. Emily noticed that the younger woman's shoulders were slumped as if under a great weight, and her eyes had the vacant, distracted look of someone who knows she should be doing something and doesn't know exactly what it is.

"I think I'll go home now. Mother's still asleep, and there isn't much—" She broke off, then added, "I need to get out of this house. I need some air. That probably sounds selfish, but…"

"Not at all," Emily said kindly. "You've had a shock, and you should go home and get some rest. Everything will be all right here."

"Will it? Right now I don't think anything will be all right anywhere. Mother looks… She doesn't look well at all."

"I know. But given her past history, her heart notwithstanding, I would say that she is a much stronger woman than you may think."

"Really?"

"I'm sure of it," Emily said firmly.

JoAnna forced an appreciative smile. "Thank you."

She started to leave, but hesitated in the archway and looked back.

"Emily, will you be staying? I mean, I thought you might go once we found out that Mother's health was all right, but…"

"I'll stay as long as I'm able and as long as I'm needed," Emily said reassuringly.

Tears welled in JoAnna's eyes. "Thank you. Mother is taking this very badly. I'm sure she appreciates having you around."

"That's quite all right. Will you be back in the morning?"

"Yes. I've already talked to my boss and told her I won't be back for a few days."

"I need to go out on an errand in the morning," Emily explained, "but I won't be very long, and I'll be here the rest of the day."

JoAnna thanked her again and then left.

Emily read for a little while longer, then set her book aside and once again climbed the stairs to the second floor. She didn't bother knocking on Abigail's door, not wanting to risk waking her. She quietly opened the door and went in.

JoAnna had been right: Abigail didn't look well at all. Her skin was pallid and her hair, half of which had been steel-gray, looked as if it were turning completely white. Her mouth hung open and her arms lay limply at her sides. All of the earlier indications that she'd been getting better had disappeared.

Emily silently crossed the room and sat in the chair beside the bed, folding her hands in her lap. She had only been there a short time when Abigail's eyelids fluttered, then slowly slid open.

"I'm so sorry," Emily said softly, "I didn't mean to wake you."

"You didn't." Her voice was hoarse and weak. "My own thoughts woke me."

"Try to get back to sleep."

Abigail's right hand went up to her eyes. "Who would've thought that one day I'd be trying to get to sleep to get away from nightmares." She sighed heavily, pressing her thumb and forefinger against her temples. "I think there comes a time in your life—there should anyway—when you look at what you've become. For some of us things turn out right and for some they turn out badly. But once the die's been cast, there doesn't seem to be any way to turn it around. You end up trapped with your lot. You realize that your life is never going to be what it could've been, and it never will, and it would probably be better if you just died."

"You mustn't talk like that."

"It's taken me a long time to realize it," she continued as if she hadn't heard Emily. "But after all these years I think I've finally realized that things are never going to work for the good in my life. I look back to when I was young, so long ago. I wanted so badly to get away from my parents, to get out of there, and what happened? I married into a situation that was even worse. Far worse." She paused and swallowed hard. "It wouldn't have been so bad if it was only me, but then I had children. Oh, God, if only I'd been a stronger person! None of this would've happened, and maybe my children would've had some chance at happiness. Maybe they would've been spared. But all we do is pass our unhappiness down from one generation to the next." She reached out and clutched at Emily's delicate hand. "All my life…all my life I've been a prisoner in one way or another. And now it will never end! If only I'd been stronger!"

Emily looked at her long and hard before responding. She wasn't much for self-pity, but she knew that Abigail had had more than her share of hardship. "You were strong," she said at last. "After your husband left, you did the best you could to take care of your children and raise them on your own. You strived to make a home for them. No matter how you feel it turned out, you can at least be proud of that."

"It was still only a prison," Abigail said with weary bitterness as she let go of Emily's hand. "And now Robert is gone. My beautiful Robert. I had so much hope for him. He was trying so hard! I never thought it would come to this!"

Emily gazed at her for some time before speaking again. "Abigail, I know this won't mean much to you right now, but I can promise you that Jeremy will do everything in his power to see that Robert's murderer is brought to justice."

For the first time, Abigail turned and faced her. "He thinks it may have been one of my children."

"He also thinks it may have been your ex-husband."

There was a long pause before Abigail's eyes widened and she let out a shocked "What?"

"There's reason to believe that your ex-husband may be in Chicago."

Abigail's reaction was almost the same as Gregory's had been. The fear on her face made it look as if the mere thought of Phillip Pearson's close proximity had taken her back to the time when he made her life a living hell.

"Why do you say that?" she asked.

"The woman that he left with, Marjorie Loughlin, is in the area. Assuming they've stayed together, it is possible— if he's still alive—that he's here, too."

"She came back?" Abigail said, her expression a mask of disbelief.

"Yes. Jeremy and I are going to talk to her tomorrow to see if she knows where Phillip Pearson is."

Abigail turned her eyes to the ceiling and lay there staring straight ahead for several seconds.

"She came back," she echoed, then closed her eyes and said no more.

TWELVE

WHEN RANSOM picked Emily up the next morning, the sky was overcast and the humidity high enough to make the detective feel as if he were wading through the air. In just the time it took him to walk from his car to the door his sports coat grew damp and his skin glistened.

Despite the oppressive atmosphere, when Emily emerged she said, "Goodness! I didn't realize how truly gloomy that house is. I haven't been out of it since I got here, you know. Do you believe that a building can take on a character of its own?"

"I don't know," Ransom replied as he helped her down the narrow walk to the curb. "Maybe. But it's probably just people's perception of it more than anything else. And atmosphere. People will associate a house with the people who live there, and the atmosphere they create, which in this case is anything but pleasant."

"Perhaps I'm just getting fanciful in my old age," Emily said with a sigh. "I've certainly felt fanciful since coming here. Abigail speaks of this house as being unhappy. She had hopes that if Robert and Leslie came here to live, that they might be able to reclaim it, so to speak, and make it a happy place."

"Abigail was unrealistic. Even if he hadn't told me so himself, after meeting Robert I would've thought he would sell this mausoleum and found a nicer spot to live. I wonder why she was so sure he'd keep it."

"Probably because he said he would, and because she loved him. We don't like to believe that someone we love would lie to us."

"I suppose."

Emily eyed him with her impish smile. "There is another reason that may satisfy your more cynical sensibilities."

"Hmm?"

"Abigail, in some ways, feels she and her family have been prisoners of their own unhappy lives for many, many years. It's difficult for someone like that to believe that someone else, especially a member of their own family, can break free."

"You mean she might have convinced herself that he would keep the house just because he couldn't break free of it?"

She nodded apologetically. "I warned you that I was getting fanciful."

Ransom helped Emily into the car, went around to the driver's side, and got in. Emily straightened her royal blue dress and fastened her safety belt.

"How is Abigail today?" Ransom asked, as he turned the key in the ignition.

"Not very good, I'm afraid. Robert's murder has been a great blow to her. And when I told her what we were planning to do this morning, it just made matters worse."

"Who can blame her? She just heard that her grandson is dead, and now she hears that her husband's mistress is back in town—and that her husband himself may be back. I wouldn't expect her to be happy about any of it."

"She talked to Gregory this morning, the first time since hearing the news about Robert, and that seemed to be even more traumatic. I must say, Jeremy, that Abigail seems very, very afraid. Before, I had the feeling that she didn't want to know who was trying to frighten her. Now it seems as though she doesn't want us to find the murderer."

"There's good reason for that. It could very easily be one of her children."

It was a long drive up to Dempster and then over to the suburb of Niles, and the trip was made longer by the fact that Ransom couldn't smoke with Emily in the car. As usual, she sat quietly in her seat, hands folded in her lap, watching the passing terrain with interest.

The Oak Tree Nursing Home was located just south of Dempster, on Harlem. It was a very uninviting, fourteen-story stone structure that looked like it had been converted from an office building for its present use, and had retained all the styleless anonymity of its original incarnation. The outer stone surface looked as if it had been dusted with gray, a sign that it was badly in need of a sandblasting that would never come.

The parking lot was half empty when Ransom and Emily arrived, and he steered the car into a space as close to the doors as possible.

"Heavens," Emily said softly, looking out through the window at the building, as Ransom turned off the engine.

Ransom looked up at it. "Not very appealing, is it?"

"Those aren't exactly the terms I would use," Emily replied, her voice sounding slightly strained.

Ransom shot her a questioning glance. "Emily? Are you all right?"

She turned to him and smiled. "Last night Abigail said to me that some people, when they see what their lives have become and know there's no possibility for change, should just die. I'm not sure I was as understanding as I should have been."

He placed his hand over hers for a moment, then gave it a gentle squeeze. "Shall we?"

The interior of the home was worse than the outside. The pale tile floor was so badly scuffed it looked like the pelt of a dalmatian. Even the walls and ceiling were badly scored and dented, as if a family of rubber-soled squirrels had been allowed to run riot around them.

Just inside and to the right of the glass doors was a large window that looked into what appeared to be a combination reception area/nurses' station/security desk. There was a hole cut in the center of the window through which one could speak to the woman behind the desk. She was middle-aged, with dark hair shot through with gray, and had a pair of overly large glasses perched precariously on her nose. A row of video screens across the front of the desk showed various areas of the home, and a row of lights on the phone in front of her flashed continuously. She flexed her fingers together anxiously as she scanned the litter of papers on her desk.

"Yes?" She said without looking up.

"We're here to see Marjorie Loughlin," Ransom said through the hole.

"Who?" She looked up at him and blinked owlishly from behind her glasses.

"Marjorie Loughlin," he repeated patiently.

The woman repeated the name several times as she placed her palms flat on several different places on the desk as if she might find the patient under one of the piles.

"Ah! Here it is!" she said, suddenly lunging for the Rolodex that sat in plain view on the right side of the desk.

"Perhaps she needs larger glasses," Ransom said softly to Emily. If he was hoping to cheer the old woman, he was disappointed. Emily stared with dismay through the window at the messy office.

The woman flipped through the Rolodex, continuing to repeat the last name, until she said, "Aha! Aha, aha, aha! Here she is! Twelfth floor." She slapped the lid shut on the card file and started to pick up sheets of paper one by one, glance at them, then put them back down without making any attempt at order, so that within seconds she was picking up sheets she had already examined.

"How do we get there?" Ransom said with exaggerated civility.

"What?" Her head came up and she looked at him as if she'd never seen him before.

"How do we get to the twelfth floor?"

"Oh! Elevator! Around the corner to the right."

They followed these directions and came upon a short, dirty hallway at the end of which was a pair of elevator doors. The one on the left sported an out of order sign, written in a nearly illegible scrawl on a piece of paper torn from a spiral notebook. Ransom pressed the button, and during the interminable wait, Emily continued to stare straight ahead, lost in thought.

At last the door of the elevator on the right slid open with a hollow, metallic rattle. Ransom and Emily got on with some trepidation, and Ransom pressed the button marked twelve. The car vibrated its way up the shaft and seemed to have stopped for over a minute before the door opened on the twelfth floor, revealing an area that was much more clearly a nurses' station than the one on the first floor.

A young Filipino woman sat behind the desk, busily processing paperwork. Ransom and Emily approached her, but she was so intent on her work that she didn't look up until Ransom spoke.

"Excuse me, we're here to see Marjorie Loughlin."

"Miss Loughlin?" the young woman said brightly. "Oh, she'll be very glad to see you!"

"She will?"

She nodded vigorously. "She doesn't have many visitors, except for her daughter. She'll be very, very glad to see you!" She beamed at them and didn't say any more.

"And where would we find her?" Ransom said with a smile.

The nurse let out a long, staccato laugh. "I'm so stupid sometimes! She's in room Twelve-twelve. I'm sorry! I should've said so!"

"That's quite all right," said Ransom, barely able to resist her infectious humor.

"It's that way. That way down the hall." She pointed to their right.

As he shepherded Emily in the indicated direction, she said earnestly, "I suspect they're very lucky to have that young woman."

"Nobody visits her except her daughter. That doesn't sound promising," Ransom said. "Here it is."

The door to room 1212 stood open. Inside, dreary, pea-green drapes were drawn across the window, blotting out any possible sunlight, and all the lights were shut off. The room was partially illuminated by the glow from a television set that was tuned to a local station with the sound turned almost all the way down. The first half of the room contained a bed that was stripped of all its linens. The walls were bare, the floor relatively clean, and the garbage can empty. Apparently Mrs. Loughlin didn't have a roommate, or had recently lost one.

The other half of the room was cluttered with the type of bric-a-brac and mementos that are the bane of nursing homes and hospitals because of their tendency to get in the way, disappear, or break. Along the windowsills there were a small wooden dog, a ceramic cat, a pair of small china dolls in ethnic dresses, as well as a variety of pictures, all of which were coated with dust. The bed had linen but was unmade, and the remnants of breakfast was on a tray on the bedside table.

Sitting in a wheelchair between the two beds was a woman whose dry, drab hair was haphazardly brushed, and whose dress had been buttoned incorrectly so that one side rode up uncomfortably. She stared uncomprehendingly at the television set, with her mouth slightly open.

Ransom glanced down at Emily and was surprised to find something close to a scowl on her face. The contrast between the two women was startling, and apparently this fact was no less evident to Emily, who seemed very displeased.

"Jeremy," she said quietly, "Would you have a seat, please?"

Without a word Ransom sat in the small visitor's chair on the unoccupied side of the room.

Emily went to the woman in the wheelchair and said, "Mrs. Loughlin? Marjorie?"

"Hello?" the woman replied, barely animating.

"Mrs. Loughlin, my name is Emily Charters. I've come to visit you. How are you doing today?"

"Hello," Loughlin said again. Her hands had been resting in her lap, and one suddenly twitched and moved up to the arm of her chair. Emily reached out and gently touched the hand. For the first time, Mrs. Loughlin turned her head and looked at Emily. Her eyes were rather dull and questioning, as if she were searching her mind for some sign of recognition, but knew ahead of time she wouldn't find it.

"Do I know you?" she said at last, her voice cracking from disuse.

"I don't think so," said Emily. There was a pause, then she looked at the woman's dress and pursed her lips. "My, it looks like they had some trouble with your buttons this morning. Would you like me to fix it?"

Loughlin nodded, and Emily efficiently undid the first few buttons of the woman's dress, the rebuttoned them correctly.

"There!" she said crisply. "Now if we could find your brush, perhaps I could take care of your hair.

Mrs. Loughlin managed a weak smile. She seemed to be aware that something nice was being done for her, but was not quite sure what it was. Emily pulled out the top drawer of the bedside table and found a hairbrush that she assumed to be Mrs. Loughlin's.

"Here we are!" she said.

She stood beside the wheelchair and slowly, carefully, brushed Mrs. Loughlin's hair back, taking great care to straighten out tangles as painlessly as possible.

"Do I know you?" Loughlin said again after a few minutes. Her face lightened and her eyes were more alive. Instead of the worry that had been there before, she looked as if she *hoped* she knew Emily.

"No, my dear, not really," Emily said comfortingly, as she continued her work. "But I wanted to meet you and talk to you." She shot a glance at Ransom that told him she was going ahead even though she knew the task was futile. "I believe that a long time ago, we had a mutual friend. A man named Phillip Pearson?"

Loughlin's lips silently formed the name.

"Phillip Pearson," Emily repeated. "Do you remember him?"

Loughlin looked up at her quizzically, shaking her head. "I'm sorry."

"No need to be," Emily said kindly. "I had heard that you knew him, and thought perhaps you could tell me where he is."

From Loughlin's expression, it was apparent that she hoped a negative answer wouldn't put an end to the care she was getting. "Who was he?"

"Oh, a man you were once quite close to."

There was a long pause, then Loughlin's face flooded with recognition. She clapped her hands together over her heart and smiled broadly. "That man! I love him so much! I don't know what I'd do without him!"

Emily looked down at her with some surprise. "Then you do know where he is?"

Loughlin fixed an earnest gaze on Emily, as if she was the one person in the world who could understand.

"That man! You don't know! He is so wonderful to me! I couldn't do without him!" Grateful tears formed in her eyes, but she didn't break down. Instead she seemed happily lost in a memory, oblivious to everything and everyone.

Emily replaced the brush in the drawer and looked over at Ransom, who was eyeing Mrs. Loughlin as if she was a treasure chest to which he had lost the key. At a nod from Emily, he rose from his chair and the two of them went out of the room, leaving Mrs. Loughlin blissfully unaware of their departure.

"Poor thing," Emily said, as they paused outside the door. "I have been very fortunate in this life. Our ages are probably not much different, but I have fared much better than poor Mrs. Loughlin."

"And better than we are right now. It's so frustrating! She sounds like she knows where Phillip Pearson is, but how we're ever going to get it from her, I don't know. It probably isn't even possible."

It was then that they were interrupted by a woman coming down the hall. She had short reddish hair and a rather pointed nose that gave an angular quality to her otherwise round face. She was dressed in a matronly brown suit and carrying a black pocketbook.

"Hello?" she said when she was not too far from them. Her voice sounded uncannily like the woman they had just visited. "Can I help you?"

"Are you by chance here to see Marjorie Loughlin?" Ransom asked.

"Yes, I am. I'm her daughter. My name is Susan DeMarco," she replied with surprise. She looked at Emily. "But...I don't know you, do I?"

"No," Emily replied.

"Are you a friend of my mother?" Her tone conveyed her prospective astonishment were the answer to be in the affirmative.

"No," said Ransom, "But we needed to talk to her, which we've just done. Is there a lounge or something around here where we could have a word with you?"

"Uh...yes. Right around here." She led them to the end of the hall where there was a small alcove in which a round coffee table and several chairs had been arranged. The three of them sat down.

"What's this all about?"

"Mrs. DeMarco, this is Emily Charters, and my name is Ransom. Detective Ransom."

"Detective?"

"Yes. I'm with the Chicago Police Department."

"What on earth are you doing bothering my mother?" DeMarco replied, her eyes wide.

Ransom sucked in his lips for a moment, then said, "Believe it or not, we thought your mother might be able to help us with a murder investigation to which I've been assigned.''

DeMarco's forehead furrowed, and a smile played about her lips. ''Is this a joke? You've seen my mother. You sure can't think she has anything to do with anything anymore.''

''Oh, no, my dear,'' Emily said. DeMarco couldn't help looking perplexed at the old woman's role in what was happening. ''It wasn't exactly with current events that we thought she could help, it was with something that happened a long time ago. We thought perhaps she might know the whereabouts of someone she knew then.''

''Mother has Alzheimer's disease,'' DeMarco explained. ''And it's pretty advanced. In five minutes she won't remember your visit, let alone anything that happened a long time ago. Maybe I can help you.''

''Your mother spoke of a man,'' said Emily. ''A man who loved her and who she couldn't do without.''

DeMarco nodded. ''My father. He was wonderful to her.''

''Your father?'' said Ransom. ''Do you mean your father or your stepfather?''

DeMarco looked completely puzzled. ''My stepfather? I never had a stepfather.''

Ransom and Emily glanced at each other.

''Your mother didn't marry a second time?'' Ransom asked.

''A second time? What are you talking about? My father only died two years ago, and that was after mother was in here.''

''And she was never divorced?''

''No! Where did you get such an idea?''

Emily cleared her throat and asked, ''Mrs. DeMarco, do you remember when your family moved away from their house in Rogers Park?''

''Of course,'' DeMarco answered. ''It was a long time ago. About thirty years, I think. I was fifteen at the time. Why?''

"Do you recall why your family moved away?"

"Of course. My father worked for a tool and die company, and they relocated to Kansas and we had to move. We didn't have a choice."

"And your mother went with you?" said Ransom.

Susan DeMarco couldn't have looked more astonished if she'd been asked if she was from another planet. "Of course Mother went with us! Where else would she have gone?"

Ransom was about to say something else, but Emily laid a cautioning hand on his arm to stop him.

"I'm so sorry," she said to DeMarco. "We were looking for someone who moved away from that neighborhood about the same time. A man named Phillip Pearson."

DeMarco shrugged. "Sorry. I don't know him."

"Hmm. For some reason, we thought the Pearsons were friends of your family."

She shook here head, still looking confused. "Not that I remember. I don't think we knew anybody by that name. Why did you think we knew them?"

"I'm so sorry," Emily said again. "We're tracing very old connections and it looks like we somehow got our wires crossed."

"Oh...that's all right." DeMarco looked as if she thought she had missed an important event.

The three of them rose and started back down the hallway.

"Your parents sound like wonderful people. How long were they together?"

"About fifty years," DeMarco responded with pride.

"Why did they come back to Chicago?"

"They always loved it here. It had really fond memories. When my father retired, they moved back." They came to a stop outside Mrs. Loughlin's room. She gave a pitiable sigh. "Fond memories. She doesn't have them anymore."

"I wouldn't be too sure of that," Emily said significantly, recalling the rapt look on Loughlin's face as she thought about "that man."

"WHY DID YOU stop me?" Ransom asked once they were back in the car.

"Stop you?" said Emily. "When Mrs. DeMarco said that her mother moved to Kansas with them. I was going to ask her something else, but you stopped me."

"What would you have said to her?" Emily said gently. "That we'd heard her mother had run off with another man at one time? That we had reason to believe that her mother was unfaithful to her father? Mrs. DeMarco was perfectly sure of her parents' relationship. I didn't think it was necessary to plant a seed of doubt in her mind when it was obvious that we were on the wrong track."

"You're right, of course. I'll tell you something else that's obvious," Ransom said as he started the car. "Jo-Anna Pearson lied to us."

"Do you think so?"

"When you asked her if she knew who it was her father had left with, she gave you the name of a woman she could've reasonably believed we wouldn't be able to locate. After all, the Loughlins moved out of state. We didn't know where they went or if Mrs. Loughlin had even retained her name. In fact, it would've been reasonable to assume she hadn't. It was only dumb luck that Marjorie Loughlin was back in Chicago."

"But I don't think JoAnna *lied* to me," said Emily. "She was quite sincere when she told me about it. I think she told me what she believed. As a matter of fact, it may be that nobody was lying about it at all."

Ransom paused in the act of putting the car in gear and looked at his elderly companion. "What do you mean?"

"Just that JoAnna was told it was Marjorie Loughlin who'd gone away with her father by one of her schoolmates. JoAnna said she herself seemed to be the last to know. I find that very understandable, don't you?"

Ransom sat back. "You've lost me, Emily."

She gave a slight shrug. "It must have been well known that Phillip Pearson was a philanderer. That sort of thing always is. Perhaps nobody knew who he really went away with. If the Loughlins happened to move away at the same time as Phillip Pearson left..." She let her voice trail off suggestively.

"Two plus two equals six, eh?" Ransom said, curling his lips.

"It can take much less than coincidence to start a rumor."

"I still think I'd better have a talk with JoAnna."

LESLIE PEARSON spent most of the morning lying in bed, staring at the ceiling. Rather than continuously running through a litany of worries over and over again in her head, she found herself curiously unable to mentally complete a sentence. She would begin with "How am I going to..." only to find the words dropping off into a void from which the end of the thought, let alone the answer to her problems, was not forthcoming.Throughout all this she would periodically run up against her own wall of disbelief that Robert was really gone. To her young mind the concept of sudden loss was so foreign that she was tempted to believe Robert's absence would somehow be explained away in some fashion other than the fact that he wasn't returning at all. And when he came back she would forgive him for having scared her so badly: She would forgive him anything just to have him back. Eventually, when his disappearance had been explained, she might even be able to laugh at how afraid she was when she thought she had been left alone.

Even in her grief, she didn't idealize Robert. In some ways he had been hardheaded and immovable, and sometimes even mean. But she'd been able to see into his heart, beyond the moments when he was unpleasant, and there she found a man who was fighting to be a better person.

And it was knowing how hard he was trying that made the occasional lapses bearable.

But then the conversation she had had with that detective when they came to tell her Robert was dead came back to her: the questions about his grandmother and all that nonsense about the house, and her remembering what Robert had said about his disappointment. Once again Leslie would find herself wondering if she had ever really known Robert at all. Could he have hidden something so dark from her?

Then her mind turned itself back to its broken thoughts of her own future, and the void would overtake her again.

The phone rang a couple of times over the course of the morning, but she had no desire to speak with anyone about anything. Condolences would just reinforce the fact that Robert was dead, while well-meaning pleasantries would deny it. Either way, she thought that speaking with anyone would only add to her pain.

It was eleven o'clock before she finally dragged herself out of bed. She moved dully through her delayed morning routine, like a ghost of herself haunting her own life. She showered without feeling the water, and a few minutes afterward found she had combed out her hair and brushed her teeth with no recollection of having done so.

After dressing, she had the vague notion that there were things that had to be done: The dishes from yesterday hadn't been tended to, and the garbage in the trash can in the kitchen was overflowing. Robert was supposed to take that out, but she always had to remind him at least twice before he would do it. Her tears started to flow at the thought that she would never again have the opportunity to remind him to take out the trash.

Still as if in a trance, Leslie filled the sink and washed the dishes. As she wiped each plate she tried to fight back the thought that it would be one last contact with Robert. When she was finished, she put the dishes and glasses away, folded the dishrag over the faucet, and laid the towel out on the counter to dry. Then she turned and looked at the garbage can. She didn't really want to go outside for fear someone would say something to her, and she thought that even exchanging hellos would cause her more pain. But she was finding some sense of comfort—if not comfort, then time filled—in moving about and performing mindless activities.

She pulled the bag from the can, spun it around once to close it, then sealed it with a twist-tie. She opened the back door, hoisted the bag in her arms, and went carefully down the unsturdy wooden steps that snaked up the back of the building.

She carried the bag down the narrow walk that ran through the overgrown backyard and behind the garage to the single Dumpster that, although large, was still too small to serve the building. All the while she prayed that she would be able to make it to the alley and back without running into anyone who would force her into conversation.

She had to set the bag on the ground in order to flip back the huge lid on the Dumpster. It fell against the wooden garage wall with a loud bang. She happened to glance down before picking up her bag and saw, sitting on top of the piles of uniform plastic garbage bags, a smallish, plain cardboard box, new enough to look pristine in its current setting. In fact, it was in such good condition that it looked rather incongruous.

Leslie's curiosity managed to partly cut through her daze. She reached in and pulled out the box, then slowly turned it around in her hands, scanning its exterior.

Finally, she stuck her finger under the flap and pulled the top open.

"Oh, my God!" she gasped, when she saw what was inside.

RANSOM AND EMILY arrived back at Abigail's house just before noon. Ransom rang the bell and they had a lengthy wait before the door was opened by JoAnna, who didn't look entirely pleased to see them.

"Emily, what did you say to my mother?" she asked as she closed the door after them.

"I beg your pardon?" the old woman replied, quite at a loss.

"Last night. What did you say to her? She seems even more upset than she did when I left. She told me it had something to do with you, but not what it was."

"It didn't have to do with Emily," Ransom interjected. "It had to do with our investigation. May we sit down somewhere?"

After a beat, JoAnna nodded and they went into the living room. JoAnna sat in the chair where Emily had done her reading, while Ransom and Emily sat on the couch.

"As you know," Ransom began, his manner almost as if he was convening a meeting, "I'm investigating your nephew's murder. Putting aside for a moment the idea that he was killed by a mugger, I have to examine the possibility that he was murdered by someone who knew him. In this case, I'm also inclined to assume that what happened to Robert might have something to do with what's been going on in this house."

"Yes, yes, I know all that," JoAnna said impatiently. "But I don't see how."

"Neither do I at the moment. But if we work from the idea that these attempts to scare or confuse your mother are related to Robert's death, then our first priority is to find out who was responsible for tormenting your mother. Now, I see four possibilities for who that person may be. I tend to rule you out because whoever it is was making him- or herself up to look like your father. That may be possible for you to do, but would probably be much more difficult than for one of the men in your family. Then there's Robert himself. He was ostensibly the only one to gain from something happening to your mother, but if he was doing it, that makes his murder much more curious."

"Unless it really was a mugger," JoAnna interjected.

"True. Then there's Gregory. He probably most closely resembles your father, but he has nothing to gain in harming your mother. He may want the house, but killing Robert still wouldn't ensure that it would come to him." He stopped for emphasis, then added, "But there's a fourth possibility, a much more troubling one: that it actually is your father doing these things, and he has come back for some reason or another and is playing cruel tricks on your mother for reasons we don't know. Which still wouldn't explain your nephew's death. But it does make it imperative, since it is your father that your mother says she saw, that we make sure of whether or not it's possible it could be him."

"You've said that before," JoAnna said with a dismissive wave of her hand. "But that's just insane!"

"Perhaps not as much as you may think," said Emily. "You see, we were able to ascertain that Marjorie Loughlin is back in the Chicago area."

"What?" JoAnna said, going pale.

"The reason your mother was so upset is that I told her we'd found Mrs. Loughlin and planned to talk to her this morning. We thought maybe she could lead us to your father."

"Well, of course Mother would be upset!" JoAnna exclaimed. The color returned to her cheeks, and she looked like she didn't exactly know with whom she should be angry.

"But, you see, there lies the problem," Emily explained, the look in her eyes intensifying. "Mrs. Loughlin disavows any knowledge of your father."

"What? Well she would do that, wouldn't she?"

"No, I don't mean that. I mean she disavows *ever knowing* your father."

"But still…"

Emily shook her head ruefully. "Oh, I'm so sorry, I'm doing this very badly. I didn't mean Mrs. Loughlin told us this, I meant her daughter. We met her daughter, you see, and she seemed genuinely amazed when we asked about your father. She told us that the reason her entire family— mother included—moved away from the area was because her father was transferred to Kansas. Her mother was never away from them, and I'm sure she would've noticed if her mother had disappeared for a time.''

JoAnna had the dumbfounded look of someone who can feel their foundation crumbling beneath them. ''But that was what I was told. You mean it might not have been true?''

''We mean it most definitely *wasn't* true,'' said Ransom, taking over. ''Now, you say that someone at school told you your father had left with Marjorie Loughlin?''

''Yes. Dave. David Berman.''

''But you don't know where he heard this?''

''No. He told me everybody knew about it.''

Ransom thought for a moment, then said, ''Miss Pearson, I'm a bit confused. If you didn't learn until later, at school, that your father had gone away with someone, what did you think before that? Do you remember anything of when your father left?''

''Oh, yes,'' she replied sadly. ''I remember the fight. There was another fight, as usual. I don't know what it was about, because I was up in bed. I told you before, there was no telling what would set him off. And I didn't get out of bed to find out what it was, I just laid there and...and...''

''You were glad you weren't the target that time?'' Emily offered softly.

JoAnna's head drooped. ''Yes. He yelled and yelled, and then I heard him run up the stairs.... I was scared that he would come into my room, but he didn't. He went into their room—his and Mother's. Then I heard him go down and slam out the front door. It was awful...but...it was more awful the next day.''

''Who told you about it?'' Ransom asked.

''Mother. She took me aside in the morning, and told

me Daddy had left, but that she would take care of me. But, you see…" She choked back a sob and tried to regain control of herself. "I could understand him leaving her, because I think I knew even then that he didn't like her. But…he never even said good-bye to me."

"And you have no idea where he really went. Gregory, your mother, they never said anything more about it?"

"No. I told you before. Talking about it made Mother cry and made Gregory so angry, I just gave up! But I don't think they knew, either. Even as upset as everybody was, I think they would've told me eventually, don't you?"

"Possibly," Ransom said. "Do you remember where your father worked at the time, or who his friends were?"

"He worked for Harris and Sons Manufacturing, which used to be on Belmont. I think they went out of business sometime in the seventies. Like a lot of companies, the father died and the sons took over, and the business went right down the tubes."

"What about his friends?"

"I was just a girl at the time. I don't think I ever paid attention to who their friends were. Mother would know."

"How about neighbors?" Ransom sounded as if his patience was beginning to wear thin.

"Well, there was the Williamses. They lived next door on the right. Mr. Williams was sort of a friend of Daddy's, I guess. He was left a widower a long time ago. He still lives next door."

"Do you know his first name?"

She looked startled for a split second, then almost smiled. "As a matter of fact, I don't. He's always been Mr. Williams to me. Mother would know that, too."

"What about the people who called the police?"

"The police?"

"Yes. Gregory told us about an incident when some neighbors called the police because he was screaming."

"Oh, yes," JoAnna replied. "Yes, when Daddy…locked him away. I think that's one of the things that made Greg-

ory so claustrophobic. Once when we were younger I got
really mad at Greg and I jammed a chair under the bathroom doorknob while he was inside so that he couldn't get
out.'' She smiled with embarrassment. ''It was a terrible
thing for me to do, because I knew how he was. He panicked. He yelled and yelled. I was about to take the chair
away when I heard glass breaking. He'd broken the window
with his fist to get out. He was that scared.''

''Do you remember who it was that called the police?''

''Oh, I'm sorry. Yes, it was Larry Whitehall. He and his
wife lived next door on the other side.''

''You know his first name?'' Ransom said with a smile.

She nodded. ''Only because my father cursed him by
name for months afterward: ''that goddamn Larry Whitehall,'' etc. etc. I don't think he ever even spoke to Mr.
Whitehall again. If you want to know the truth, secretly I
used to thank God for the Whitehalls. It made me feel...I
don't know, a little safer knowing somebody was listening.''

''Do you know where the Whitehalls are now?''

''Yes. It was only two or three years ago that they moved
away. They thought their house was getting too much for
them to keep up. They bought a condo in Evanston, I'm
afraid I don't know where.'' She paused, then said, ''Mr.
Ransom, do you really believe my father has come back?''

''Truthfully? I think it's very unlikely. It's not unusual
for an abuser to seek out the object of his abuse, but its
rather unusual for one to be so long about it. Frankly, the
one thing that makes me entertain the possibility at all is
that you and Gregory and your mother all seem terrified at
the idea of your father coming back. It's as if the three of
you wouldn't put it past him to have done something like
this. That, more than anything else, leads me to believe that
however unlikely, your father *might* be involved. But I still
think it's a long shot.''

The doorbell sounded just as Ransom was finishing this,

and JoAnna rose and left the room in answer. A few seconds later she showed in Gerald White.

"If you're finished with me, I'm going to go back up and sit with Mother."

Ransom replied with a nod and JoAnna left the room.

"Good afternoon, Miss Emily," Gerald said as he took a seat.

"Good afternoon, Detective White. And how is your wife and those two little girls of yours?"

"All three of them are getting bigger every day," he said with a laugh.

"What do you have for me—" Ransom broke off with a glance at Emily. "—us, Gerald?"

"Nothing good. Nothing we didn't know before. Everybody's been telling us the truth about finances. Neither Gregory nor JoAnna Pearson are exactly rich, but they aren't hurting, either. They're well enough off to make jumping through hoops to get this house a pretty strange thing to be doing. Robert Pearson is the only one that was hard up for money."

Ransom let out a frustrated *"Humph!"* "So once again, our chief suspect is the victim."

"What did you find out from Marjorie Loughlin?" Gerald asked.

"Absolutely nothing," said Emily. "She had never heard of Phillip Pearson."

"What? That's weird," said Gerald as pasty ripples formed across his forehead. "What does it mean?"

"Only that the rumors at the time were wrong." She clucked her tongue and shook her head with disgust. "Honestly, I feel I'm being very stupid."

"About what?" said Ransom.

"About Marjorie Loughlin. There's something about her that's just not right...."

"You mean, besides the fact that she didn't run off with Phillip Pearson?"

"Yes." She pressed her fingers together. "It's something

on the edge of my memory. Something that was said about
Marjorie Loughlin. I have a feeling now that it meant something, only I can't remember what it was. I just don't know
what the matter is with me!'' She lowered her hands and
shrugged. ''Oh, well, I suppose if it really was important
it will come back to me.''

''What do we do now?'' Gerald said to his partner.
''We've got nothing but dead ends.''

''I know,'' Ransom replied with a weary sigh. ''Robert
Pearson is dead, killed with the proverbial blunt instrument
that was not found at the scene of the crime, so unless we
manage to find a witness who happened to be in an Ed-
gewater alley in the middle of the night, we probably have
no hope of pinning the murder on anyone.''

''Do you have any idea who could've done it?'' Emily
asked.

''The obvious and least far-fetched suspect is Gregory
Pearson, merely because he was the only one we know of
who had a squabble with Robert, and because he was in
the area the night of the murder. But when it comes to
alibis, nobody's doing well. JoAnna was home alone, as
was Leslie.'' Before Emily could ask it, he added quickly,
''And no, I don't believe for a minute that Leslie did it.
But whoever murdered Robert, there's probably no way for
us to prove it. He was killed in the way that is most difficult
to deal with—he was just bashed in the head with something. Most killers are too artful. They try to devise some
clever, foolproof method of killing their victims while
maintaining an alibi, and in the end leave a trail leading
directly back to themselves. The safest way to kill someone
is to just club them over the head somewhere, exactly as
was done to Robert. This killer may be very bright.''

Emily looked up suddenly and said, ''Or very stupid....''

''What do you mean?''

''Oh, I'm not sure I know what I mean,'' Emily said
with a sigh. ''Now, what do you intend to do next?''

Ransom thought for quite a while before answering. ''I

suppose with nothing else to go by, we might as well go and talk to the neighbors, Mr. Williams and the White-halls.''

"What good will that do?'' Gerald asked.

"I'm sure I don't know, Gerald,'' Ransom replied somewhat irritably.

"Perhaps it will provide you with more insight into the family,'' Emily offered. "Oftentimes neighbors end up knowing quite a lot, especially ones that have lived next door for so many years. They may even know who Phillip Pearson went away with.''

Ransom let out a single laugh. "We can always hope!''

THIRTEEN

RANSOM AND GERALD proceeded down the front walk and over to Mr. Williams's house. They could have cut across the lawn and stepped over the low hedge that separated the properties, but Ransom feared that Williams might object to them traipsing across his lawn, and didn't want to run the risk of antagonizing someone from whom they hoped to get information.

The walk leading up to the front door of the house was wide, and a wooden ramp covered the left third of the staircase. As they neared it they could see that the wood was rotted, so Ransom figured that Williams's late wife must have spent her last days in a wheelchair. As they had come up the walk, the curtains in the front window fluttered and parted about an inch. A withered eye peered out at them as they went up the steps and rang the bell.

The curtains closed and after a wait of almost a minute, the inner door opened. The man who greeted them had a shriveled, reddened face and was slightly stooped. He wore a shiny gray suit, desperately in need of pressing, a white shirt, and a tie.

"Yes?" he said, his startled eyes riveted on Ransom.

"Mr. Williams?"

"Yes? What do you want?"

Ransom displayed his badge. "I'm Detective Ransom, this is Detective White—"

"I seen you next door," Williams exclaimed, his face opening with excitement. "I seen you coming and going. Lots of comings and goings lately…."

"There's been a little trouble next door. Could we speak with you for a minute?"

"Sure, sure," he said. He unlocked the screen door and Ransom pulled it open, but instead of admitting them, Williams came out onto the porch, hurriedly shutting the inner door behind him. But he didn't get it closed before Ransom managed to get a look over the old man's shoulder into the living room. It was a shambles, full of what looked like stacks and stacks of old newspapers. Ransom was rather relieved that they hadn't been invited in.

"We'll make it quick," said Ransom. "We don't want to delay you."

"Delay me from what?" Williams blinked at him.

Ransom motioned to the man's suit. "Weren't you going out?"

"No, I'm retired. I was just watching some television." He seemed entirely at a loss as to what Ransom was talking about.

"I'm sorry. All right, then, you said you have been seeing a lot of comings and goings lately. Do you mean at night?"

"What? No, no, I sleep at night. I meant during the day. I seen you come...." He turned to Gerald. "And I seen you come." He turned back to Ransom. "I seen the old lady, too. The one you took out today. Has she moved in there?"

"No, she's just visiting for a while."

"What's the matter over there, anyway? What kind of trouble they had?"

"Well, it didn't actually happen there," Ransom explained. "But Mrs. Pearson's grandson was killed."

"Oh, I see, I see." The old man rattled the change in his pocket and shifted from foot to foot.

"So we've been looking into a little of the family history," Ransom said matter-of-factly. He wanted to sound assured enough that Williams didn't ask for an explanation of what one had to do with the other, which would have taken unnecessary time.

"I lived here next to them for a lot of years," Williams

said, his use of the past tense making it sound as if he were eulogizing himself.

"That's what the family told us. So, maybe you could help."

"Sure, sure. I'll try. What do you want to know?"

"I understand that you knew Phillip Pearson."

"Phillip? Phil? Oh, yeah, I knew him." Williams's face lit up. "He was a tartar!"

"A what?" Gerald asked. He was leaning against the railing with his pencil poised over his notebook.

"A tartar," Williams repeated. "Never knew what he would do! He was a good friend, but ho ho ho, don't ever cross him!"

Gerald's forehead furrowed as he made a note.

"You sound as if you liked him," said Ransom.

"I did. We used to drink together. Oh, Phil had a temper, he had. But what's that? It's just a sign of life."

"Mr. Williams, we're trying to locate Phillip Pearson. Would you have any idea where he is?'

"Phil? He's gone. Left nigh onto…nigh onto…"

"Thirty years?" Ransom offered.

"Yeah, that's it. Thirty years ago if it's a day," Williams nodded, continuing to rattle the change.

"You don't know where he is now?"

"No. Wish I did, now that the wife's gone. She never did like Phil too much, but he was a friend to me."

"Did he ever say anything to you before he left his wife?"

There was a pause in the jingling. "About what?"

"About his plans. About leaving his wife or who he was going to go away with?"

"Hundreds of times! Hundreds!" Williams said as he went back to shaking his change. "He talked about leaving her all the time! When he finally did it, the only surprise to me was that it took him so long!"

"So he told you when he was leaving?"

Williams shook his head. "Just left! But he was always

talking about it. Said he was crazy to marry that woman. Said she was always harping on him about something, and when she wasn't harping, she was buying something, and when she wasn't buying something, she was whining about how he treated those kids! As if there was anything wrong with the way he did that! Thing that's wrong is the way people raise their kids *now*. They'd just as soon run you down as spit on you! Phil knew how to raise kids. You didn't see *his* kids getting out of line.''

I'll just bet you didn't, thought Ransom.

"And when they did get out of line, whew! Watch out! He'd give them what for and they'd wail like babies!''

From the rapacious grin on the old man's face, Ransom got the unpleasant feeling that he had found his neighbor's exploits entertaining.

"Mr. Williams,'' Ransom said, adopting a more formal tone, "do you have any idea who Pearson went away with?''

"No, no.'' Williams looked almost disappointed. "Could've been any one of a dozen women. Ol' Phil didn't exactly care which inkwell he dipped his pen into, if you know what I mean.''

"Do you remember any of their names?''

There was another pause in the jingling as Williams searched his memory. "No. Nope.''

"How about Marjorie Loughlin? Does that name sound familiar?''

"Can't say it does,'' Williams said.

Ransom stared at him for several seconds, then said, "Thank you,'' and went down the stairs with Gerald trailing not far behind.

The startled old man called out, "Anytime,'' at the detective's retreating backs.

"That wretched old fool!'' Ransom said through clenched teeth when they reached the sidewalk. "Discipline! As if what was being done to those kids was discipline.''

"Where to now? The Whitehalls?"

"We may as well."

Gerald made a quick call to directory assistance for the Whitehalls' address and phone number, then called the Whitehalls, who sounded understandably astonished by the nature of his call, and readily agreed to a visit from the detectives.

"What's wrong with you?" Gerald asked as he opened the door on the driver's side of his car. He almost always drove when the two of them were together, so there was no need to discuss which car they would take.

"I don't like this case."

"Why? Because Emily's involved?"

Ransom opened the passenger door, then stood facing his partner across the top of the car. "No. Because the whole thing seems so damn backward to me. We don't usually investigate before there's been a murder. I have a sort of 'cart before the horse' feeling about this whole thing that is very unsettling. I don't like it at all."

With this he dropped into his seat, slammed the door, and pulled out a cigar, all at once. Gerald got behind the wheel as Ransom unwrapped the cellophane.

"You know, it's only going to take us a few minutes to get there," said Gerald.

"Then I'll smoke fast," Ransom said, barely moving his lips.

THE WHITEHALLS LIVED on Sherman Avenue in one of the large, semi-elegant buildings erected during the fifties, apparently by someone who thought the idea of a family living in an apartment was rather chic. To Ransom it was little more than an upper-class version of a tenement. Like most, it hadn't been able to escape the condoization of the seventies and eighties and, in fact, due to the spacious apartments and desirable location, had been one of the first to go.

Gerald pressed the button beneath the Whitehalls' mail-box, and the security door buzzed before he had even re-tracted his finger.

"It seems we're expected," Ransom noted wryly. Prob-ably the only thing more troublesome to him than a reluc-tant witness was one who was overeager.

Once inside, they found a tiny elevator next to a carpeted staircase. They got in, closed the gate, and Gerald pushed the button for the fourth floor. The elevator gave a slight lurch, then quietly slid upward.

"I get the feeling this was an afterthought," said Ran-som, referring to the elevator as Gerald pulled the gate open.

"Right down here, fellas," a hearty voice called from off to their right.

A man with a pleasant, round face and thick salt-and-pepper hair stood halfway out of a door at the end of the hall. One hand was clinging to the jamb as if he might topple over if he released it.

"Mr. Whitehall?" said Ransom as they approached.

"Yes, yes!" the man replied, "We've been waiting for you!"

Not surprising, thought Ransom, *given the fact that we called you only fifteen minutes ago to tell you we were coming.* He introduced himself and his partner.

"Did you find us all right?" Whitehall said.

"Yes."

"Did you get a parking space?"

"We didn't have any problems."

"Good! Good. Come in, come in!"

He stood aside and let the detectives enter, then closed the door behind them.

"The wife is waiting in the living room. We're just all in a dither! Detectives! That's certainly something you don't see every day! At least, *we* don't!"

Whitehall led the way down a long hallway with a par-quet floor and numerous paintings, mostly portraits, on the walls. The hallway opened into a large living room filled with furniture that could best be described as fifties-modern: a wood-framed couch and matching chairs covered in what looked like maroon burlap; a pair of floor lamps with perfectly round, unadorned shades; and a pair of easy chairs in one corner facing a console television set. Between the chairs was an ashtray stand so clean it was evidently just for show. The room looked like a museum tribute to *The Jetsons*.

Mrs. Whitehall was standing in the center of the room when they came in. She was a handsome woman with the same rounded face and the same gray and white mix of hair as her husband. Apparently through decades of marriage the Whitehalls had grown to resemble each other both physically and in their mannerisms. When she saw the detectives, Mrs. Whitehall flashed a smile identical to that of her husband. If Larry Whitehall had not introduced her as his wife, Ransom might have taken her to be his sister.

"This is Martha, my wife," said Whitehall, who then turned to the woman in question and added inconsequentially, "These are the detectives."

"Ransom and White," said Ransom.

"This is just so…so…" Martha Whitehall produced a disbelieving smile and shook her head. "Just so incredible! Nothing like this has ever happened to us before. Well, we've traveled a lot, but this is the first time we've ever been questioned by the police! It's so exciting! I don't know what to offer you. Do you want some coffee?"

"No, thank you," said Ransom. "We're fine."

"Oh, of course!" Martha said as her cheeks turned a deep pink. "That was silly of me! You're on duty."

"That just means they can't have booze," her husband laughed, "not coffee."

"Oh, of course!" she said again, blushing more deeply. "I don't know what I was thinking. You can have coffee, can't you?"

"Yes, but we don't need any right now, thank you."

"Well, sit down, sit down," Larry said expansively. He laid a hand on the center of Ransom's back to guide him to one of the chairs by the couch. Ransom tried not to flinch. Gerald sat in the chair at the opposite end of the couch.

After the Whitehalls had seated themselves side by side on the sofa, Larry said, "Detective White said on the phone that this has something to do with Abigail Pearson?"

"I hope nothing's wrong with her," Martha said earnestly. "Abigail's had more than her share of troubles in this life. I just hope she knows that things will be better in the next one."

"I'm sure she does," said Ransom quickly, hoping to stem the flow of any excess religion. "Actually, it has to do with her grandson. I'm afraid he's been murdered."

"Oh, no!" Martha exclaimed with motherly compassion. "Poor Abigail. How awful! What happened?"

"That's what we're trying to find out."

Larry said, "Well, I don't see how we can help. We haven't seen hide nor hair of any of the Pearsons since we moved up here." He turned to his wife. "Isn't that right, honey?"

Martha nodded vigorously. "That's right. We did invite Abigail over just...not long after we moved. She didn't come, of course."

"Why 'of course'?" Ransom asked.

"Well, we were next door to them—what?—forty years, give or take a few, and in all that time I don't think any of the Pearsons set foot in our house more than once."

"That's right," Larry added. "Heck, I don't even think we could be much help even if we still lived right there next door. They never had much to do with anybody, so I can't say we knew them very well even then. You don't think Robert Pearson was killed by one of the family, do you?"

"Probably not," Ransom said, thinking it expedient. He didn't want to explain the reasons he thought the family *could* be involved. "It was probably just random. But we have to be thorough. That's why we came to you. We thought maybe you could help us fill in some of the background on the Pearsons."

"Well, I'm not sure I like that," Larry said so jovially it belied his words.

Martha chimed in, "What if we said something perfectly innocent and it gave you the wrong impression about them?"

"I don't think you could give us the wrong impression," Ransom said smoothly.

"But, like I said, we haven't had any contact since we moved away," said Larry, "so there's nothing really we can tell you about what's going on with them now."

"Actually, we're looking for information about Phillip Pearson."

"What?" Larry said with a hollow laugh. Despite his outgoing demeanor, it was clear that the subject of Phillip Pearson dampened his enthusiasm. "Phillip? Phillip's been gone for…what?" He looked to his wife for help.

"Twenty years now," she said.

"No, thirty, I think," Larry said, sounding as if he'd been testing his wife's memory. "It's been at least thirty."

"Oh, you're right!" Martha patted his knee proudly. "It *was* thirty, at least."

"So what could he have to do with anything going on today?"

"That's part of being thorough," Ransom said self-effacingly. "We want to make sure he doesn't have anything to do with it. We understood that Phillip Pearson was a rather difficult person to like."

"To like?" said Larry. "He was difficult to like, to know, to understand, and even to ignore. But I see what you're saying. The usual suspects and all that. If somebody in that family had been killed back then, I'm sure Phillip would've been the one who did it. But now? Huh!"

Ransom glanced at Gerald, who sat directly across from

him with his hands resting on his knees, like a schoolboy in church. It had been decided ahead of time that he wouldn't take notes during this interview, partly because Ransom believed it would make the elderly couple nervous, and partly because he had very low expectations of receiving any useful information from them.

He looked back at Larry Whitehall and said, "I understand that you were forced to call the police once."

"Oh, yes!" Martha answered for him. "That was just terrible! Wasn't it terrible, Larry?"

"Terrible," he agreed. "Poor kid, screaming in the attic. You should've heard it!"

"We thought he was finally killing poor Gregory!"

"Finally?" Ransom said with one raised eyebrow.

"He mistreated those kids something fierce," said Larry. "Always yelling at them…"

"…and the words he used!" Martha took up the thread. "Stupid, and idiot, and all sorts of degrading things! It's a wonder either of those children could hold up their heads and look anyone in the eyes, their self-esteem must have been so low."

"And he hit them, too," said Larry. "He managed to keep it out of sight, mind you. He didn't give them black eyes or anything like that. But you could hear him yelling, and then he'd break off and then whichever one of the kids he was yelling at would start squealing bloody murder, and then he'd just yell at them for crying."

"It was very hard…." Martha's voice broke. She put her knuckles up to her mouth and tears welled in her eyes.

"It was especially hard for my Martha to listen to," Larry said sympathetically. "We couldn't have children of our own. It was hard to hear someone blessed with children treat them so badly, like they didn't know what little treasures they had."

Martha nodded and wiped the tears from the corners of her eyes with the back of her fingers. "He treated…he treated Abigail much the same way. I saw her sometimes in the backyard when I was hanging out the wash, but how do you ask somebody about that? Even making small talk was difficult. If her husband was home, she always had one eye on the back windows, like she was afraid he might look out and see her and get mad. So how could I ask her about how he was treating her? I just tried to let her know I was there for her, if she wanted. It made me feel very lucky, though, every day." She gave an adoring look at her husband. "Lucky to have my Larry."

"Thank you, honey." He patted her hand and for just a moment their heads tilted toward each other's. He turned back to Ransom and said, "The children never talked to us, either. Much as Martha tried to reach out to them. They were scared, too, I guess."

"But all that changed when Phillip Pearson left, didn't it?" Ransom asked.

The Whitehalls looked at him, both of them obviously confused. Martha was the first to speak. "Oh, no. It didn't. I think when you've been afraid for so long, it just doesn't go away. Even when the reason you're afraid does. Whenever I saw Gregory after his father left, he'd say hello but he wasn't really cordial."

"That was his daddy's doing," said Larry. "I think Gregory was mad at us because of that time I called the police. I probably got him in even bigger trouble. I should've thought of that before I did it. But what can you do?"

"Nothing," his wife answered sadly. "Absolutely nothing, because you have to do what's right, even when the consequences aren't that good." She looked to Ransom. "Isn't that right?"

"I think you were right to call the police, yes. I'm just sorry they didn't do more about it."

"They certainly didn't do much," Martha said scoldingly. "They came and talked to us for a bit after they went over and saw the Pearsons. The police told us this was just 'a family thing'—that's what they called it, isn't it?"

"Yes," Larry assented.

"'A family thing,' and that everything was all right now. It didn't help when we told them that there was 'a family thing' every day over there. I don't think they did anything at all."

"I'm sorry that happened," Ransom said. "How did JoAnna take all of this? Do you have any idea?"

"JoAnna was a little better to us," Martha said. "Sometimes I gave her some cookies to take home and sometimes I'd just chat with her. She always seemed sad to me, though, and I felt bad for her. I tried to reach out to her, didn't I?" She looked to her husband again.

"Of course you did, honey, of course you did. But you can't make up for all that damage that her father did."

Martha continued. "She was always reticent with us. I don't know if she blamed us for making things worse. She never said much of anything. I tried, though."

"If it makes you feel any better," said Ransom, "JoAnna told us how much she appreciated you for calling the police."

"Really?" Martha's face brightened noticeably. "She did?"

Ransom nodded. "She said that after that incident, she always felt a little safer."

"Do you hear that, honey?" Martha said, turning her freshly watery eyes to her husband. "Do you hear that? You *did* do some good for them."

"I'm glad of that," Larry said, sounding as if he'd just been relieved of a lifelong worry.

Ransom crossed his legs. "Do you remember when Phillip Pearson left his family?"

"Only from the quiet," Larry said.

Martha nodded. "I would've known he was gone, even if nobody'd told me."

"Who did tell you?"

"Abigail herself did, oh, I guess a week or so after he left. I saw her in the backyard. I asked her how she was doing, and she told me I might as well know that her husband had gone.''

''She did?'' Ransom said, betraying a bit of surprise.

''She said he'd gone away and now he was someone else's problem, and she pitied her.''

''It was unusual for her to be that open with you, wasn't it?''

''When Phillip was there, yes. I guess she was kind of relieved he was gone and wanted to talk about it.''

''*Kind of* relieved,'' Ransom repeated slowly. ''I should think she'd be a good deal more than that.''

''It's like Martha said,'' Larry chimed in. ''I don't think you ever get shy of the effects of having been abused like that.''

''No, you don't,'' his wife agreed. ''I didn't see her very often after that, but she never did look like she felt safe, even after Phillip left.'' She squeezed her husband's hand. ''I hope he hasn't come back. I can't imagine what it would do to that poor family!''

Any further discussion with the Whitehalls was interrupted by the chirping of Ransom's cell phone.

''Excuse me,'' he said, extracting the phone from his jacket pocket. He flipped it open and said, ''Hello?''

''Hello, Jeremy? Is that you?'' Emily's voice came through as tentatively as it always did on the phone.

''Yes, Emily. What is it?''

''I need you to come at once!''

''What's wrong?'' he said as he uncrossed his legs and sat forward in his chair.

''It's not an emergency…. Well, actually, it may be one, I don't know. You need to see it for yourself. I hate to interrupt you like this, but please do come as soon as you can.''

''I'll be right there,'' he said. As he rose he snapped the phone shut and stuck it back in his pocket.

''I'm sorry, we have to go.''

Gerald was on his feet in a second, and the two of them

started toward the door before either of the Whitehalls had a chance to get up.

Ransom paused at the entrance to the hallway and turned back to Martha. "By the way, did Abigail tell you who it was her husband went away with?"

"Did she..." Martha looked away and furrowed her brow as she tried to remember.

Wanting to get to Emily as soon as possible, Ransom was about to tell her to forget it when she said, "You know, she *did* say who it was but...it's been so long ago, I just don't remember. And it wasn't a name I knew."

"Could it by chance have been Marjorie Loughlin?"

"That's it!" Martha exclaimed. "That's the name!"

RANSOM SMACKED THE BUTTON for the elevator with his palm, then before the elevator even started to move, he said, "Let's take the stairs."

"What's wrong? What happened?" said Gerald, moving swiftly down the steps after his partner.

"I don't know. That was Emily. Something's wrong at the Pearsons'."

"We were wasting our time here anyway."

Ransom shot him a glance over his shoulder. "Were we?"

"Yeah. We didn't get anything we didn't know out of all that, did we?"

As they came out onto the sidewalk and hurried to the car, Ransom said, "I find it very interesting that the Pearsons weren't more relieved that Phillip Pearson had gone. I would think that after all they went through with him, they would have jumped for joy."

"But that's normal, isn't it? I mean, people that are abused, aren't they always looking over their shoulders as long as their abuser's alive, even if he's in jail?"

Ransom hesitated for a split second before getting into the car. "Perhaps you're right."

His tone was so odd that Gerald grimaced. There were

times when he would prefer that Ransom didn't agree with him.

It took them less than ten minutes to drive back to the Pearsons' house. Ransom was out of the car before Gerald had switched off the engine. He walked quickly up the front walk, and Emily opened the door just as he reached it.

"What's happened?" he asked.

"Come into the kitchen. I'll show you."

He followed her down the hallway, and Gerald brought up the rear after shutting the front door. When they came into the kitchen, they found JoAnna Pearson sitting at one side of the table, and Leslie Pearson at the other. Lying on the table between them was a small cardboard box. Leslie looked up as they entered. Her eyes were vacant and her face very pale. She had the expression of someone whose world had collapsed from an aftershock rather than from the earthquake.

"It looked new," she said without preamble. "That's why it caught my eye."

Ransom greeted the two women, then looked to Emily for an explanation.

"She touched the box and some of the things inside when she found it, but I was careful not to touch it, or to let anyone else, either."

"I brought it over when I found it," said Leslie. "I didn't know what else to do. But you said finding out who was doing...you said it would help you find who killed Robert."

Ransom placed his fingers gingerly on opposing edges of the box and slid the top off. Leslie looked away as if she couldn't bear to see it again. JoAnna folded her hands prayerfully, touching her fingers to her lips.

Inside the box was a gray wig, assorted tubes of light-colored makeup, and a small container of white powder. There was also some sort of adhesive and bits of latex that looked unpleasantly like peeled skin.

"Where did you find this?" Ransom asked.

"In the Dumpster behind our building when I took out the trash. It was just sitting there on top of the trash. The thing is, it looked so new...it didn't look like it belonged there. That's what caught my eye. That's why I opened it." She was silent for a long while, then said sadly, "I guess this means it really *was* Robert who was doing those awful things to Grandma. I just don't...believe it."

"And you shouldn't, my dear," Emily said crisply. "Because this means exactly the opposite."

All eyes in the room turned to the old woman.

"What?" said Leslie.

"For the time being you will simply have to take my word for it, because it wouldn't be possible to explain until the case has been solved. But you may take my word for it that your husband was not involved in anything that went on in this house."

"Do you mean it?" Leslie asked hopefully, her voice beginning to tremble.

"Of course I do."

Leslie covered her mouth with her hands, closed her eyes, and wept. After allowing a decent interval for her to collect herself, JoAnna rose from her chair and laid a comforting hand on the young woman's shoulder. "Come on, Les, I'll take you home."

Leslie touched JoAnna's hand with her own, then got up.

"Just a minute, Miss Pearson—" Ransom said to JoAnna, but before he could finish Emily cut him off.

"No, Jeremy. It will be quite all right."

He hesitated for a moment, then gave a nod to JoAnna. She led Leslie out of the room and out of the house.

"You're sure?" said Ransom once they'd heard the front door close.

"Oh, yes. Very," Emily said gravely.

"I get the feeling that you know something we don't," said Gerald.

"I know that I've been very, very foolish in this whole

business. I knew that the minute I saw these things." She gestured at the exposed contents of the box.

"So," said Ransom, "the idea of Phillip Pearson returning was just a boondoggle, and now we're supposed to believe that Robert was the one breaking in here pretending to be his grandfather...and that when we confronted him, we scared him off and he threw these things away."

"Yes, that's what we're supposed to believe. But that was a very bad mistake," said Emily. "The killer should have disposed of these things someplace where they couldn't be found. That way, with Robert dead and the 'visitations' stopped, everyone would have been left to assume that Robert had been the one doing them. Instead, the killer tried to directly implicate Robert."

"Implicate him? In the break-ins? But why?" Gerald asked, his face a mask of perplexity. "The important thing here is the murder, not the break-ins, isn't it?"

"Oh, no, Detective White. It was because the break-ins weren't successful...and I daresay because we came onto the scene...that Robert was murdered." She stamped her foot once with frustration and rubbed her right fist inside her left palm. She looked truly vexed. "I don't think I shall *ever* forgive myself for how foolish I've been in this matter!"

"Emily," Ransom said, trying to hold his patience, "you're not making any sense. Would you please explain what you're talking about?"

"I knew it the minute I saw the contents of the box. I should have known it when Abigail told me what she'd seen the second time, but as I said, I've been slow and very stupid."

"Not half as slow as I'm being right now," said Ransom.

Emily pointed at the box and said, "Banquo!"

"What?"

"All along I kept thinking about the three witches and the idea of stirring up trouble, when I should have seen that the really important aspect of the case was Banquo."

"Emily…"

"There's really no time to explain it all right now. You must get to Gregory Pearson as soon as possible."

"Why?"

"Because Abigail called him this morning. I'm sure she told him that we were going to see Marjorie Loughlin. You have to get to him right away! I'm sure something terrible is going to happen to him, if it hasn't already."

"You know all of this from seeing the contents of this box?"

"Yes," Emily said insistently. "Jeremy, you really must hurry!"

"Wait…I know that finding the box in Robert's Dumpster looks suspicious, but it still is possible that Robert was the one who put it there, and he was the one breaking in for the very reason we thought: to try to scare Abigail to death and get the house."

"No, it couldn't possibly have been Robert. It *had* to be Gregory," Emily said emphatically.

"Why?"

Emily narrowed her eyes. "Because Gregory is the only one who *knows*." As quickly as she could, she told them what she was thinking. As they listened to the explanation, Ransom's jaw became more fixed, while Gerald's mouth dropped open.

"You're kidding!" said Gerald, once Emily had finished.

Ransom looked at his partner sharply. "No, she's not. And she's right, we'd better get to Gregory Pearson!" He turned to Emily. "Are you sure you'll be all right here?"

"I'll be perfectly safe now," she replied.

EMILY WATCHED through the living room window as Ransom and Gerald went to the car and drove off. Her feelings were somewhat ambivalent: on the one hand she hoped they would get to Gregory before anything happened to him, while on the other she thought it might be best if they

were too late. With a sigh she relinquished the outcome to
Providence, then went upstairs to Abigail's room.

Emily found her hostess lying on the bed, with some of
the pillows she had formerly used to prop herself up scattered to the sides. Although some of the color had returned
to her cheeks, Abigail looked as if she had aged another
ten years overnight. Emily pulled the bedside chair up
closer, sat down, and folded her hands. She sat gazing at
Abigail like an elderly Grand Inquisitor.

"Abigail," she said softly but firmly.

There was a long silence, then Abigail's eyelids fluttered
open.

"I thought you should know that something was found
at your grandson's apartment building. It was a box containing some theatrical makeup and a wig, the items necessary to make someone able to appear to be your husband."

"No," Abigail said quietly, her eyes opening wider.
"You mean...you mean it was *Robert* who was trying to
scare me?"

Emily shook her head. "I think you know that's not
true."

"You..."

"In fact, you know who it was, don't you? That would
explain many, many things. It explains why you never
spoke of changing your will, even when Robert seemed to
be the only one with a motive for pulling these 'little
pranks.' I think you know that Gregory was the one trying
to scare you. I think you've known that ever since Jeremy
investigated and assured you that you weren't losing your
mind, that someone really *was* coming into the house at
night."

Abigail swallowed hard. "He wasn't trying to kill me.
You have to believe that."

Emily nodded. "It's all about this house. Or rather
what's inside this house. You started it all when you decided to leave the house to Robert, because you were so

happy that he was going to give you a great-grandchild, and the house was the only thing you had to give him. And, I suppose, you really did feel that the abuse that had been handed down through the generations was finally dissipating, and Robert and Leslie might be able to, as you put it, reclaim this house. But I don't think you would've left it to them if you thought he would sell it. At least, not while Gregory was alive. It's unfortunate for everyone involved that you were blinded by two things: first by your belief in Robert's veracity, and second, if you will forgive my putting it so bluntly, you were blinded by your own stubbornness. You were annoyed at Gregory's attitude, and that only made you more determined to do what you intended. But his attitude was understandable, wasn't it? He was terrified, and it was you who frightened him into action."

Despite her weakness, a certain hardness crept in around Abigail's eyes. "He had no right to the house."

"But that's not the point, is it? He was afraid for his own safety. I blame myself for not seeing it all sooner. I suppose it was the peculiarity of the midnight visits by an intruder that looked like your husband that drew my attention away from the most important aspects of those appearances: *The intruder looked like he was dead.*" She paused and sighed. "That is, of course, where I was most foolish. Even though I was rereading *Macbeth*, I missed the significance of Banquo's ghost, when he returns in later scenes to haunt Macbeth. Gregory wasn't trying to frighten you by making you think that your husband had returned, or that he had died: He was trying to make you think you were seeing a ghost."

Emily stopped and looked down, waiting, but Abigail said nothing.

"I assume," Emily said matter-of-factly, "that Phillip is buried in the cellar."

There was a very long pause. Abigail stared into Emily's eyes. Then she turned her head and released a long, low sigh that seemed to rattle up from her chest.

"Phillip was a brutal, brutal man," she said slowly. "He destroyed me, and he destroyed my children. Even when he was dead, we were never free of him. He passed his brutality on to his son and to a lesser extent to his grandson. There was...probably...something mentally wrong with him. Maybe if it happened today, we'd be able to get some help for him. But not then. Not back then. Nobody would listen. Nobody knew or wanted to know what went on inside this house." She suddenly looked back at Emily. "Gregory didn't *mean* for it to happen. You have to believe me! He was trying to protect me."

"I do believe you," said Emily. "Now, why don't you tell me what happened?"

"A scarf..." Abigail put her hand up to her throat, rubbing it absently. "It was because of a scarf."

"I beg your pardon?"

"I saw it in a store. It was blue silk, and so pretty. And not *really* expensive. I swear it wasn't. I wanted it. I knew I shouldn't have bought it. I knew it even as I paid for it. But my life was so ugly, you see, and every now and then I would see something I thought was beautiful, and sometimes I would buy it. Most of the time I resisted, because you never knew what would set Phillip off. But there were some things I knew were risky: anything that looked like extravagance, anything that was unnecessary, anything..." Her voice trailed off sadly.

"Anything that made you happy," Emily said.

Abigail swallowed again. "Yes. I wore it home. It was so lovely, and so soft, I didn't remember that I had it on. Phillip was very late home that night, probably out with one of his women. When he saw the scarf, he flew into a rage...just as usual. But this time it was worse. He ended up grabbing the scarf. He twisted it around my neck. I was choking.... My face got very hot and tight.... I couldn't breathe...and then Gregory came in. He was fourteen or fifteen at the time, and he'd long since started to show signs of his father's rage. When he saw what was happening, after all the years of abuse we'd suffered, it was just too much. He grabbed his father by the neck and...and...choked him to death.''

"I see," said Emily. "And then?"

"The basement floor was still unfinished. We decided to bury him there.''

"Why didn't you just call the police?"

"The police?" Abigail said disdainfully. Some of the feistiness reappeared in her face. "The police had been called before, and they didn't do anything except make everything worse. And Gregory was terrified, you see. He was afraid that even if the police believed us, he would've had to go to jail. And that would've killed him. He was *so* afraid of being confined." She paused and started to absently pick at the blanket that covered her. "After it was done...after we buried him...within a few days, Gregory finished the basement floor, to cover up...completely. But he didn't know what he was doing, really, and the floor is a mess.''

"And he knew that if the house was sold, the floor would be dug up, and most likely the remains would be found.''

Abigail nodded.

Emily said, "JoAnna never knew about any of this?"

"No. She was in bed. The next morning I told her that her father had gone away, and she was never to ask about him again. She did once, but after that she knew to let it drop.''

"And you were so understandably upset by what had happened, JoAnna found it easy to believe you were telling the truth." Emily leaned forward slightly. "But why did you bring Marjorie Loughlin into it? That was very unwise.''

Abigail had managed to retain her composure up until this point, but when Emily touched on the subject that had started their downfall, she gave way to tears.

"We were so frightened, Gregory and me. We were so frightened, you see. And we had...*him* here. Phillip was always so noticeable that we were afraid someone would miss him. It so happened that the Loughlins had just moved away. We didn't know them well, we just knew of them. I don't think anyone around here knew them. They lived three blocks away, and even back then they might as well have lived in a whole different city. We *might* have known them if their children had gone to public schools…at least, my children might have met theirs. But we didn't.''

"You took a very great risk, didn't you? It might have gotten back to someone who did know them, and then back to the Loughlins.''

"But you see,'' Abigail said, wiping the tears away, "we thought it sounded more…plausible, I guess, if we said we knew who he'd gone away with. I didn't tell many people. I was afraid to talk about it with anyone. But if it *had* been found out that he hadn't gone away with Mrs. Loughlin, I thought I could say that I had *thought* it was her, and that I didn't really know who it was.'' With a certain amount of pride, she added, "After it was all over, after Phillip had been taken care of, Gregory was a rock. He seemed to be able to take care of everything. He called Phillip's employer. He pretended to be his father, and told them that he quit. He told them he'd found a better job.''

"They didn't recognize his voice?''

"No, no…. He called the personnel office. Of course, they hadn't spoken to Phillip very often, and Gregory was enough like his father to get by. If he'd had to talk to Phillip's supervisor, it might've been a different story, but Phillip was as much trouble at work as he was at home. His supervisor never called to check on him. I think that, like us, they were just glad that he was gone.''

Emily sat back and shook her head in amazement. "That was all a very bold plan.''

"There was no plan. We weren't bold, we were desperate! I was so afraid that people would ask me about Phillip that in time I barely went out of the house at all.''

"So you became a prisoner in this house.''

Abigail let out a choking cry and began to sob. "Yes! Yes...."

Emily considered the woman and the mess that had been made of her life for some time, while allowing Abigail to give free rein to her grief. At last, Emily said, "Gregory really didn't understand, did he?"

Abigail calmed slightly and turned her watery eyes to her. "What?"

"The *real* reason you didn't want him to have the house. You didn't want him to become a prisoner, too. Isn't that right?"

Abigail nodded as she renewed her sobs. "I never...never thought that he would kill Robert! How could I think he would kill his own son?"

Emily didn't point out that he had killed his own father. "What have I done? Now it will all come out! Gregory will go to jail, won't he?"

"I don't think so."

Abigail sniffed. "You don't?"

"You called him this morning and told him that we'd found Mrs. Loughlin, didn't you?"

"Yes...yes, I had to warn him. What do you mean, he won't go to jail?"

"Unless I miss my guess," Emily said, folding her hands in her lap, "the chain has finally been broken."

IT TOOK Ransom and Gerald over half an hour to reach Gregory Pearson's town house. On the way, Ransom tried to reach him by phone to no avail. They double-parked directly outside Pearson's home and emerged from the car in unison.

Gerald rang the bell, but there was no answer. As he pressed it a second time, Ransom leaned over the railing and looked in through the front window.

"Oh, Jesus," he said softly. He turned to his partner. "Break it down."

The two of them put their shoulders to the door. On their

third try, they could hear the wood splinter and crack, and when they hit it the fourth time the molding gave way and the door swung open with a loud crash.

Gregory Pearson was on the couch. Spasms had left his body contorted: His knees were turned inward and his heels turned out; his head drooped to one side, and his mouth hung open. His arms were outstretched, palms up. Long slits had been cut lengthwise along the undersides of his arms. The couch was soaked with blood, and a razor blade glinted in the pool on the floor. From the condition of the body and the blood, it was apparent that Pearson had been dead for a few hours at least.

"Well," Ransom said somberly, "it seems that Mr. Pearson is free now."

FOURTEEN

"YOU HAVE TO REMEMBER that these people were not criminals," said Emily as Lynn Francis poured out a cup of tea for her from the old teapot that Emily cherished. She was glad to be back in her own home, and even more glad to be surrounded by friends.

Ransom had finally been successful in his attempts to get Emily to leave the Pearsons' house, explaining that the Pearsons—or what remained of them—would be busy with the police for a while, and would probably prefer to be alone now, anyway. He had expected more resistance from her, but now that the case had been solved and they knew that Abigail wasn't in any danger, Emily said that she was rather anxious to "shake the dust of this case and this family" off her feet and return to the comfort of her own home. Lynn had been there to welcome her.

It was later that evening. Gerald White had gone home to his wife Sherry and their two daughters. The two ladies had been joined by Ransom. They sat at the table in Emily's kitchen which, even as the summer dusk set in, was a good deal more cheerful than the one at the Pearsons' house.

"When you say they're not criminals, I assume you're forgetting the two murders," Ransom said wryly.

"Not at all," she replied primly. "I simply mean that they weren't operating out of a criminal intent, they were working from a place of desperation and fear. Always fear. Gregory hadn't meant to kill his father, and I really do believe he was trying to protect his mother. I think Abigail told me the truth about that. But they didn't think the police would believe them, and Gregory had a mortal fear of going

to jail. But they weren't criminals. They didn't know what
to do, so they did what they thought was the safest thing:
They buried the body in the basement, without realizing
how disastrous the results would be.''

"How do you mean?" Lynn asked as she took a sip of
her tea.

"Well, they had to account for his disappearance, or at
least they felt they had to. If they had, say, taken the body
to the lake and thrown it in, it would eventually have been
discovered, and even if the police had suspected that one
of the family had murdered him, there probably wouldn't
have been enough evidence to do anything about it. Isn't
that true, Jeremy?''

"Possibly."

"So in their panic and fear of being discovered, they
kept the body, not realizing that that would be the very
evidence against them.'' She turned to Ransom suddenly.
"You know, you never told me what the next-door neighbors had to say. The ones that had called the police.''

"The Whitehalls? They only told us what we already
knew: that Phillip Pearson was an ogre, and that they were
glad when he left. Oh, they also said that Abigail was the
one who told them that Phillip had left with Marjorie
Loughlin.''

"Ah!" Emily said knowingly. "You see, they were
mounting a campaign of disinformation. It was the thing I
was trying to remember about Marjorie Loughlin that I
thought might be important. You said it yourself: that one
of JoAnna's classmates—someone at school—had told her
the name of the woman her father had supposedly run off
with. You were remembering it wrong, just the way I was.''

"What do you mean?"

Emily leaned forward. "JoAnna didn't say one of her
classmates, she said *one of Gregory's friends.* She said
something about school at the same time, and I'm afraid I
got the two things jumbled in my head.''

"But I don't understand," said Lynn. "Why did they

give a name at all? Didn't they know what a risk they were taking?''

"They thought that that risk outweighed the others,'' Emily explained. "They were terrified that if they just said Phillip had run away with some woman, it would sound too vague and raise suspicions. They thought if they gave a name it would sound much more plausible. It *was* a risk but, as Abigail said, if anyone ever challenged her over it, she could say she'd simply been mistaken about who it was he'd gone with.''

"The real problem became the house,'' said Ransom, taking up the story. "Gregory was not exactly good at building. He did a terrible job laying the floor in the basement. It was the first thing I noticed when I went down there. It was so uneven you could see the flaws with the naked eye. After all, he was only about fifteen at the time and he didn't know anything about construction, and he didn't exactly have time to learn. But even if he could've fixed it, I don't think they would've wanted to sell the house. The chances were just too great that new owners would do something—remodeling or what have you—with the basement and find the bones. As long as Gregory was alive, that was a danger to him.''

Lynn asked, "Why didn't he just move the body? He had all those years to do it.''

Emily answered, "I don't think either he or Abigail had any idea of what to do with it. The average person would most likely be rather at a loss as to how to dispose of a body. And he probably felt safe as long as the house stayed with the family. By the time the possibility of it being sold arose, it was too late. JoAnna was at the house every day. He couldn't have broken up the floor in the basement without her finding out, and till his dying day, he protected his sister. You have to remember that these were not criminal people. They weren't even particularly resourceful people. They were like children trying desperately to hide their

wrongdoing from authority. And they'd learned from a lifetime of hard experience to be truly terrified of authority."

"But why all that crazy business of Gregory dressing up
like his father and trying to scare Abigail? That just doesn't
make any sense."

"That's where I was very, very stupid," Emily said,
curling her lips. "When Abigail saw the 'apparition' the
second time, she said she'd seen her husband, but he was
dead. She explained later that she meant she thought he
looked dead, but that was only after she'd had time to calm
down and realized the danger of what she'd said. I
should've known then what was happening. Someone was
trying to scare her by making her think she'd seen a ghost,
and making everyone else think she was going out of her
mind. She thought it was a ghost because she knew her
husband was dead. When Jeremy told her that he'd found
evidence that a real person had been in the house, she knew
immediately that it was Gregory, because he was the only
other one who knew Phillip was dead."

"You see, he really didn't want to kill anyone," Ransom
said. "He just wanted to make everyone think his mother
needed to be put away. As her executor, he would get control of the house. Robert didn't get it unless Abigail *died*.
With control of the house and JoAnna having no further
reason to visit there, he would've at least had some time
to try to do something about his father's remains."

"But Gregory killed his own son!" said Lynn.

"Yes," Emily said, shaking her head sadly. "Once
again, out of desperation. He killed Robert when he realized
that the house would go out of the family, and the only
way to ensure that that didn't happen was to kill the person
who would inherit, even if it was his own son. He was *that*
afraid that if the house was sold, the truth would come out
and he would go to prison. And he might have been right,
you know. Times have changed since the murder happened,
and it's likely that it would've looked much more suspicious to the modern mind that the murder was covered up,

than it would if they'd just told the truth about it to begin with.''

"How did he manage to kill Robert?''

"We don't know exactly,'' said Ransom. ''But my guess would be that he told Robert he had something important to tell him that he didn't want Leslie to know about, and persuaded him to join him somewhere near Robert's apartment. When Leslie told us about it, she said that she'd asked Robert what was going on, and he'd said he would tell her when he got back. She thought he was just upset and didn't want to talk about it until he'd gone for a walk. What he really meant was he didn't know, but would when he returned.''

Emily released an exasperated sigh.

"What's wrong?'' Lynn asked.

"I just think that that's another area in which I was rather foolish. I misunderstood what I heard.''

"What do you mean?''

"When I overheard Abigail telling Gregory that he should tell Robert about his grandfather, I believed she was saying that if Robert knew how Gregory had been treated as a child, he might understand why Gregory had always been so hard on him.''

"That makes sense,'' said Ransom. ''And it's what Gregory told us he said to Robert.''

"Oh, is it? Yes, well, that may be what he said. But I don't think that's what Abigail was really telling him. And I suppose that should be a lesson to me about eavesdropping.''

"You're losing me again, Emily,'' Ransom said lightly.

"I'm sorry. What I'm trying to say is, I don't think she meant that Gregory should tell Robert about how his father mistreated him, but *what had happened* to Phillip, so that he would know the importance of keeping the house. But Gregory was just too afraid to let the secret out, even to his son. And the way he killed Robert was another example of his not being a criminal. It was one of those cases where not being artful worked to Gregory's advantage. When Robert met him, Gregory just bashed him over the head and dropped the body in the alley." She looked to Ransom. "I suppose now your people will go over his car."

"Um hm."

"Of course, Gregory's real mistake was planting the box containing the disguise in the Dumpster behind Robert's apartment."

"You mean because it might not have been found?" said Lynn.

"No, that part was a calculated risk," Emily explained. "He believed if it was found it would definitely implicate Robert. If it wasn't found, Robert would still be implicated because the visitations had stopped. But Gregory would've been better off if the box of makeup had never been found."

"Why do you say that?"

Emily leaned in toward her. "Because the box contained the makeup necessary to make it look as if someone was dead. Robert had no way of knowing that his grandfather was dead. So rather than prove Robert's guilt, it proved his innocence."

Ransom added, "And although Gregory tried to wipe the tubes and things free of fingerprints, there aren't very many place in Chicago to get theatrical makeup. Most likely we could've traced it to him."

They fell silent for a while, then Lynn said, "You know, the thing that puzzles me the most is that knowing all of this, knowing how Gregory had reacted about the house and how much trouble it was causing, why didn't Abigail just change her mind about leaving it to Robert?"

Emily clucked her tongue. "There were two reasons for that. You know, when we came onto the scene, Abigail was being terrorized and we mistakenly believed her to be a timid woman. She's not really timid; she's actually quite forceful in her own right. And with over thirty years of frustration over the effects of the tyranny and iron hand of her husband, she wasn't about to be bullied by her son. And she's a rather obstinate woman. It was because Gregory was so adamant that he should have the house, even though Abigail knew his reason to be valid, that firmed her resolve that he shouldn't have it. The other reason is a bit more palatable: Abigail, despite everything, loved Gregory. All of her life she has been trapped in that house, and deep in her heart she didn't want the same thing to happen to him. I suppose we'll have to believe that she thought Robert would retain the house, but if the truth be known, I don't think she really cared. I think she was tired of their family being held hostage.''

''Well, there's one thing you can explain to *me*, Emily,'' said Ransom with a smile. ''When I first came into this business, you said that Nedra Taylor, Abigail's maid, might prove to be a key player in this case. Would you mind telling me why you thought that?''

''She *was* a key player,'' Emily said, putting her cup down on its saucer. ''Because she wasn't doing her job.''

''You said that before, but what did you mean?''

''Just that Gregory was coming in and doing those strange things with the furniture the night before Nedra was to be there each week. It was supposed to be a sign that Abigail's mind was going, and that she shouldn't be left on her own. Nedra did say something about it to JoAnna once, but it upset the poor girl very badly. You see, Nedra really cares for Abigail. She didn't want to see anything bad happen to her. So after the first time she just put the furniture back where it belonged and said nothing to anyone about it, even to Abigail. She was trying to protect her. What she ended up doing was flying in the face of Gregory's plan. You see, he expected her to keep reporting on Abigail's supposedly bizarre behavior, but she didn't do it.''

''Ah! I see,'' said Ransom, pushing himself back from the table and crossing his legs. ''Well, I started out on this case as an unpaid advisor, and for all the good I did, I still probably shouldn't draw a paycheck. You were the one who put this whole thing together.''

"Nonsense," said Emily, reaching over and patting his hand. "You're the detective in this family."

He pursed his lips. "Emily, if I didn't know better, I would think you were making fun of me."

"Not at all."

Lynn took another sip of tea. "What do you think will happen to Abigail and the other Pearson women now?''

"I doubt very much if they will prosecute an elderly woman for covering up for her son's crime—the original one, I mean. Especially given the circumstances," said Ransom.

"They may be all right," said Emily doubtfully, "but I don't know. Perhaps now that the men of the family are gone, the new generation will have a chance."

"Emily!" Lynn exclaimed with surprise.

"Oh, I'm not condoning murder," Emily explained quickly. "But Abigail was right about one thing: abuse keeps getting passed down through the generations, even if it becomes dissipated. Who knows how long it would take to work itself out? Maybe now at last Abigail has a chance to be free."

IT WAS TWO MONTHS before the furor had died down. The media had gotten hold of the story of the house where the husband had been buried for over thirty years and covered the family scandal in all its lurid detail. Camera crews were on hand outside the house when the body was removed.

JoAnna'a visits stopped when she learned the truth. She didn't exactly blame her mother—she knew what a brute her father had been—but she couldn't bring herself to re-visit the house that had served as her father's tomb for so many years. She didn't entirely cut off communication, though. She made infrequent phone calls to inquire after her mother's health, and took up where Gregory had left off in doing what she could to alleviate the financial burden of caring for the house.

Abigail offered Leslie the opportunity of staying with her rent-free in the house, but Leslie declined. Like JoAnna, she couldn't bear the idea of living in a place that had been a grave, and that had so many unhappy memories connected to it. She found the atmosphere of the house abhorrent and sickly the one time she visited it on the occasion of Abigail's offer. But there was another reason that Leslie refused. Though she would never admit to it, she inwardly blamed Abigail for Robert's murder. She believed that if her grandmother-in-law had been able to see reason—if only she'd given in to Gregory—Robert would still be alive. Not long after the business was over, Leslie gave up her job and moved back with her parents to take care of her child.

Once the dust had settled, Abigail saw no reason to hang onto the house any longer, and in fact was anxious to be rid of it. She tried many real estate agents, all of whom agreed they could list the house, but in an uncharacteristic bit of honesty one of them told her the chances of selling the house were very limited.

"It's not a very desirable property," the woman had sniffed while going through the house. "And then there's its history. I don't think anyone will want to buy it. Maybe you should wait a few years…until people forget. Maybe then you'll have more luck."

A few years, Abigail had repeated to herself, her heart sinking.

One night, about six months after the truth had come out, Abigail was in her bed, lying against pillows. The book she'd been reading lay by her side. The branch from the tree outside scraped lightly against the window. For a second she thought to remind Gregory it needed to be trimmed, but then she remembered that he was gone. She might try to find someone else to do it, but didn't know where to begin. With a sigh she decided she would probably just have to learn to live with it. She reached over and switched off the bedside lamp, pulled the blanket up, and rested her hands on her chest.

And when she closed her eyes, all she could hear was the steady ticking of the grandfather clock in the hall below.

THE
VICTIM
IN
VICTORIA
STATION

A DOROTHY MARTIN MYSTERY

JEANNE M. DAMS

A charming, quick-witted woman of a certain age, Dorothy Martin once more finds herself embroiled in a most puzzling crime.

The victim: a fellow American, her seat companion on a commuter train to London. Dorothy is convinced he was poisoned, yet the authorities' response to her interest is emphatic denial: there was no man, no body, no crime.

Undaunted, Dorothy plunges ahead and not only discovers the victim's shocking identity, but a deadly game of corporate rivalry. Donning a wig and polishing her phone skills, she takes a temporary job in a London software company—and boldly enters the hornet's nest....

Available December 2000 at your favorite retail outlet.

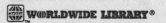

Dead Man's Fingers

Barbara Lee

A Chesapeake Bay Mystery

Maryland real estate agent Eve Elliott has left Manhattan for a more peaceful life along the shores of the Chesapeake. Once there, Eve discovers greed, corruption and murder rock the calm waters of Anne Arundel County.

Both Eve and her aunt/business partner, Lillian, find themselves scapegoats in a heated controversy over zoning. Development scams, crooked politicians and unhappy wives with dangerous secrets add fuel to the fire. Soon, sinister threats and the murder of an attractive, ambitious environmentalist warn Eve she's digging too close. Now the murky issues are becoming frightfully clear: her life...versus a killer's deadly intent.

Available December 2000 at your favorite retail outlet.

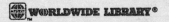

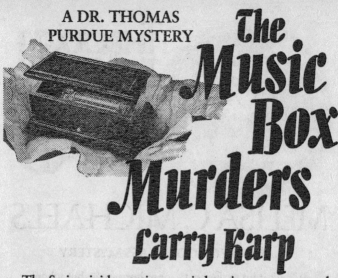
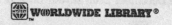

THROUGH THE EYES OF THE DEAD

MELISA C. MICHAELS

AN AILEEN DOUGLASS MYSTERY

Chalk it up to the heat…or to hormones, but when
San Francisco P.I. Aileen Douglass catches the sexy
young Gypsy man trying to hot-wire her car, she doesn't
call the cops. Instead she gives him a lift to Oakland…
and lands herself in a twisted case of murder.

Nick inhabits a dangerous world, as Aileen quickly
learns, when she stumbles across a dead fortune-teller,
then dodges a hail of bullets. Next, Aileen's only paying
client is murdered, her office ransacked and
her partner drugged.

And she discovers these cases are connected…
by a missing $100,000.

Available December 2000 at your favorite retail outlet.

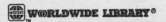

WMM370